"Nobody ever talks about the guy biological clock, but it was ticking loud and clear in me. And I did not have a lot of time left."

I am not going to blame it all on the job. This job was always the dream. To get paid to go to ball games? It's the greatest job a person can have. But I have paid a price. Twenty years on the road catches up with you. It sure as hell makes it even more complicated than it already is to hook up with a woman. Unless you're talking about a pretty low-maintenance type. And women you pick up in saloons after you've filed your stories might be fine for some guys, but it isn't the solution to the emptiness gnawing at me.

So there I sat. And I decided. Enough. I had to get ahold of my life. I had to stop wishing for something I wasn't willing to take any risks to try to get. I wanted some roots. I wanted some connection.

I wanted a kid.

THE DADDY CLOCK

The Daddy Clock

Judy Markey

Bantam Books

New York   Toronto   London   Sydney   Auckland

This edition contains the complete text of the original
hardcover edition.
NOT ONE WORD HAS BEEN OMITTED.

THE DADDY CLOCK
A Bantam Book

PUBLISHING HISTORY
Bantam hardcover edition published January 1998
Bantam paperback edition / November 1998

Library of Congress Catalog Card Number: 97-37372

ISBN 0-553-57743-3

Published simultaneously in the United States and Canada

Bantam Books are published by Bantam Books, a division of Bantam
Doubleday Dell Publishing Group, Inc. Its trademark, consisting of the
words "Bantam Books" and the portrayal of a rooster, is Registered in U.S.
Patent and Trademark Office and in other countries. Marca Registrada.
Bantam Books, 1540 Broadway, New York, New York 10036.

PRINTED IN THE UNITED STATES OF AMERICA
OPM   10 9 8 7 6 5 4 3 2 1

To Tom, my beloved co-conspirator in life

The Daddy Clock

Charlie

I'm telling you, they were amazing tits.

And there I was, ravenously devouring them at the precise moment my mother showed up.

Granted, they were only fantasy tits, attached to the fantasy female starring in my dream. But when Sophie started shaking my shoulder and whispered, "Chuckie. Papa wants to see us now," I was one unhappy guy about leaving them.

So okay. It is not good form to have dirty dreams in the intensive care waiting room when your father might be dying. The public hard-on potential alone should be enough to deter a guy. However, given the current status of my sex life, that dream could arguably be the high-light of my fall season.

Daylight had started to creep through the blinds of the waiting room. The tan vinyl couches and pallid green walls had the look of a bad hangover. There was a little too much of yesterday left in it. Yesterday's newspapers, yesterday's coffee cups, and yesterday's occupants, all in assorted modes of pacing or sleeping or staring dourly at the TV.

"Chuckie," my mother nudged, "come ON!"

Christ, I hate being Chuckied. I am forty-four years old, and my name is Charlie. Charlie Feldman. No one gets away with Chuckie-ing me anymore. No one but the fabulous Sophie. Who, like all mothers, acknowledges only under duress that I am an adult. Her preferred vision of me still involves little brown corduroys and cowboy suspenders.

Of course even the most cursory reality check should alert our Sophie to other signs of my being full-grown. Such as the fact that I am six feet tall (okay, five-eleven), weigh one hundred eighty pounds, and am beginning to gray in a way that I don't exactly pull off as distinguished. Further proof that I am a certifiable adult is the fact that I have spent nearly twenty years covering sports for the *Chicago Sun-Times*. Unfortunately the assholes masquerading as editors have refused to give me the column that I, like all sportswriters, feel I deserve. Even so, I have won some national writing awards, and my byline is not unknown.

Except maybe to Sophie. Who does know it. But doesn't read it a lot. Sophie has a hard time getting into sports. Abe, on the other hand, the one currently on the respirator and who maybe has seen my byline for the last time, reads every single word. Twice. Maybe three times. The old man can hardly get enough of my dazzling prose. Part of it is that my younger brother Roger is a podiatrist. There is not much conversational follow-up when you tell people your son is a podiatrist. But when you tell them your son is a sportswriter, you can have a conversation for days.

Abe and Sophie have been married forty-seven years. Most of that time was spent behind the counters at Feldman's Children's Shop, formerly of Rogers Park, subsequently of Skokie, currently extinct. Since then, they have happily divided their time between Florida winters and Chicago summers, causing Abe to marvel, "Who ever thought I'd be living year round in white shoes?"

However, right now Abe was the only person in the room without white shoes. He was surrounded by three nurses on monitoring duty when Sophie and I pushed open the door. It was six-thirty A.M. on Sunday, and Sophie and I had been at the hospital since four the afternoon before. Roger and his wife Elaine had left at ten last night to go home to their three kids.

I had no one to go home to, and nothing to do. At least if I spent Saturday night at the hospital, I could do nothing in the company of a few other people. There was the usual waiting-room problem of who controlled the TV, but fortunately the Cubs were on, so everybody seemed willing to settle in and suffer together. Nothing like having a relative in intensive care to put another crappy Cubs season into perspective.

I hadn't seen the old man since four in the morning, and wished like hell that waxy, gray look he had would go away. "Dad. Hey, Dad," I whispered from the foot of the bed, "you're looking great. How ya doin'?"

Abe looked like he was trying to be doing good. It wasn't that easy. I'm sure all he wanted was for it to be the way it was. The way it was Friday before he collapsed with a massive heart attack. Or the way it was three years ago when he and Sophie went to Roger's kid's bar mitzvah. Or the way it was thirty years ago when he and Roger and I would sneak away from the store, take the El down to Wrigley Field, and play hooky for the day. I bet Abe didn't care which "way it was" he went back to, just so it would be anytime but now. Now he must be scared shitless. I was.

There hasn't ever been a whole lot of talk in the Feldman household about dying. But now, if we got through this part without the dying really happening, we would never be able *not* to think about it again. We all knew that.

"Abe-y," whispered Sophie, "it's Chuckie."

"Mom, he knows. Right, Dad? She just can't believe that she finally has you where she's always wanted. With all those tubes down your throat so you can't tell any of those lousy jokes."

Abe almost smiled. But it was more than he could handle. His eyes closed immediately. Sophie and I spent the rest of our allotted five-minute visit standing in a conversation-less holding pattern. And hoping the next time we'd be allowed in, we'd get a little more of Abe back.

As the morning progressed, the hospital began to take on more of a full Sunday look. Pre-church and post-church families with straight-from-the-supermarket cellophaned carnations started streaming in. This group to see their dying father, that group to see their dying grandmother . . . The thing I noticed most was that they all arrived in groups. Sunday is always a big group day. When you're alone, you feel Sundays in a tough way. Tougher even than Saturday nights. At least Saturday nights are dark. You can hide. Or you can hang out with a buddy. Granted, in my case, I'm usually hanging out with a bunch of guys in face masks at some hockey rink. Or I have for the last three years. That's when they took me off baseball, and I started covering the Blackhawks. But even during the summer when I'm off, Sunday is the day that you notice your oneness the most. Everybody shows up in some version of a unit. Nuclear families, extended families, divorced dads with their kids, divorced moms with their kids, divorced dads with their kids and girlfriends, divorced moms with their kids and boyfriends, straight couples with no kids, gay couples with no kids, and kid couples who you hope like hell are smart enough not to have kids. Just about every kind of demographic mutation always seems to show up full-force on Sundays.

Except singles. Single guys, anyway. Single women get together on Sundays. But not us guys. Not guys my age. No way am I going to call up a guy and say, "Let's get some brunch and watch the game at the bar." For Chrissakes, I'm forty-four. My friends aren't available for games. My friends are married. Or they are divorced. But on Sunday they all have some version of family or fatherhood to deal with.

Like Bobby. Bobby Tuckerman was my best friend all the way through Senn High School. Then after college, when I came home from Michigan and he came home from Madison, we shared an apartment for two years. Bobby was in dental school, and I worked nights at City News Bureau, so we figured out how to squeeze our alternate sleep schedules into a cheap one-bedroom place on Belmont. Until we hit a triple snag. I got switched to the day shift, Bobby fell in love with Sherry Lowenberg, and Sherry wanted to move in. The solution was real clear. So long, Charlie. That was okay with me. I wasn't crazy about Sherry. She was a world-class complainer. So I moved out, Sherry moved in, they got married, and now they were the proud owners and operators of Jennifer, Joshua, and Jason Tuckerman, ages seventeen, fourteen, and eight, respectively.

I started out pretty involved with their kids, in an Uncle Charlie way. But once Bobby and the family went suburban out there in Deerfield, I've been less inclined to show up in their lives. Bobby and I still talk on the phone regularly, but the one-on-ones with each other have definitely dwindled. Part of this has to do with the half-hour drive between us and my being out of town so much. But it's also his wife-driven social schedule, the kids' gymnastics tournaments, and soccer coaching. It isn't that I begrudge Bobby any of this, but it does make it tough to relate. Tough to connect to this parenthood club that he and most everybody else seems to belong to. But me.

Christ. I hate how that sounds. I hate guys who gripe. It makes me seem like some mope vying for a spot in the Lonely Guy Hall of Fame. But waiting rooms do not bring out the best in a person. They make a person think all sorts of who-is-going-to-be-sitting-in-the-waiting-room-for-me thoughts. It's a little tough not to notice that you are careening toward fifty and seem to be the only son in the room who hasn't had the opportunity to be a fine father too.

I looked over at Consuela and Romero Gomez. They had been in the waiting room since midnight when their ten-year-old boy was brought in after a car accident. It looked like he was going to be okay, but it had been touch-and-go all night. I wondered what it was like to feel the naked, raw terror I had seen on their faces for the last eleven hours. Jesus, I envied them their connection to something more important than themselves. I wondered what it felt like to be welded to another person by the intensity of your feeling toward a third person.

Watching the Gomezes clinging fiercely to each other made me feel as if I were at a drive-in movie all by myself. How hard was it to fall in love with a person, make a kid with that person, stay in love with that person, have fights with that person, raise your mutual kid with that person? How hard was it to stop living in chronic float?

God, that was precisely how I'd felt the last time I'd been in a hospital waiting room. Even though then I was sitting there with my arms around Janice. That was five years ago, and Janice and I had been together about three years by then. Janice was a terrific woman, but one of the big attractions had definitely been Timothy, her seven-year-old son. When things would get scratchy between Janice and me, I had no problem envisioning a life without her. But without Timothy? I always knew that would involve a lot more bleeding. Man, I loved that kid. And the great thing was that it had been mutual. Which wasn't any big victory. Timothy's dad was a real asshole.

But at least he was a long-distance asshole. He had moved to Milwaukee after the divorce and married the woman he'd been fooling around with. And when he showed up in the waiting room after Timothy's emergency appendectomy, Janice and I were dumbfounded.

I remember she bolted from the couch, saying, "Ben! You didn't say you were coming down! What are you doing here?"

"How's he doing?" the guy asked, completely disregarding both me and her question.

"Okay I guess. He's still in recovery. They said he'd be up soon."

"When?"

"Soon," snapped Janice, clearly unnerved at the sight of her bald ex-husband, and clearly incapable of doing any sort of introductions.

Since I had no intention of evaporating, I stood up and stuck out my hand to him and said, "Charlie Feldman."

"Yeah, I know," he said, throwing an undefinable glance at her. "I used to read your stuff. Still covering the Sox? Fisk is having a great season, huh?"

Jesus. Even I knew you had to be a real putz to talk ball while your kid was under some surgeon's knife.

"Mrs. Lindsay?" said the doc, coming through the door. "Timothy is just fine." And then since I'd been the one in there with Janice for the past six hours, he nodded to me and added, "You and your husband can go in and see him now."

There wasn't even time for Janice to say, "This isn't my husband." The ex-husband did it for her.

"Oh," said the doctor. "Well, yes. I'm sorry. So then you are Timothy's father?"

"For seven years," said the guy who hadn't shown up much during the last five.

"Well then, you two can go in now," said the doctor.

And there I stood. Superfluous. Uncategorized. And ripped apart that you could love a kid for half his life, but you weren't shit in a waiting room.

And here I was five years later back in the waiting room and no closer to being in my permanent life than before. I was still waiting for it to happen. The wife, kids, two-car garage life. Not that I had been doing much to make it happen these past five years. Janice and I had lasted another two years before she went to her high school reunion and hooked up with the old boyfriend. Six weeks later she and Timothy moved to L.A. It was brutal. I was really fucked-up for a while. And then with hockey keeping me on the road nine months of the year . . .

Dammit. I am not going to blame it all on the job. This job was always the dream. To get paid to go to ball games? It's the greatest fucking job a person can have. I love sports. I love the commitment and the intensity of the athletes. And at some naive level, this job has always made me feel that I've had it better than most. For twenty years I have been immersed in a world that I find consistently compelling. Not everyone can say that. But

I have paid a price. Twenty years on the road catches up with you. It sure as hell makes it even more complicated than it already is to hook up with a woman. Unless you're talking about a pretty low-maintenance type. And women you pick up in saloons after you've filed your stories might be fine for some guys, but it isn't the solution to the emptiness gnawing at me.

So there I sat. In the waiting room, in the middle of everyone else's extended family. And I decided. Enough. I had to get ahold of my life. I had to stop wishing for something I wasn't willing to take any risks to try to get. I wanted some roots. I wanted some connection.

I wanted a kid. A girl, a boy, a baby. Now.

Of course, even if I started right that minute, even if I walked out of the hospital, fell drop-dead in love with a woman, and we made a baby right there in the parking lot, I'd still be somewhere around sixty-four when the kid graduated from high school.

Christ, it was depressing to do those "even-if" mathematics. But it was hard to stop doing them. It was hard not to wonder where your life was going when you were on the road with guys who were your age, but had kids going to college. Or when you were on the receiving end of Christmas cards with snapshots of kids going from babies to braces in what seemed to be three years. Well, those things had happened to me, and they had me adding and subtracting like crazy.

But not multiplying.

Truth was, I wanted a kid bad. Nobody ever talks

about the guy biological clock, but it was ticking loud and clear in me. It had been for years. And I did not have a lot of time left. Not at forty-four. Nor did I have a lot of options.

Because unlike a woman, who could go to a sperm bank, select the father of choice, and then ride off into the sunset of single motherhood, the system doesn't work that way for us guys. A man who wants a baby can't purchase an egg. It's more complicated. Eggs come from wombs, and wombs are attached to women. And women don't like to give up babies. That's one of the great things about women. So, at some level anyway, a man who wants a baby is going to be very involved with his co-babymaker. And as long as you're involved, it might as well be with someone you like. Love even. Guys don't want to just have a baby. Even when we want one as bad as I do. We want a package deal. We want the full catastrophe, not parenthood without a partner. That would scare the shit out of me. Nope, no way was I about to walk into this baby-having business alone. But I most definitely wanted to walk into it. I was ready. I was sure. And my daddy clock was ticking big-time.

Now, I am not a religious man. But I'll tell you one thing. Sitting in that waiting room, right down the hall from where my old man might be dying, I found myself cutting a deal with God. "Okay," I said, "if You let Abe live, I will do my level best to get my life in order. I will stop procrastinating. I will get off my ass. I promise. I know I've let a lot slip by. But I know I can still put together a life here. Honest, God, I'll do all the things I haven't done in years. If You let Abe live, I'll get an answering machine that works every time. I'll learn to like sushi. I swear it, God, I will even date . . ."

And then I had to laugh. What the hell was in the deal for God?

Lacy

THE NEXT DAY

Oh, swell. I mean, I really do my best to keep it together, it was only 7:45 on a Monday morning and I'd already nearly lost my cool.

I mean, I had purposely come in to the office early to get organized, and do you think I could find one single thing? Over the weekend, the paper's features and sports sections had moved down to the third floor so our new computers could be put in upstairs, and nothing—not even my "Lacy Gazzar" official desk nameplate—was where it was supposed to be. Shit.

The place was a wreck. All the desks were piled high with boxes and my desk was crammed into a corner, though if I sat on six phone books and craned my neck, I could grab a teensy view of Lake Michigan.

"God," I mumbled, crawling under the desk to plug

in my lamp, "this is a hell of a price to pay for getting some modern technology into this paper."

"I'm sorry? What did you say?" asked this sports guy whose desk was jammed up against mine in our new, unimproved, editorial reconfiguration. Oh, Christ, I knew I was supposed to know him. After all I'd been at the *Sun-Times* eleven whole years, but for the life of me I could not remember his name. It was something like Harry, or Herbie, or Charlie—one of those old guy names that had gotten stuck on a regular age guy. I'd kind of been surprised by that when I first saw him at a Christmas party a few years back, because from his by-line I'd just assumed he was some geezer with ear hair instead of a lean, kind of cute guy in jeans and a camel blazer.

He was wearing the same sort of blazer today. "Sorry," I said, "I'm just bitching to myself. This is just so frustrating. I don't even want to think what it's going to be like today with the phones. Have you tried yours yet?"

"Only to call out," the guy said.

He had sandy graying hair, sort of like Harrison Ford, but I couldn't quite nail the color of his eyes. Charlie, that was his name. Charlie Fineman? Fleckman? Feldman. That was it, Charlie Feldman. He wasn't much further into the unpacking than I seemed to be.

"If you want, we can test the phone," he said, "what's your extension?"

"Great. Five-four-three-three."

He punched it in, and miracle of miracles, my phone

rang. I picked it up and like a robot I chimed, "Advice Ladies . . ."

He smiled at me. He had excellent teeth, and a dimple too.

"Oh. So you're the one that runs that 'Advice Ladies' office."

"Yeah. But 'runs' isn't exactly the verb—I mean, it's not the verb I'm paid for."

"What verb are you paid for?"

"*Assist*, of course. I'm the proverbial editorial *assistant*."

I said that somewhat more snottily than I actually felt. I mean Adrienne and Ruthie, the two women I work for, aren't *that* horrible. They're horrible to each other, but then, they *hate* each other—almost as much as they hate the readers that write to them for advice. But they are never horrible to me. And even though they are the ones getting paid all the bucks for giving advice, they let me do some of the letter writing sometimes. The deal is, though, that I never publicly cop to it. Partly because of the reputation thing—their advice column is syndicated to sixty-seven papers—and partly because they think I am awfully young to be explaining to people how to live their lives. And chronologically that is true, since I am only thirty-five. But neither of them has ever even had kids, so in some ways I know a whole lot more about life, considering all the years I've spent in the Mom biz.

And Mom biz was what I needed to take care of now that I knew the phones worked. "Hey, thanks for testing the phone. Now I can at least call my kid and wake her up for school."

"Your kid?"

He said it weird, like I'd just said "now I can call my gorilla," I don't know. Anyway, Jessica answered after only two rings. "Hi, babe, just checking to make sure you saw the note about getting the gas."

"I did. Thanks for the fresh o.j. You want ten dollars of unleaded?"

"No, babe, get regular this time. We only have to put in the fancy kind every other time."

"Okay. I'll probably do it after school."

"Thanks, hon. You're the best. I love you."

"Love you too. Bye."

"Bye."

The Charlie guy was kind of staring at me. "Can I ask you something?" he said.

"Sure." I pushed back my hair. My hair is a big problem. It's all black and curly and wild, and the combs Dolores—that's my mom—had brought over yesterday were not doing the job. They were cute though, with the ceramic pizzas on them and all. Anyway, I scooped my hair back—playing with it is a big habit of mine—and said, "Ask away. I'm Lacy Gazzar. Rhymes with 'bizarre.' "

I never understand why people don't smile at that. It's not like I'm sensitive about having a weird name or anything. I kind of like it. But he had that usual blank did-she-really-just-say-that look on his face. Then he said, "Charlie Feldman."

"Yeah, I know. You're a sports guy—baseball—right?"

"Not anymore. Hockey. The Hawks. You ever read our sports section?"

"Not much. Some Bulls stuff—I love the Bulls—but no, mostly I don't read sports. Don't take it personally or anything. Do you read our advice section?"

"Nope. But don't take it personally. I'm too busy reading everybody else's sports sections. At least the hockey guys anyway."

"What do you do the rest of the year?"

"What rest of the year?"

"When it's not winter."

He looked at me like I'd said the "gorilla" thing again. "That's the big misconception. Hockey is not exactly a winter sport. I'm writing preseason stuff right now. The regular season starts in three weeks, on October seventh. Then, depending on the play-offs, we go all the way through June. I have exactly three months a year when I am not up to my ass in hockey."

"Oh."

I wasn't sure what to say next. I knew hockey was the sport that had a lot of Canadians with no front teeth in it, but I didn't have any Canadian-with-no-front-teeth questions.

He didn't mind though, he had a question for me instead.

"Here's what I want to ask you. I know it's personal, so if you don't want to answer, it's okay."

Just then someone called, "Hey, Charlie," from across the room. Other sports types were drifting in to start dealing with the disruptiveness of being jumbled in with us features department people. There was this sort of first day of school feeling everywhere, because we were all going to have to start living in this new scrunched-together classroom. He waved to the guy, and then turned back to me.

"So what did you want to ask?"

"Well, I know this sounds stupid, but you were just talking to your kid, right?"

"Yeah, my daughter Jessica—there's a picture of her somewhere here in this mess," I said, opening my drawers to unearth it, but unable to come up with anything. "Why?"

"Well, it's just that it sounded like she was pretty old. Like she could drive or something."

"She can. She's eighteen."

"Eighteen?"

God, I always have such mixed feelings about this part—the part where people always tell me that I look too young to have an eighteen-year-old daughter. I do. I was. And that's what I told Charlie. "Yeah, I'm thirty-five now, but I was seventeen when I had her. I was one of those babies having babies that we always do stories on, only I thought I was pretty grown-up, because I got the guy to marry me."

"Are you still married?"

Apparently he was not the kind of guy who noticed things like rings. "Nope. Tony walked out when Jessica was twenty months old. Are you married?"

"I was once. For about two years in the late seventies. She left me. For a proctologist."

Yikes, that sounded like the opening line to a bad

stand-up routine. But the guy wasn't kidding. "Uh, well, do you have kids?"

His phone rang just as he was saying, "Nope, no kids," and then I heard him say, "Really? He's out of the woods? God, that's great, Mom. Just great."

He talked a few minutes longer but by the time he hung up, his whole face had changed. It was almost jubilant.

"Damn, that is great," he said to no one in particular—except I was the most convenient human around. And then he just erupted with personal info. He told me all about his dad's heart attack, and how he didn't even realize how scared he'd been until this moment, and about how yesterday he had cut this deal with God—not that he was religious or anything—saying that now he would really jump-start his life . . .

And then he stopped, looked at me funny, and said, "Lacy? You really give advice to people?"

"Well, yeah, sort of. But you can't go around saying that—it could cause me some major aggravation with my bosses."

"Listen," he said, leaning forward so I could finally see that his eyes were blue, a real smoky blue, "I don't know you at all. But maybe you're a good person for me to talk to about something."

"About what?"

"About some pretty important stuff, at least for me. Listen. I'm not hitting on you or anything. I don't do that with people in the office. And I am so out of practice that even if I did do it, you'd know it, because I do such a crappy job of it. But would you have lunch with me tomorrow? I'm going to the hospital today, but tomorrow could you go to lunch around one?"

Now I thought it was pretty weird that this sports dude I didn't even know forty minutes ago was asking me to lunch. I mean if I had been flirting with him, that would be one thing, but I had been strictly business. But he seemed so urgent or something. So I said, "Well, sure. Yeah. Are you okay?"

"Why? Doesn't anyone ever take you to lunch?"

"What kind of remark is that? Sure they do. I asked because you sound so intense."

"Well, I feel intense. I'm at this kind of significant moment in my life. And I know I don't know you, but you seem like a person who cuts through the crap. Who's practical. I just think you might be good to talk to."

"Actually I can be great to talk to—so yeah, lunch is fine. But you've made me kind of curious. I hate not knowing what I'm walking into—give me a hint."

"What do you mean?"

"Well, I just mean if you have a problem you want to talk about, I'd like to have a preview, you know, at least the headline. I mean maybe I'm not the right person for your particular problem, and you'd be out six, seven bucks for lunch. Because if it's about substance abuse or something, I'm not all that sympathetic with these twelve-step programs. I think they just take one addiction and substitute another, and that everyone sees himself as this colossal victim, and that . . ."

"It's not about substance abuse. It's something else."

"What else?"

"I want a baby."

"A baby? How old are you?"

"Forty-four."

"You want to start at your age with a baby?"

"Well, actually, I'd rather start at your age with a baby. But I don't seem to have that choice. I'm stuck with my age. Is one o'clock tomorrow still okay?"

I told him straight, "Better make it twelve-thirty. You want a baby at forty-four? It sounds like there's a lot you don't know about babies."

It took me four more hours to get my damn desk set up.

Charlie

THE NEXT DAY

Luigi's front room was packed and blaring. It was the kind of place I always wound up in. Short on decor. Long on ambience. The whole joint felt warm and red. Old red. Old red carpet, old red bar stools, and those old red-and-white oilcloths over the tables. The place was beat-up and real. And in the twenty years I'd been going there, Angie, who was responsible for the best manicotti this side of Naples, had never failed to find me a table.

"*Carlo-mio*," she said, hugging me as soon as we walked in, "*come stai?*"

"*Bene, Angie, bene. Tu? E come vanno i bambini?*"

Lacy looked a little freaked. "You're an Italian Jew?" she asked.

"No. I'm a Jewish manicotti addict. But don't tell my mother."

She laughed. She looked different today. Less

hassled. Less ready to pounce if a person said the wrong thing. Not that I'd said the wrong thing. Not yet, anyway. But Lacy struck me as a pretty reactive type. "Let's not get started on mothers—not if yours is Jewish and mine is Italian."

"I like my mother," I told her. "But she could win the Winter Olympics of worrying."

"Yeah? How do you figure it's a winter sport?"

"More to worry about."

Angie returned from table scouting and directed us to a corner booth in the back room. "It's better back here. Quieter," I said. The place was still pretty noisy for quieter, but you couldn't do much about that. The El ran overhead, and that kicked up the decibel level if you wanted to be heard. Lacy nestled back into the leatherette booth. The sun angling through the window bounced off the glossy blue-black of her hair. Today she had pulled it all up in a ponytail. She looked about nineteen. Great. Just great. I'm about to solicit advice on putting my life together from a person who looks like she cannot legally get a beer. Right.

Not that there was anything terrible about sitting across a table from this woman. She moved like a swimmer—great body, everything smoothly extended and strong. Her legs were long and she must have known they were terrific, because she hadn't attempted to put much skirt on over them. I know you're supposed to notice the eyes first, but when a woman puts a pair of legs like that in front of you, the protocol is tough to follow. Lacy was pretty too. Overdone, but pretty. Green eyes, creamy skin, and a wide, disarming smile. I couldn't tell about her breasts. She had on some sort of slinky maroon undershirt or something showing beneath her suit jacket. I could never figure that part out. You know, how simultaneously with the women's movement, it got to be okay to let your underwear peek through. Not that I minded. I just didn't get it.

I was also at a loss how to begin our conversation. I have never been a great one for opening lines. But she wasn't so hot at it either. "So?" she said, unfolding her napkin.

"Uh . . . Do you want a drink or something?"

"Nope. Just the house salad and some iced tea. How about you?"

"The manicotti. And a beer."

And then there was thunderous silence.

"So this is pretty odd, huh? My asking you to lunch and all."

"A little, I don't know. I guess it's odd—but nice."

"Yeah. Well."

"Charlie? Maybe you should just tell me about it. You know like you started to do yesterday," she said, rearranging her forks and spoons in some order that worked better for her. "I don't want to rush you, but I do have to make it back to the office in an hour."

"Well," I started, "this is a little hard to just dive into, but as I said yesterday, it's been bothering me a lot that I'm a guy without kids. I'm sure some of this was brought on by my dad's heart attack, but it isn't as if I haven't had these feelings a real long time."

"Like how long?"

"I don't know. A long time. I think you operate on the

assumption that you are always going to . . . you know, marry, make babies, and be a family. Even if you don't, by the time you are thirty or thirty-five or even forty, you still think that you are going to do it. But once you're veering toward forty-five, you're damned surprised that you haven't. And you begin wondering if maybe you won't. It makes you sad and frankly, it scares the shit out of you."

I didn't do this kind of thing much. But the feelings really were so damn close to the surface, I barely had any skin on over them.

"I'm not even sure that I can articulate this. But it's a yearning. This intense feeling in my gut. That I have all this really great stuff, like love, and knowledge, and insights that I'm dying to give to someone. Someone I can indulge, and hang out with, and douse with the very best parts of me."

I stopped. Jesus. Where did all that come from? Two beepers went off at the next table. Christ, the nineties sucked sometimes.

"God," said Lacy, ignoring the beeper-creeps, and never looking away from me, "I've never heard any guy talk about this, which doesn't mean you're the only guy to feel this way—I'm sure you're not—it's just that . . ."

"Listen, I *know* other guys must feel like I do. But the thing is, we never do talk about it. I've been best friends with a guy since high school and I'm still sitting here talking to *you* about it. Not him. It's a hard thing to acknowledge. But you read all this shit in magazines about women and their biological clocks, and I'm telling you, guys have this terrible sense of time ticking too. I'm surprised there hasn't been an *Oprah* show on it."

"Maybe there has been."

"If there had been, my mother would have taped it for me."

"Why? Have you talked to your mother about this?"

"I don't have to. She has her own world-class grandma clock ticking. Despite the fact that my brother has three kids."

I'd thought a lot about Sophie too in the past few days. About how for all her occasionally nudgy mom moments, she really has never once laid any "can't you find a nice girl and settle down" shit on me. And I have never given her credit for that.

"Do you think that's part of it?" Lacy asked. "Making your parents happy?" She pulled a bread stick from the basket and then pushed it toward me.

"No not really. And it's not some propagation imperative of the family name theory either. This is more of an inside-me thing. I keep getting zapped with these images."

"What kind of images?"

Jesus, this was hard to talk about. Particularly to someone who was so young. And so odd. What was with the long fingernails with the rhinestones on the tips? And that dark pink stuff around her eyes? Wasn't eye shadow supposed to be blue or something?

"Charlie? What kind of images?"

"Oh, sorry. I just have these images I walk around with. Visual hits of fatherhood that come and go and leave my stomach all wrung out. They're not exactly conventional ones. I'm not talking about some slow-motion scene from *The Natural* where I am teaching my six-year-old to pitch."

"What's the matter with that?"

"Nothing. It's just so fucking predictable. It's such a dad/son cliché. I don't know what the parallel one might be for a mother, you know some moment where you are teaching your daughter this core female skill? I'm not saying girls can't throw balls, but some mom/daughter moment that a guy can't horn in on. Do they have that for women?"

A slow smile crept across Lacy's face. "Sure. Shaving your legs."

"Huh?"

"I don't know if that's exactly considered a Hallmark card moment for the rest of America," she said, leaning toward me, "but one of my absolute favorite memories is the night I showed Jessica how to shave her legs. She was so solemn about it—maybe she was eleven—and we had this big ceremony with bubble bath and shaving cream. Only we got very stupid and wound up having this huge shaving cream fight, which made me go all weepy because I realized that as much as she was struggling to be a grown-up, she still was a kid, and I was too, sort of, and that . . . Oh, shit. I'm sorry. You probably don't need someone doing great moments in parenthood with you right now."

"Hey, it's okay. I asked you. I don't resent you for having a kid. It's a major part of your life," I said, signaling the waiter to take our orders. I was ready for a beer.

"Yeah. I know. More than half of my life has been

spent being a mom. Not many thirty-five-year-olds have that as a personal statistic. It's going to be weird when she goes next year."

"Where's she going?"

"College. She's a senior."

A senior. Christ, it was all so out-of-sync. This woman was a parenting vet, and I wasn't even a goddamn rookie. She had done her life in fast forward, and I had done mine in slo-mo.

"Does she know where she wants to go?"

"Well, it depends on who offers her money. "

"Is she smart?"

"Pretty smart—I mean she's a solid B student—but the scholarship we're hoping for is for softball. Jessica is an incredible pitcher. She was co-captain of the team last year, and will be again. Her coaches think she could get a full scholarship."

"She's that good? What's her record?"

"Last year it was eight and two."

"No shit? That's impressive. Where's she hoping to go?"

"Well, her first choice is North Carolina. After that, maybe Vanderbilt. Maybe Northwestern—though she's not crazy about the idea of being only twenty El stops away."

"So then what happens to you?"

"Me? I guess I better order," she said as the waiter showed up. He brought us the Moretti and iced tea while she continued. "Well, I'm going to start college too. Actually Jessica and I took our SATs together. She killed me in math, but I beat her in English. I have a fabulous vocabulary."

"You took those tests again?"

"Not 'again.' I didn't get my GED until Jessica was about four. I loved school . . . I just couldn't afford to go back—no time and no money."

"And now?"

"Now? Well, I'll have both. Once Jessica leaves I'll have plenty of time in the evenings. And I'll have some money too, if a scholarship comes through for her."

"Where are you going?"

"I don't know yet. DePaul. Loyola. It depends. I want to study psychology. The advice gig sort of whets your appetite for that."

I was about to ask her about her job when she said, "Charlie, did you ask me to lunch to get my life story, or did we just get sidetracked?"

"Sidetracked," I said, thinking about how you work alongside people for years and never even consider how many stories and emotions are packed into their lives. To look at the woman, all five-five and I'd guess one hundred fifteen pounds of her, you would have no idea about SATs, and eighteen-year-old children, and softball scholarships. It was fucking amazing.

Lacy started back on me as the food arrived. "So, you were telling me about these images you have, these dad moments."

"Jesus, I don't know, I feel real stupid now."

"No, really, I'm interested."

"Well, there are lots of them. I'm not sure. But one is the icebox."

"Icebox?"

"Refrigerator. Sorry. Anyway, whenever I'm in my kitchen I always feel that it's so stripped. It's like a motel kitchen. When I go to other people's houses, there are drawings and finger paintings and soccer schedules stuck all over the icebox. I hate that my icebox is naked."

"Yeah. I guess I've never thought about that. Mine is pretty jammed with stuff from Jess's life. Has it always been empty?"

"Once there was a drawing from my nephew. He must have been about five. On top it said, 'our family' and there were all these stick figures in a line. He was in the middle with my brother and his wife on either side, then there was his sister and brother, one set of grand-parents on one side, the other set on the other, the dog, the gerbils, the goldfish, and then someone must have said, 'What about your Uncle Charlie?' because there just at the edge I was stuck on. Right after the two gold-fish."

"Jeez. How did that make you feel?"

"Glad they didn't have three goldfish."

Lacy laughed. "How could you bear to even leave it up?"

"I don't know. He gave it to me. And anyway, the woman I had been going with a few years before had given me this broccoli magnet so I could finally use it to hold up the drawing."

"Is it still there?" she asked, sopping up the extra olive oil in her salad with some of Angie's herb bread.

"Nope. Everything's gone now. Even the magnet. It's a completely naked icebox. I know that's probably a stupid image to symbolize the emptiness in me, but it does." When Lacy didn't say anything, I added, "Plus, it's not just the kid part. It's also this guilty feeling that I just didn't get my life organized in time to have the relationships I wanted. And now that I want to get organized, it feels like there aren't that many relationships to be had."

"Do you have an image for that too?"

"Yeah, I do. My brother and I used to call it making a kid sandwich. I wonder a lot what it would be like to lie there with a kid in between me and some woman. A wife. You know, just a kid in pajamas sound asleep between us, because maybe he or she had a nightmare, or something."

"Charlie, can I say something? I mean relationships are nice, but have you ever thought about just an open-faced sandwich?"

"What do you mean?" I asked, setting down the fork that still hadn't made much of a dent in the manicotti.

"Well, I'm just saying, and I'm sure this has a lot to do with being a single mother and all, but you don't necessarily have to have a wife if you want to be a father—a good father. You could do this alone."

"Are you crazy," I said, nearly choking on my beer. "I have a friend, my college roommate from Columbus who got divorced. Like you. Only *he* got the kid, not the wife. And it was not only hard. There were years when it was almost *impossible* for him. Once he was even hospitalized with an ulcer. No way do I want to do this alone. I mean no offense, I'm sure you're a great mom, but frankly the prospect of being a parent all alone scares the

shit out of me. Too much to handle. Jesus, I can't believe you're even suggesting it. I mean I know you've
done it, but face it, it wasn't by choice."

She flashed me a look. "No, it wasn't. But it also
hasn't been terrible. The money thing is terrible, especially when the father of your kid is an incredible dick
about money, but sometimes I wonder if it hasn't been
simpler for Jess and me there just being the two of us."

"Single parenting is a lot easier for women. If that
makes me some male chauvinist pig, then sorry. I'm sure
there are plenty of guys who make great single dads, but
I don't see myself as one of them. Christ, I'm on the
fucking road most of the year. No way could I do it."

"So maybe what you really want is a baby and someone to stay home with it. Maybe you don't want a family?"

"Where do you get off saying that?" I looked at her
hard.

She looked back equally hard. "I'm just saying that
you are forty-four years old. And for whatever reason,
you haven't hooked up on a permanent basis with any
woman yet, except for the one who wound up with the
proctologist. So maybe you aren't that good at adapting
to someone else. It's an observation, not a judgment. It's
not such a terrible thing, either. I don't know if I could
do it anymore, after being on my own for so long."

"Christ, that is so typical."

"What's typical?"

"Your response to my being a forty-four-year-old single guy."

"What do you mean?"

"I mean when people hear that, they assume there is something really fucked-up about you. That you have some secret deviant behavior. Like maybe you microwave gerbils. Or have sex with green leafy vegetables."

"I didn't say any of that."

"Yeah, but you were wondering what was *wrong* with me. Admit it."

"I was thinking that you were probably set in your ways, that's all."

"Well, maybe I am. But I'm not rigid!" I must have been yelling because the beeper table guys had suddenly turned to listen. Lacy shot them a look—as if they were the ones with the shit manners.

"Listen," she said, sliding her napkin off her lap and folding it into little squares, "maybe this wasn't a good idea after all. You know, getting into all this. I understand where you are coming from. I mean I'm sure that people *do* make assumptions about you when you're forty-four and single. I guess in some way I did—it's hard not to."

"I'm telling you, when you're my age, you are less suspect if you've been divorced four times and left a string of kids across America than if you're like me. Battling all these bullshit assumptions is one of the reasons I haven't dated much of late."

"What's 'of late'?"

"Since the second half of the nineties."

She smiled. She even picked up my Moretti and took a gulp. "Okay, so what can we do here?"

"I don't know. Maybe you've done all you can do by just listening."

"No, Charlie, come on. Let's get you on your way to something you want. I mean if you really do want it."

"I do. I just don't know where to start."

"Well, start with some women you think would be interesting."

"That's the whole point. There isn't anybody I know. And the people I know, know women I don't want to know. Believe me, I've been fixed up with them."

"Ohhhhhhhkay. Then let's move to Plan B. Advertise."

"Are you nuts? I've never run a personals ad in my life. You've got to be desperate to do that. And I'm not desperate. I'm frustrated. I'm confused. Shit. I'm about to go on the road for nine months. That would make a great ad. 'Single white male looking to start family. Gone all year, except summers. Available to stay home full-time with kid June through August.' Maybe I should marry a lifeguard."

"You could do worse, at least she'd know CPR."

"Yeah, and with a guy my age, she'd probably figure she'd need it."

"I'm serious. You can meet a lot of pretty cool people through the personals."

"Yeah, right. Have *you* ever placed an ad?"

"Once. It was actually pretty fun to get all those letters, or you can get voice-mail messages too. It's very civilized. I have a girlfriend who dated someone for two years that she met in the personals."

"Then what?"

"Then she stopped dating him."

"That's a success story?"

"Charlie, not everyone is looking for the full 'family values' package. For her, two years of Saturday night dates was fine. I really think if you advertise in the personals, women would respond."

"Women is a very large category. And anyway, I have some real demographic constraints."

"What do you mean?"

"I mean I don't even know what age bracket makes sense for me. There really isn't one. Women in their forties are biologically ineligible. Women in their twenties listen to bad music and want to go rollerblading. And women in their thirties are plain impossible."

"Thanks a lot."

"Well, either they are hell-bent on some career track and don't want to have a kid; or they are hell-bent on a career track and want to have a kid, but are determined to do it alone; or they are divorced and the mother of someone else's kids who are never going to like me much anyway, and then if I make a kid with their mom they would get jealous and hate the kid, and what kind of environment is that for my kid to grow up in anyway?"

"Is that all, Charlie?"

"Yeah, that's all."

"Good. Because I wouldn't want you to have a defeatist attitude, or anything."

"Is that what that sounds like?"

"Yeah. Maybe you should ask yourself, you know, if you really do want to go for it."

"I do, but advertising is such an admission of being socially inept."

"So who do you know that's so damn ept? Trust me,

Charlie, using the personals is not an admission of anything. Except that you're looking for something you
haven't found yet. You want a baby? You want a wife? If
you want it, it's out there. It's gotta be. Anyway, if you
decide you want to do an ad, let me know. I'd be happy
to help you write it."

Christ. The idea of writing advertisements, screening
the responses, and going on weeks of coffee dates knot-
ted up my guts. So I asked her straight out, "Lacy, you
don't know anyone do you? You know, who might, kind
of be looking for what I'm looking for?"

"Charlie, almost everyone in America is looking for
what you're looking for. You seem like a nice guy.
You're nice-looking. You've got a good shot at it, I'm
sure. Come on," she said, sweeping the bread crumbs
from her skirt and standing up, "I've got to get back."

I looked at my watch. It was almost two o'clock. Lacy
pushed back her chair, grabbed her purse from the floor,
and thanked me for the lunch. I put twenty bucks on the
table and followed her through the front room. She was
a nice size to follow. All her sizes were nice. Once we
got outside she turned to me, put her hands over those
big green eyes to shade them from the glare, and said,
"Really, I'm serious. If you want, I'll help you write it.
It's kind of fun."

We waited to cross the street until one of those ma-
niac bike messengers blitzed past. "Okay. Thanks. I feel
like a jerk. Like one of those guys who spills his guts to
someone on an airplane to Cleveland. This was just like
that."

"No, it wasn't. The food was much better."

Lacy

LATER THAT NIGHT

Damn! I had forgotten to take them off again. My stupid black sling backs were always getting caught in the AstroTurf on our porch, and they were ripping the staff to shreds.

Not that AstroTurf was exactly my fave when it came to a welcome home look, but Jessica and I were rental trash so we didn't have a big vote on these home improvement items. Actually, Jessica and I were semi-suspect from the minute we moved to Bridgeport five years ago. Not only were we the only Italians in a solid block of Irish, but we'd moved into a nuclear family neighborhood without the regulation nucleus—we forgot to arrive with an actual father, thereby providing Emerald Avenue with its very first single parent household.

Sure, the bungalow we moved into had belonged to

another single parent, but Brian O'Connell had become single via the approved program—Mrs. O'Connell died. By then the O'Connell kids were grown and out, but Brian stayed in the bungalow and would have been in it today, had he not met the extremely complicated and alluring Dolores DeVito—my mother.

Ma's courtship with Brian took forever, at least by her standards. She'd already had a couple of husbands, so there wasn't a whole lot of down time between father figures as I grew up. But she and Brian must have "dated"—her word, not mine—at least three years before she decided to marry him and move him into our trailer in "Hill and Valley Mobile Estates."

Yeah, I know the term "Mobile Estates" is pretty weird, but it wasn't nearly as weird as the idea of Brian's moving in. Not that Jessica and I didn't love him. But we three females had been in there a full four years with no resident guys. And Jessica, who was then a highly hormonal twelve-year-old, had a pretty hard time coping with the idea of a man in the midst of three generations of mousse. Oh, yeah, that was the other thing, Dolores is the proprietor of Coiffures de Dolores, and she was always into messing with Jessica's hair. Jessica was sure that once Brian invaded, our full pajama-party motif was going to disappear. But it was also time for the two of us to move out, anyway. Dolores had housed Jessica and me for a whole, mostly happy decade, and she was entitled to get her trailer back to whatever version of domestic bliss she was signing on for this time. So the neat thing was that Brian offered to let us rent his bungalow—for almost nothing.

Jess and I had never really lived in our very own detached two-bedroom, and scared as she was to move and change schools, no way were we about to turn down the offer. Dolores couldn't move there, she wanted to be by the shop, so we accepted Brian's offer. And on Labor Day five years ago, Jessica and I each slept in our own bedrooms for the very first time since there ever was a Jessica and me. It was a pretty cool moving day.

Not that there were a whole lot of welcome-to-the-neighborhood covered dishes brought over—word must have gotten out that we were something less than a regulation family. Of course, over the years most of the neighbors have managed to defrost a bit, though they still get a little undone seeing women mowing the lawn. Maybe they'd have liked it better if Brian had run the stupid AstroTurf all the way to the sidewalk.

Opening the front door, I could hear approximately eight thousand more decibels of Springsteen than was absolutely necessary—and I like Springsteen a lot. I yelled back to the music emanation point, "Grown-up alert. I'm ho-ome. Can you turn it down, hon?"

As usual, with the music that loud the yelling was futile. So I dropped my purse and blazer on the Naugahyde couch, and headed back to Jessica's room.

"Oh, hi, Mom. Nice look for the office," Jessica said, eyeballing my Victoria's Secret cranberry camisole. I just kissed her. I was not about to get into an outfit discussion considering the huge fashion chasm between us. Jessica is devoted to granny dresses, and I'm a little partial to black leather.

I stuck out my hand to pantomime the turning down

of a volume knob and she lowered the music. I was always a little startled when I studied my daughter. She looked like such an advertisement for clean living— olive skin that never needed a drop of makeup, straight blond hair that stayed sun-streaked all year long, and the no-braces-required smile, which thank God had showed up again, once she'd gotten past sixteen.

"So. How was school today?"

"Fine. How about you?" she asked. "Save anybody from suicide or sleeping with their brother?"

"Jess. I love you, but you are an incredible wiseass. What's for dinner?"

"Tandoori chicken."

That was the deal we had. Ever since Jessica had turned fifteen and gone on her No Red Meat campaign, I had put her in charge of cooking. "Look," I'd said to her, "you're the one who says there are a thousand ways to cook chicken. I figure there are only two—KFC regular and KFC crispy. That's it. So I'll be in charge of those two and you be in charge of the nine hundred ninety-eight others."

"Mo-om. I don't want to do this," she had said.

"No, I mean it, Jessica. You don't want to eat hamburgers or spaghetti and meatballs, then that's cool. But I do not want to spend my time coming home on the bus reading *Woman's Day* articles on 'Fun Things to Do with Eggplants.' I am just not interested in expanding my recipe repertoire. I have cooked for fifteen years, and it would be nice to kind of retire. Anyway, you're home earlier than I am."

"What about during softball season?"

"During softball season, I'll cook. We've got too much riding on softball. So what do you say, hon?"

"I don't know. It makes me nervous."

"It's mindless, Jess. Don't worry, if it doesn't work out, we'll figure out the next thing. I just want you to at least try it."

So she did. And the great thing was, she began to love it. Suddenly, stuff that I had never heard of in my life—like this herb called cilantro and these little gray-greenish things called capers—began creeping into our kitchen. Occasionally there was a huge fiasco, but for the most part Jessica was happy because I did all the dishes, and I was happy because the food was pretty damn fab. And here was the best part—not having to plan dinner kind of made me feel like a guest in my very own home.

Just like I did tonight, when Jessica said, "We're not eating until seven. I have a calculus test to study for, and I want to get it done before dinner so I can chill out later in front of the tube."

"What's on?"

"A rerun of *Clapton Unplugged*."

"Really? Maybe I'll watch too."

"Cool," she said sort of flatly.

"What's the matter? I won't watch it with you if you mind."

"No, it's not you. It's cool if you want to watch. It's just that Richie is coming over to have some big discussion or something. I don't know. I don't want to talk about it right now. I've got to study."

"Okay, hon," I said, instantly anxious to know the

details of her teen crisis. Richie, Jessica's boyfriend for the past two years, was an okay enough kid—cute, like a puppy or something, but not particularly ambitious. Certainly not someone who in the long run could keep up with the likes of Jessica, either in terms of intelligence or resourcefulness. And even if this was the mom in me speaking, so what? It was true.

Back in my room where the shades were still down and the bed was not exactly made, I pulled on my jeans and my old "I Knew Elvis Before He Was a Stamp" T-shirt. I considered hanging up my clothes, but then I figured if I started with today's outfit, I'd have to hang up yesterday's and the day before's too. But if I left it all piling up there, then I'd have something nice and constructive to do on the weekend. So I grabbed my "Fuchsia Forever" nail polish—I've just gone back to it for toes only—headed into the living room, clicked on Tom Brokaw, and hit the mute button.

I like to watch the news this way. It makes all the bad stuff—floods and murders and world calamities—less jarring. Also it's fun to guess what Tom might be talking about during the intros, and then to find out if I am right when the pictures come on. Tonight, Tom, who generally has on a particularly outstanding tie, was wearing a splashy one that actually verged on bad taste.

Taste happens to be a topic I take pretty seriously, in spite of having been raised in a trailer park by a woman with a large inventory of see-through plastic spiked heels. I mean it's not that I don't know that things like shag carpet, foil wallpaper, and Hummel figurines are not the way to go. The problem though is that we are renting the house furnished, so right now we are pretty much stuck with the decorating decisions of the dead Mrs. O'Connell—Dolores being the live one—and the dead one was definitely partial to tree-slice coffee tables and La-Z-Boys. But I have my file of dream rooms, and someday, when I am a practicing psychologist, there will be this place with white silk couches, black lacquer tables, and big art, just like Cher had before she decided to invest the greater part of her fortune in monthly collagen shots.

The polish on my left foot was still sticky when the doorbell rang. I figured it was Richie coming to see Jessica and I got ready to vacate the premises in the name of teen love. But when I hobbled to the door, I found Steffi standing there. Steffi is my best friend. She did not look one bit happy.

"Hi! What are you doing here? Are the kids all out for dinner?"

"Do not mention the word 'kids' to me," she said, stomping into the room.

"That's a little bit tough to do, Steff, you seem to have four of them."

Steffi Ranalli has four kids in the hardest possible way a person can. Steffi has quadruplets—two boys and two girls. And Steffi, who works in the Mayor's Office of Special Events, has raised them all by herself ever since their dad walked out on their third birthday. Having Steffi for a friend has always helped me put things in perspective, because no matter how bad it is at my house, it is easily four times as bad at Steffi's.

"I don't suppose you have a beer or something?" she asked. Steffi is this truly great-looking redhead, who would be gorgeous if she'd just put on some foundation and mascara and accessorize a little. I've told her that for years, but she's not that good at following my advice. She says that things like rhinestones on my nails cut into my fashion credibility. I personally feel her aesthetic sensibilities are narrow.

"Sure I do, hon," I said. "Come on into the kitchen."

"God, it smells great here. What's Jessica cooking?"

"Tandoori chicken. It's Indian, or maybe Pakistani, I can't remember. I think she's working her way through the U.N. We have Miller Lite and Old Style—what do you want?"

"Whichever is bigger, stronger, and faster-acting."

"Jeez. What's the deal?" I asked, handing her the Old Style. "Why are you out on the streets alone with four fifteen-year-olds dying of hunger at home?"

"Fifteen-*and-a-half*-year-olds."

"Right. I forgot."

"God, I wish I could. In fact, their being fifteen and a half is the entire reason that I'm not home with them at this very minute. I am telling you, of all the ages they have been, this one is the worst." We sat down at the kitchen table and I moved the place mats from this morning's breakfast aside.

"You say that about every age. Is this because of the learner's permits?"

"It's *always* because of the learner's permits. Their

entire lives now center around cars and driving. It is making me crazy. I am one woman, with one car, and four kids constantly on my case to take them out to practice."

"I know. It must be a nightmare."

"Please. I am venting," she said, plopping her feet up onto a chair. "I am so furious. I just got home and within the first five minutes each of them tried to corner me to see when I could take them out driving. All of a sudden they have all these mandatory errands to do—this one *needs* mousse, that one *needs* a new CD. I don't know, I had a shit day at work today, and tonight I really lost it."

"What happened?"

"They just all converged on me at the wrong time, and I exploded. I mean I just went completely ballistic, and all of a sudden I'm screaming, 'I can't take it, I'm going to kill myself!' "

"Yeah?"

"Yeah. And do you know what Ryan said? He said, 'Mom, when you decide where you want to do it, can I drive you there?' "

I loved it. So did Jessica who had banged through the kitchen door to check out the chicken and caught the tail end of Steffi's tirade. Jessica slipped an arm around her shoulder and said, "Don't worry, Mrs. Ranalli, they'll shape up. Once we get our licenses, we chill out. Honest, ask Mom. Hey, I saw Melissa today at her tennis practice. Her backhand is awesome."

Melissa is Steffi's girl-jock quad. Steffi has a boy-jock quad named Ryan, a boy-artist quad named Billy, and a girl-thespian quad named Julie. "That's the thing about those fertility drugs," she always said, "when those little chemicals split your eggies four ways, none of your eggie parts go in the same direction."

Steffi and I had hooked up ten years ago in a single mom support group that we immediately abandoned once we found each other. She lived up here in Bridgeport, though, so it was predominantly a phone relationship until we moved in five years ago, and our kids all wound up at the same school.

"That's nice to hear, Jess," said Steffi, opening the cupboard under the sink and tossing her beer bottle into the trash. "Maybe if I'm ever speaking to Melissa again, I'll tell her you said that. It will mean a lot, coming from one of the school's major jocks."

"No, really," said Jessica, who like every woman in America never knows what to say when someone gives her a compliment.

"What's happening with North Carolina and the scholarship deal?" Steffi asked. "When are you supposed to hear?"

I tried to signal Steffi not to pursue the subject. It was not a topic Jessica could bear talking about right now— at least not with me. It was too terrifying because of the potential rejection. So I was amazed when Jessica responded in a totally civilized tone, "Well, if I'm lucky I'll get a letter of intent from them mid-November, asking me to commit. As a pitcher there's a chance it can happen. Otherwise I may have to wait until April like everybody else. I'm pretty freaked about it."

I was pretty freaked about it too. The whole question of where and how we were going to pay for college could be solved with one letter from Chapel Hill, North Carolina. I hated the fact that so much was riding on someone else's decision, especially someone in smelly socks in an athletic office halfway across the country. But if the smelly socks guy came through, Jessica would be taken care of, the six thousand dollars I'd saved for her college education would be freed up to help pay for mine, and I'd be zooming toward Chapter Two of my grown-up life.

"Well, babe," said Steffi, throwing her purse back onto her shoulder, "you know I've got my fingers crossed for you."

"Thanks, Mrs. Ranalli," Jessica said as she pulled open the refrigerator and took out some lettuce and tomatoes for the salad.

"Jess, I'll help you do that. Steff, want to stay for Tandoori night?"

"No, I just needed to cool off," she said, hugging each of us. "I'm going home to my kids now. I might even speak to them."

"Don't do anything rash," I said.

Salad making was kind of quiet between us. I kept waiting for Jessica to bring up the Richie crisis, but it didn't seem to be on her agenda. I really do try to be respectful of Jess's need to be a private person. But sometimes it just tears me apart not to be privy to every single one of my own kid's thoughts. I hate that she has so much of her life away from me.

"Why are you looking at me like that?" she asked when we sat down at the table.

"Like what?"

"I don't know. Kind of intense. Maybe kind of sad. What's going on?"

"I don't know, hon. Maybe I'm practicing missing you for next year. You know, putting myself twelve months ahead and wondering what it will feel like without you."

"God, Mom. Did you get one of those empty nest letters today? The ones where the kids have all gone and the mom is a complete mess?"

"No. Actually, it might be something else. I had lunch with this sportswriter guy I've never really talked to before, but I've always figured he was a jerk."

"What's his name?"

"Charlie. Charlie Feldman. He covers the Black-hawks."

"And he's a jerk?"

"Well, actually no. He isn't. He's kind of sweet. Very decent, and I don't know, just sweet."

There was a long and steely look beamed across the table at me. Jessica has almost never liked anyone that I liked. And you could just tell she was thinking, "I do not need, in the middle of my senior year, to have my mother go all melty over one more future ex-boyfriend." I did not appreciate the silent hassle. I have been very careful in the last few years not to spin out on any ill-fated romances. I'm not saying I've exactly avoided them, but I have been very careful not to let anyone really intrude on my heart or my head while I've been monitoring this child toward adult life. So I did not need any looks from across the table, thank you.

"Cool your jets, Jess. It is nothing like that. Not even

close. He . . . Charlie was just telling me about how much he wants to have a baby, and wants to be a dad."

"Why was he telling *you*?"

"Because sometimes people tell me things. You know I'm a good listener."

"How old is he?" she asked, reaching for the rice.

"Four-four. And his dad almost died in the hospital this weekend so he's got a lot of what's-it-all-about questions. And he's not married."

"Is he cute?"

"God. I don't know. Yeah. I guess. He has all his hair, so he looks pretty young and he has a very good smile and this chipped tooth. I don't know. I didn't notice. It's just that we had a real intense talk, and it made me think a lot about having a baby—the power and the scariness of it all."

" 'Scariness'?" The phone rang then, but we let the machine in the living room take it. That was the dinner rule—no interruptions. For twenty minutes a day no one could get to us. "Were you scared of me? I mean, I know you and Dad were really young, but it is weird to think of you as scared of me. Were you?"

"Are you kidding? I was terrified."

"What of?"

"Of everything. You were so pink and bald and needy—and you didn't talk! I mean I knew babies didn't talk, but I'm a very verbal person, you know. It made me crazy not to know what it was you wanted all the time."

"Wasn't Dolores a help?"

"She wasn't around a lot when you were little. She

was busy at the shop. And she was furious at me and your father for getting pregnant."

"Was she mad at me too?"

"No, she was crazy about you. But I didn't want her around a lot, either. First of all she'd always glue these stupid little bows onto your four wisps of hair. You looked like a miniature Mr. Clean who cross-dressed. And second of all, because it felt important to prove to her that I could be a wonderful mother even though I was so scared."

"But what was scary about it? I don't understand."

"Everything. You'd never been a baby before and I'd never been a mom. We were both so new at our jobs."

"I didn't have a job."

"Yes you did. Your job was to show up. My job was to be in charge of everything else. It was not all that fair a division of labor."

"Good thing you don't hold a grudge, Mom."

"Yeah, well, it wasn't fair. You were allowed to cry a lot more than I was."

Charlie

EARLY OCTOBER

"Charlie, how come your living room always looks like a basement?"

That was what Janice had asked me six years ago just after I'd moved into this apartment. I should have been pissed, but she had a point. Even though I was paying $1100 a month for this place, the centerpiece of my living room was still an old metal desk that I have lugged through my life. I like the desk. It was Abe's. And I sat at it for years in the backroom of the store, listening to Cubs games on the radio and drawing out the plays on paper.

No doubt the basement look is also enhanced by the brown wooden file cabinets I've always used as end tables. All my furniture is in assorted shades of brown. I have trouble committing to a color. A couple of women in my life have felt this was related to a hesitation to commit to relationships. But hell, women think everything is related to that.

Anyway, looking around my apartment now made me think of that evening with Janice. The place was still a mess. "I don't want to hurt your feelings or anything," she'd said, "but this room is like all those basement rooms guys have, the ones my mom called 'Man's World.'"

"'Man's World'? What the hell is that?" I asked, not all that sure that Janice's decorating observations were going to be a big assist to our having a nice romantic dinner. I had outdone myself that night making a terrific meal of grilled salmon, sautéed spinach, and scalloped potatoes. Cooking was something I didn't do often, but I did do it well. And enthusiastically.

"Man's World was what Mom called the place Daddy disappeared to down in the basement. He had a ratty desk and moldy old couch down there and it was filled with sports memorabilia and putrid cigar butts. Daddy said all men need a Man's World because women make the rest of he house so off-limits. Your living room isn't that extreme, Charlie, but it does have a definite Man's World feeling to it."

"Well, shit, Janice," I said, determined not to let her spoil the evening, "I'm a man."

"I know, honey. And I don't mean it in a critical way," she offered in that critical way she thought the disclaimer masked, "but you are in a two-bedroom apartment on the twenty-fifth floor, and it *still* looks like the basement. Only it's the basement in the sky."

Actually, I liked that description. I hated places that

were crisp or formal. So the basement in the sky was fine with me. It still is. It's my place, with my things. There are some good antique maps on the wall, some great drawings I've picked up over the years of park benches from around the world, and a gorgeous wide-angle photo of the old Comiskey Park when Bill Veeck had it. Way before they built this bullshit stadium that feels like a mall. Last year I did cave in though and got myself a new couch. Not brown. I went wild. It's tan.

At the moment though, I had yanked all the pillows off that couch because I'd lost the damn envelope to my Visa bill and I was hoping it had slipped between the cushions. I had to leave in three hours—I was headed to Toronto with the Hawks, and one of my rituals before going on a road trip was to pay all my bills, do all my laundry, toss my old newspapers, and water my two lame ficus plants.

I do this not because I'm leaving town for a couple days. I do this in case I die.

I am not embarrassed about this. Millions of people feel the same way. One night, when I was sitting around a hotel bar with three of the other beat writers after a game last year, each of us admitted that we all straighten out our lives before taking off on these road trips, because at some dumbfuck level we're thinking maybe we might croak. In fact, Maggie Richman from the *Detroit News* told us about the time her brother moved in for a week while she was out of town, and in addition to paying her bills and stuff before she took off, she had to empty something she called "the nasty drawer."

"What the hell is that?" asked Roger Murphy, the *Tribune* guy.

"A drawer all single women have, Murphy. It's where we stash our sex stuff—the vibrator, a couple of juicy books, maybe a video. I'm telling you, all I could think of was what if my plane goes down? The brother inherits my place, and then *shazam!* one day he pulls open the nasty drawer and learns much too much about his baby sister. God, I think I'd die twice." We three guys left the bar pretty quickly after that. I don't know whether we were more threatened by the topic of death or vibrators.

After ten minutes I gave up on the Visa envelope. But I did manage to get all the bills paid, leave a note for my cleaning lady, and grab the *Chicago Reader*. That's the paper with all those singles ads in it. It had been almost a month since I'd had lunch with Lacy, and the two times I had gone into the office to pick up my mail and my paychecks, she hadn't been around. It's funny, life with a laptop really does unlink a reporter from any sort of home-base feeling. And while there is a freeing aspect to that, it compounds your sense of isolation. I was bummed she hadn't been around, but relieved too. I hadn't done squat about writing a personals ad and I was feeling pretty lousy about it. I figured maybe I'd have a chance in Toronto.

• • •

It was nearly one in the morning before I set foot in my room at the Royal York Hotel. I was beat. I kicked off my loafers, stepped out of my clothes, and I could see myself reflected in the full-length mirror. There aren't a lot of mirrors at my place, so it was only on the road that I ever got a look at what everybody else had to look at when they looked at me. Not that too many people had seen me lying around in boxers of late. Even so, I'm still pretty fit. The belly is almost flat and the shoulders are okay. Abe still looks pretty good too, so I'm sure some of it is due to genetics, and some of it is due to the twenty-minute workout I've been doing every morning for the last fifteen years. I hate to admit it, but the motivation is as much vanity as it is health. Hell, I have to do something to minimize the contrast between me and the remarkable physical specimens I've spent my life confronting in locker rooms. Most of those guys are in amazing shape.

Tonight's game, the third of the season, had put me in a pretty good frame of mind. It ended early enough so I could easily file for the first edition by the 10:15 deadline. Plus, I'd gotten some great quotes down in the locker room for the second edition story. I'll tell you, it sure didn't hurt when the Hawks won. Plowing into a locker room with a bunch of other reporters to ask "So where did it go right?" was a hell of a lot easier than plowing in and asking, "So where did it go wrong?" Sometimes I feel that I put so much effort into massaging my questions for the players and coaches that it's no wonder I wind up depleted when it comes to small talk with women.

I checked my messages on the new machine at home, and there was one from Bobby asking me to call him tonight if I got in early. Up until a year ago, I never got in early on game nights. After I filed I'd always decompress over some beers with the other beat writers. Lately though, I head back to the hotel and order room service like tonight. There's just too much bullshit and one-upmanship going on at the bars. Too much of an opportunity to watch some of the guys get stupid with a couple of beers in them and a couple of women near them. Christ, I've been on the road long enough to have pulled every dumb sportswriter stunt a million times. And I know that of all the options available—getting loaded, getting laid, getting both—nothing beats the payback of a good night's sleep.

Bobby's voice mail answered, so I left him a message and was two-thirds through my pizza and one-third through a bad Clint Eastwood movie when he called back.

"Hey. Where were you out to so late, Robert?"

"Nowhere great. I was walking the dog, Sherry and Jennifer are on the great college search out East."

"Jesus, is that starting already?" I said, feeling the onset of a daddy clock pang. I still hadn't said word one to Bobby about any of this fatherhood stuff. In a sense, Bobby was part of my problem. Or at least part of what I was reacting to. I knew that if I told Bobby that I was feeling so out of sorts with my own life, the guy's first response would be guilt, and his second would be pity. And I didn't want to deal with either. Not that we hadn't talked about some of this before. But then that was before the waiting-room epiphany happened. And before the Lacy discussion happened. And before I committed to do something about all of it. Once I stopped procrastinating.

"Yeah, it's started already. I could puke."

"Why?"

"Partly because I can't believe it's gone so fast, and partly because I can't believe how fucking expensive all these places are. Christ, when I went to Madison I think my parents paid twenty-two thousand dollars total for my education. Some of these schools you can pay twenty-two thousand and the kid still isn't a sophomore."

"Well, good thing you're a rich successful oral surgeon, my man."

"Yeah and good thing you're the hotshot sportswriter being paid to attend games most people would kill to get tickets for."

"Yeah, right."

"Right."

Bobby and I had been doing this for years. Pretending to be envious of the other's chosen profession. But the truth is I would no more want to put my head down rancid mouths every day than Bobby would want to pry half-literate sentences from guys who chase a piece of rubber around some ice.

"So how is Abe doing? Sophie sent us a thank-you card for some flowers the other day, and she said he was really bouncing back. He already looked pretty good that afternoon I stopped up to the hospital."

"Yeah, I heard you were there. Sorry I missed you.

My day was running late, because I'd gone out to lunch."

"I thought you didn't do business lunches."

"Well, it wasn't exactly business."

"Oh? Don't tell me. It was a date?"

I hated the question. But I knew he didn't ask it for his data files—he asked it for Sherry's. Sherry had fixed me up with two of her divorced girlfriends in the past few years, and from my end, neither one of them had been a go. Sherry was not exactly thrilled about that. Once she even called me and asked, "Well, are you going to call her again or not?"

"Call who?"

"Trish. She said you had a nice time."

"It was okay," I told her. "Trish seems like a very nice person."

"So, are you going to call her?"

"Sherry, we're not in high school here. If I were going to call her, I think it would be good form to make sure that *she* knew about it before *you* did."

"You're not going to, are you? Jesus Christ, Charlie, she said you said you would."

I had to work hard to stay calm. "Sherry, I did not say I would call her."

"Well, you didn't say you wouldn't, and if you knew at the time that you wouldn't, why didn't you just say something to her?"

"Like what? 'Don't take this personally but I won't be calling you again'?"

"Yeah, maybe."

"Jesus, Sherry. People can't deal with that. A city-side

reporter I know told me that a guy brought her home once and said, "Thanks. It was nice meeting you. But I probably won't be calling you again.' She was devastated. Listen, I am really sorry you think that I sent some sort of mixed signals to your friend, Sherry. But dating is very complicated, and I'm just doing the best I can."

Since then, Sherry had been pretty chilly to me. On the other hand, she was still interested in my dating stats, and she now sent Bobby out as a stringer. But tonight I wasn't biting.

By the time I got off the phone with Bobby, there was no point in watching the end of Clint Eastwood. None of those old ones was as good as *Unforgiven* anyway. His character was amazingly complex. Cold-blooded, wise, sad, and tender. It was a strong movie. I saw it at home one night on cable, but it was always a movie I wished I had seen and talked about with a woman. Women see things through such a different prism.

Women.

Okay, that's it. Your waffling days are over, bud. So is all your damn whining. It was bite the bullet time.

And with that, I pulled the damn *Chicago Reader* out of my duffel bag. It wasn't a paper I read very often. It didn't have a sports section. Not that I'm narrow. I do read novels and magazines. Mostly the *New Yorker* because I am always hacking around with short stories. But if I picked up a newspaper, I wanted it to have a sports section. However, the *Reader* had a vast personals section. Hundreds of people advertising themselves, their hopes, their needs, their urges. Everyone seeking an other-based solution. Men Seeking Women, Women

Seeking Men, Women Seeking Women, Men Seeking Men.

Some of it was coy—*"This personal isn't for you. It's for a friend of yours who doesn't read the personals."* Some of it was confusing—what the hell was an *"ISO brunette"*? And some of it was unnerving—*"350-pound freelance magician looking for male companionship; no priests need apply."*

Jesus, I thought, I can't do this. And then I started writing.

Lacy

LATE OCTOBER

I decided to read the ad a third time.

I needed the time to figure out the nicest way to tell
Charlie that he had not exactly crafted the most seduc-
tive presentation.

*Decent, middle-aged SWM looking to bore people with
stories of our kids' soccer games. The problem is that we
don't have the kids yet. This is because we haven't met yet.
I'm a 44-year-old sportswriter interested in starting a family and sharing a life with a tolerant, lovely, 30–38 SWF.
I am not looking to be a stepparent. I am sensitive, stable,
mature, and don't phone my mom every day. I love my
work, and make possibly the world's finest meat loaf
(though I consider myself flexible and would be willing to
try yours). If you would like a regular guy with no dis-
eases, not a lot of hang-ups, and a good attitude, I would
like to hear from you.*

"Well, what do you think?" he asked from the other side of the table. We were sitting in one of the claustrophobic "interview rooms" at the paper. They'd originally been built so you could run an interview privately, away from the noise of the city room. Only today, typewriter clacks are pretty much muffled by computers, and interviews can be held anywhere since everyone has laptops. So now the rooms are always empty, except for a couple of folding chairs and the big tables in the middle. Actually, they would have been excellent for office sex, but people just don't seem to be doing that anymore.

Charlie was taking a noon plane to Detroit. He sat at the table fiddling with the zipper on his duffel bag, and he seemed very wired—maybe he was nervous about what I'd say after reading the ad. He looked good though. In fact, when I followed him down the beige hallway into the room, I realized there was a very good reason he always wore jeans . . . and I was looking at it. Actually he looked good from the front too. His hair had gotten longer in the six weeks since we'd had that weird lunch—some of it was curling over the collar of his shirt and he just had a nice real-*guy* look about him.

"I've been walking around with this ad for a couple of weeks," he said, cracking his knuckles. I swear I have never understood why men do that. Or why they spit out car windows.

"I meant to show it to you sooner. But I'd start messing with it and then last night I decided to stop operating in a vacuum, and take you up on your offer to help. I promise not to get pissed off if you think it's too bullshitty."

"That's not the problem, Charlie. Actually, it's not bullshitty enough."

"How do you mean?"

"Well," I said, taking a deep breath before plunging in—I didn't want to hurt the guy's feelings—"there's some good stuff in here, there really is. But on the whole, it's a bit too straightforward."

"I don't get it."

"See, the thing is, you've got to look at the big picture. For the most part, this is going to appear on a page that is virtually a sea of lies—well, not lies, exactly, but half truths, or maybe bent truths. Personals are not meant for whole truths. And most important of all, personals are written in code."

"Well, I thought I got that. The SWM thing and all."

"Yeah, well, first of all you aren't an SWM, you're a DWM."

"What? You can't call me divorced. I was married to Marcy for one minute. It was a mistake. It doesn't count. It was like the one bad shot, the mulligan you get on the first hole."

"Are you talking about golf? I don't play golf, Charlie."

"Well, in golf they let you have one bad shot that you don't have to count. It's called a mulligan. Marcy was my marital mulligan. I really don't want to have to pull her into this, and have to dredge up all that stuff about the proctologist."

"You dredge it up anyway. You told it to me. It's there. It's part of your past," I said, pulling the damn tortoiseshell comb out of my hair and then scooping everything back behind my ear again. It was only ten in the morning and the new ceramic accordion earrings I'd ordered from Home Shopping were already killing me. I only allow myself to watch it half an hour a week, but turning off that set sometimes kills me, their stuff is so great. These earrings were only $17.95, and even though they hurt like hell I didn't want to take them off in front of Charlie. I hate my earlobes—actually, I hate earlobes per se unless they are on babies. They're the only people with the right size earlobes. Charlie was about to go into another denial about his divorce, so I said, "That's not the kind of code I mean. I mean more the one where people say one word but really mean another."

"Like?"

"I don't know, like take the word 'petite.' "

"Like, 'looking for a petite woman'?"

"Yeah. Exactly. Because 'petite' sounds like a word describing a woman, but in the personals it's really a code word that says, 'I am a very short guy.' A short guy will never say he's short, but he will say he's looking for a petite woman."

"Christ."

"Let's take a whole ad. It's easier to explain if you have the personals section with you. Do you have one?"

Charlie dug through his scratched leather duffel and pulled out an edition he must have been carrying around for weeks. Outside in the hallway a ladder or something had just clattered to the floor, and you could hear the remodeling guys swearing about having to try to do their work at the same time we were trying to do ours. The whole computer installation thing was taking much longer than originally scheduled and no one was being that good a sport about it.

"Okay," I said, "pick out an ad and read it, then I'll tell you what it means."

"Okay. Here's one. 'Thirty-nine, athletic, handsome, social drinker, romantic friendship first,'" he said, looking up—God, he had really nice eye crinkles.

"Well, it could be a lot of things. The worst-case scenario would be that the guy is about forty-six, he once spent about three weeks on a StairMaster, his mother tells him he's gorgeous, he's been thrown out of every bar on Division Street, and what was the last thing?"

"'Romantic friendship first' . . ."

"Yeah, he's willing to wait all the way till the end of the date before he tries to have sex with you."

"For Chrissakes, Lacy, you can't be that cynical. You are the one who told me to do this."

"I still think you should do it, but we have to take the ad you've written and put it in sort of singlespeak. People expect a little hype in it. We tell this to readers all the time when they write in to complain that someone has misrepresented themselves in personals."

"What do they write in and say?"

"You know, stuff like, 'This woman's ad said she was attractive, and then when she showed up, she was missing three front teeth.'"

Charlie pushed back his chair and started pacing back and forth in the little room. "Holy shit! Is that for real?"

"Sometimes, but we always say that you have to expect that people embellish a bit. People pitch themselves in terms that are, you know, applicable on a very good day, or after half a bottle of wine . . . or with, I don't know, some low-wattage peach lighting. All I'm saying here is that there's a serious amount of enhancement involved in these things."

"Then what's the point?"

"The point is, for starters, Charlie, you gotta say the word 'attractive' in there up front. I mean you leave that out, and people are going to think you're Jabba the Hutt."

"Lacy," he said, leaning across the table to me, "a guy can't just describe himself as 'attractive.' It's awkward. It's . . ."

"Charlie, you *are* attractive. Don't make me sit here and compliment you. You have to put it in—you can't just start out with an ad that says 'decent.' "

"What's the matter with 'decent'? It's a fine description of me. Both looks-wise and as a person."

"Charlie, these are commercials. Would you buy a car that says 'it's decent'? 'Decent' is a last-resort word. When I was in high school that's how you'd describe someone who finally asked you to the prom when no one else would, and he wasn't so gross that he made you throw up. 'Decent' means he's presentable, but barely. Girls are not beating down the door to get to decent. Sure, they want decent—as in integrity and kindness and all—but it is not your lead."

"Oh, yeah? What is?" Charlie said more testily than was necessary if you ask me. I mean, I was doing the guy a favor here.

"I'm not sure. But I know 'attractive' is in it."

"How about 'reasonably attractive'?" he asked, coming over to my side of the table and looking down at the ad again. He smelled good—not cologne-good, just guy-good.

" 'Reasonably' makes it a much larger category than many women are prepared to deal with, Charlie. 'Reasonably' could make it possible for a person to show up with those three missing teeth. Trust me on this."

"I don't know, maybe this whole thing is a big mistake."

"No, it's not. It's a good way to meet people. You just have to craft your message and pace it a certain way. For instance, I think putting the having a baby part at the beginning is a bit overwhelming—maybe we could re-work it to kind of build to it, and put a bit more about you up top."

Charlie had this dejected look on his face, like little kids get when they are the last to be picked for kick ball. "Listen, a lot of what you wrote is really good," I said, patting the chair so he would sit down next to me and we could start marking up the ad. I took a pencil out of his pocket. I love guys in light blue oxford cloth shirts— they smell so ironed. "This whole thing about the meat loaf and 'I love my work' is very good. But we've got to separate the 'I am sensitive' from the 'I am not looking to be a stepparent' . . . it sounds like a bit of a conflict. In fact, you might pull 'sensitive' out altogether. It kind of translates to 'wuss' these days."

"You're saying I have an out-of-fashion attribute?"

"*Being* sensitive isn't out of fashion. Advertising it is. Maybe we could think of something else."

" 'Sense of humor'?" he said, leaning back and tipping the chair toward the wall.

"Oh, God, no. Never. People who put in 'sense of humor' are people who think they have one because they laugh at everything, or because they buy whoopee cushions. No, definitely leave out 'sense of humor,' and definitely leave out 'like to go for long walks.' Everyone says that stuff."

"What about *Seinfeld*? Every third ad I read, the person says they love to watch *Seinfeld*. Call me old-fashioned, but I am not about to build a relationship on mutual television shows."

"Why? People build relationships on less."

"You're very young to be such a skeptic," he said, tipping his chair back to level ground, looking me right in the face.

"Yeah? Well, I used to be a younger skeptic. Maybe it has something to do with seeing my mother have three husbands." Now I was the one who had to get up and pace back and forth to nowhere. "Or with reading about a thousand we-have-nothing-in-common letters a month. Or with a quick review of the left-field selections from my personal dating life for the past fifteen years."

"Are there more than ten?"

"Ten?"

"Left-field selections."

"Don't get me started," I said, reaching into my purse for some gum. "Want some?" He shook his head. "Anyway, we're doing you, and we have to get some kind of snappy lead going. How about 'husband trapped in bachelor's body'?"

"Please," he groaned. "Let's not bring bodies into it."

"Why? You have a nice build. You look nice in those jeans."

"Uh, thanks. I'm not that good with compliments. But anyway I really don't want to put the word 'body' in the lead. Then women will think that I'm body-focused, either on my own body or on theirs, and one of the upsides of being forty-four is that I am finally past that."

"Oh, come on." I walked away from him, stopped, and I know it wasn't nice, but I looked back over my shoulder at him, with my hands on my hips like that old Betty Grable pose and I said, "You notice a woman's body."

He laughed. He got it. "Notice? Absolutely. But I do not make any decisions or value judgments about a woman based on that. I've known too many women who have tormented themselves over imagined physical imperfections or inadequacies. Women make themselves crazy over this stuff. How come women don't believe that men are basically very, very accepting?"

"Because we can't tell the difference between a guy who is accepting and a guy who has low standards."

"God, you're tough, Lacy. How come you're so tough?"

"How come you can't tell the difference between someone who's tough and someone who's terrified?"

He didn't have to give me such an odd look. Like I was so hard to figure out or something. Hadn't he met any perfectly nice defensive women who had been burned before? I didn't think we were such a small category.

"Okay," I said, sitting back down so we could make some headway, "let's try and think of a new lead . . . something snappy."

"We could always go with 'Womb with a View' . . ."

"Very funny, Charlie."

After we'd fiddled with the ad another ten or fifteen minutes, he looked at his watch and said, "Shit, I've got to get going. The plane leaves in an hour.

"I'll call this in for next week's *Reader*," he said, stuffing the paper and the ad back in his duffel. But as he put on his leather jacket he said, "You know, Lacy, I could save a lot of time and money here, if maybe you would consider some of this."

"Consider what?"

"Well, you said I don't make you throw up."

"Throw up?"

"You know, you said I was better than decent. You said I should use the word 'attractive.' And you can probably tell that I'm a pretty good guy, right?"

"Yeah . . ."

"Well, I'm just saying it would be so much simpler if maybe *you* would go for it. You know maybe *we* could go out. See how it went. I like you. You seem real straight and real capable. You understand what a reporter's life is like. And you already know how to mother. And this time it would be a lot easier because you'd have a partner—four months of the year anyway. You could even quit work and go to school . . ."

Charlie stopped. My face must have gone white or something.

"I'm sorry. I didn't mean to scare you," he said. "I was

just kidding. Or maybe I wasn't. Maybe I was fishing. Or panicking. I don't know. I shouldn't have said anything. It was stupid. I apologize."

I smiled at him and said it was okay. But as I watched him go to the elevator, I came a little unglued. It was just so out of the blue. I didn't even know this guy. But one thing I did know was this—I am definitely out of the mom business! No ifs, ands, or buts on that one. I am eleven seconds from freedom, and no way would I sign on for a return engagement. Not even if Mel Gibson, or Brad Pitt, or anyone else asked me. And certainly not for some midlife crisis hockey writer, no matter how cute he was.

Even so, the whole discussion made me feel funny. Going home on the Halsted Street bus that night, I started thinking about what it actually would be like to just be home and be able to *savor* having a baby. And it made me remember how much I had loved being pregnant. And it made me aware of just how long it had been—like never—since someone had said, "How would you like to spend the rest of your life with me?" It was amazing. I mean this guy had sort of made me a lifetime offer, and he didn't even know how I looked naked.

Charlie

EARLY FEBRUARY

Bobby and I were in his den. The newly decorated den.

This fact had been slammed home by Sherry, who greeted me at the door with, "Hi. Take off your shoes if you lie down on the couch. We just got it last week, okay?" Sherry was a charmer. She was also one of those women who gave meaning to her life by chronic redecorating. From what I could tell, the den's new theme was cowboys and Indians.

"No, Chas, it's called Southwest," said Bobby. Indian rugs were everywhere, a gigantic painting of some tribal chief hung over the couch, and you needed the moves of a quarterback to avoid the blitz of potted cactuses all over the room. Bobby generally went along on this stuff, but this time he had insisted that a huge fifty-three-inch TV be allowed to intrude on the overall Roy Rogers look. That tube must have really offended the aesthetic sensibilities of Sherry and her current decorator autocrat. I'd bet big bucks that Sherry was still hoping to throw a teepee up around it.

"Man," I said, kicking off my Nikes so I wouldn't incur any wifely wrath, "I haven't seen this much turquoise and orange in a room since Howard Johnson's."

"Don't say 'orange' in front of Sherry. She'll tell you it's 'salmon.' "

"She's a hard woman to argue with, my man."

Unless you were a teenager. Because ten minutes after I walked in, a world-class brawl ensued between Jennifer and Sherry over something called "the college essay." It appeared that Sherry, an English teacher whose career had spanned the entire first year of her marriage, couldn't keep her well-manicured hands off Jennifer's prose. Several white-hot words flew between the two of them in the kitchen, and the last thing I heard before Bobby closed the den door was, "God, Mom, you are such a bitch!"

"Jesus, they have been at each other for weeks," he said, taking another hit of his beer. "Don't ever have kids, Charlie, the payoffs are too few and far between."

I didn't say squat. Where was I going to start? How the hell did I explain that I'd spent the past couple of months holding auditions for the role of future mom of my future kids? I still hadn't figured out how to tell Bobby what I'd been up to. The dad longings had not gone away. But it did feel good to at least be *doing something* about them. I wasn't Mr. Family Guy on a Kodak Christmas card yet, but I *was* working on it.

The number of women who had responded to my ad

blew me away. In the past three months I had probably talked on the phone to thirty women and had gone out with about five. Most of them were relatively nice and bright, and at least for a few dates had seemed like genuine possibilities. The problem was, I wasn't looking to "date" someone. I was looking for a lifetime partner. And if all this effort was only to wind up with two people who sounded like Jennifer and Sherry bitching at each other in the kitchen, it sure as hell gave me pause.

Bobby passed me the nacho chips. Today was our annual post-Super Bowl Sunday event. The two of us had been watching the Super Bowl together for twenty-five years. Even in college, we called each other long distance so we could watch one quarter together. It was a holdover from when we were kids. Our moms made us each come in at dark every night, so then we'd sit in our separate living rooms with the phone at our ears and watch the same TV show. Most of the time we barely exchanged a word other than "cool" or "didja see that?" It used to make our mothers crazy. But then women have a tough time understanding the inherent inarticulateness of male friendship. I wrote about that two years ago in a piece that ran in *The New York Times* "About Men" section. About how silence and presence works for us in a way that words do not. Women don't get that guys can be close without talking. They don't get the power of hanging out. I was very proud of that piece.

In fact, part of the piece was about our Super Bowl ritual, because it's a tradition that's important to both Bobby and me. So important, that now even though I was usually working or traveling on Super Bowl Sunday,

Bobby would tape the game and then wait to watch it or watch it again, with me. Usually it was only a day or two later, but this year it was Super Bowl Sunday plus seven. Both of us had seen enough of the game in the intervening week to make this mostly a fast-forward presentation, but even if we only hit the high spots, we were still making an effort to keep up the tradition.

A door slammed, Sherry steamrolled in, plopped down next to Bobby, and said in a slow, steely voice, "I should just kill her . . ." And then turning to me she added, "Charlie, don't ever have kids."

Maybe twice in one hour was a sign. Who knows? But I figured if I didn't tell them then, it wouldn't get any easier. I'd have preferred to tell Bobby alone. But what the hell, Sherry was going to hear anyway, so I plunged in. "You know it's real odd you say that. Because for the past few months I have been thinking of almost nothing else but having a kid."

"What?" Sherry asked in a way that made me wonder how the hell I was going to explain this without sounding like a real asshole. "Charlie, are you involved with someone?"

"No, not yet. I know this is going to sound strange to you two, because you've got me pegged as this permanent bachelor, but I am busting my ass right now to get sprung out of that category. Something happened to me when Abe was sick. I just realized that having kids is something I really want in my life. I always have, but I am forty-four. There's a real time crunch now, sort of like a woman with her biological clock."

"Oh, come on, Charlie. It's not the same," said

Sherry, never short on opinions. Then getting up to drip some of her bottled designer water into a cactus, she added, "A guy can become a father even in his sixties. Not that I don't think it's time for you to hook up with somebody, but there are all these late-in-life dads these days. Look at Warren Beatty and Clint Eastwood."

"For Chrissakes, Sherry, those are movie stars. Those are people with publicists. I'm a regular guy. I have to be realistic. If I wait much longer to do this, by the time my kid stops drooling, I'll probably be starting. I'm telling you this clock thing is plenty real."

Bobby motioned me to follow him into the kitchen. It was one of those kitchens you couldn't leave a dirty dish in, everything was white. While I dumped my bottle in the recycle bin, Bobby pulled out two more.

"Jesus, Chas," he said, handing me one, "are you really serious about this?"

"Dead serious."

"You are blowing me away, man. I mean you have always been terrific with our kids, but I always figured you were happy to walk away from the whole domestic scene," Bobby said, putting another six-pack in to chill.

"Yeah, well, maybe I was. And maybe I just thought I was. I'm not so sure. But at some level, there has always been this chronic sense of missing out on something. Something important. Listen," I said, examining a magnet off his refrigerator that was Jason's photo in the shape of a football, "it's not like I am saying to myself, 'I've been to eighty-seven of Joshua's games and dammit now it's my turn.' I *liked* going to Joshua's games. Or I wouldn't have gone. You know that. But wanting a kid comes from something more than that. It's a way of finding and exploring a part of me that I know is there, that will deepen and change all the other parts of me. I don't know." I added as we headed back to the white couch, "it's like having a kid would force me to be the best version of me."

"There's a lot of 'me' in all that," Sherry chimed in.

"For Chrissakes, Sherry," snapped Bobby.

"No, that's a fair shot. Even though it *was* a shot. I'm not going to deny that some of this comes from a selfish place. Hell, it's scary to think of dying alone in a hospital room with no one hanging around the bed. So you bet there's the part that says having a kid makes it possible to fill the room. There's also a part, stupid though it is, that makes me believe that if I have a kid, then I am keeping a piece of me, and Abe, and Grandpa Max still on the face of this earth. And while that's not central to my motives, it is a comforting thought. Despite some of the horror stories you guys have told me over the years about teenagers."

"Yeah," said Sherry, "but I'm telling you, Charlie, this chapter is really the worst. You must know other people going through this college thing."

"Not a lot. I know one woman. Her daughter is going to North Carolina next fall."

"She's already in?"

"She got a softball scholarship. I hear she's a terrific pitcher."

"Well, an athletic scholarship is not on Jennifer's horizon," huffed Sherry, who had switched from plant watering to pillow straightening. "I don't even know if college is, considering how she is dragging her size-four butt on all these applications. So, speaking of applications, is this something I should tell some of my divorced friends? You know, in case they are interested in applying now that you are seriously looking to marry and have a family?"

I had to grin at her. "Sherry. We've been through this before. I am not the solution for any of your friends. We know that. Plus, most of your friends would probably find me even less appealing than usual, once they found out I want to *start* a family. They've already done that, right?"

"Well, that's true. Much as they are dying to date someone, I think the idea of starting over in the sandbox would make you a hard sell. So what are you doing? You're not dating a twenty-nine-year-old, are you?" she prodded, ever eager for details.

"Truth is, Sherry, I'm doing something I never thought I'd do in a million years." Then I proceeded to tell them about the ad. And the responses. And some of the less-than-magical social encounters I'd had these past few months.

I told them about my date with Donna, the massage therapist, with the mynah bird who could say "empowerment." Forty-five minutes into our one-and-only date, she asked if I wanted to strip so she could demonstrate Rolfing on me. I knew my resistance to drop trou made her think I was a world-class mope, but it seemed pretty clear to me that sayonara was inevitable anyway.

Then I told them about Tory. She was one of those people who got very intense about food. I went out with

her twice, and both times she insisted on making reser-
vations at three restaurants, so we could decide at the
last minute where we felt like going. I hate that shit.
The worst part was that she wasn't even going to call the
other two restaurants to cancel once we decided. The
other worst part was that she would reach across the table to taste my food. It was one of those deals where
there were more worst parts than best parts.

Jason cruised in for a couple of minutes looking for a
videotape, so I spared them my brief and traumatic encounter with Suzanne, the gynecologist. Whatever
made me feel I could deal with a person who saw more
pussy on any given day than I had possibly seen in my
lifetime escaped me the minute I met her. Granted it
was not all that evolved of me to back off from someone
based on her job, but I had to be a realist. Dating a
woman with that kind of expertise is more pressure than
your average, hell, even your above-average guy can handle.

I did tell them about Ellen, though. She was a labor
lawyer I had gone out with five or six times. There were
two standout facts about Ellen. She had an amazing
body and she insisted on doing all the driving. I didn't
mind except that she would never park in a parking lot.
She had to drive the fucking car around for twenty minutes until she found a free place on the street. She also
carried one of those little flip-out phones that really
bummed me out. Also, she talked a lot about her "personhood." I'm not that good at dealing with a person's
"personhood."

"But you're not giving up are you?" asked Sherry who had now turned her energies to aligning the blinds.

"Definitely not. Tomorrow after the Hawks' morning practice, I have a lunch date with a veterinarian. A vegetarian veterinarian. I am determined to keep plugging away at this, but it's been grueling as hell. It's like having two jobs, but you only get paid for the easy one. In fact, Ellen the lawyer had a license plate that said WORN OUT. She was really pretty funny about it. She said she bought it for herself on her thirty-sixth birthday as a present for having endured two decades of dating. Two decades. Christ. I've only put in three months."

"Well," said Bobby, finishing off his beer, "you've been dating for two decades, more or less."

"Yeah, heavy on the 'or less.' At least until my ad ran."

When I got home that night, I called Lacy. All the dating talk had depressed me. Lacy had proven to be a terrific antidote during these past few months, sitting on the other end of the phone and laughing at my stories. I'd gotten to know some more about her too, about growing up in "Hill and Valley Mobile Estates." About having two stepdads in a thirteen-year period, and no memories of the biological one who died in a car crash when she was six months old. And about how bust-her-butt determined she was to get a college degree under her belt within the next six years. I liked Lacy's energy, and there were moments when I was stunned by her candor. Sometimes it was like talking to a guy. The woman was completely without guile. She was fucked-up and regular at the same time. Fucked-up enough to be interesting. Regular enough to be real easy to talk to. It was a great combination.

"I was wondering where you'd disappeared to," she said when I called around nine. "The last I heard from you, you and the lawyer were headed to someone's dinner party. How'd it go?"

"I don't remember. I only remember we left earlier than she wanted. But I had a plane the next morning, so I needed to get back."

"Back where?"

"Back home."

"Whose home?"

"What is this—the big 'her place or mine' question?"

"Yeah, I think so. Considering that the highlight of my sex life these days is when my panty hose get a run in them going upward, I've got to live vicariously. Of course, you don't have to answer if you don't want to, Charlie."

"No, it's okay," I said, opening my bedroom curtains so the whole Chicago skyline shimmered through. "My sex life isn't a lot hotter. We went back to her place."

"And?"

"And? Lacy, for Chrissakes."

"And?"

"And . . . well, let's just say since all this AIDS stuff, dry humping seems to have made a big comeback."

She laughed. She had a great laugh. It was belly-anchored. "Yeah. I know, but in a sense, don't you really love that? It's so yesteryear, and so hot. God, dry humping—maybe I'll have to take the plunge and jump into the ring too."

"What ring?"

"The dating one. Maybe instead of just getting twice-weekly reports on your dating life, I should run an ad, and get going on my own. Jessica will be gone in eight months and I'm going to miss her. Maybe a new guy would be a nice distraction."

Okay. I had no claims. But it bummed me out big time when she said that.

Lacy

MARCH

Honest to God, I was seriously considering charging Jessica and Richie rent for the living room. It had been nearly eight weeks since I'd been able to get in there. Not that I was exactly crazy to be around them, given that they were breaking up and lurching through all these melodramatic death throes.

But the thing is, when their deal had been less rocky, they always seemed to want me to hang out with them. I'd always thought that was pretty amazing, considering that at Jessica's age—well actually a couple years before Jessica's age, since I was already Jessica's mother at Jessica's age—all I'd wanted was to get as far away from Dolores and the current stepfather as possible, so I could mess around with Tony. Boy, once I saw Tony Gazzar the first day of high school, my heart and hormones went up for grabs.

However, for whatever reason—chalk it up to softball, or AIDS, or whatever—Jessica's deal with Richie always seemed a lot less physically intense. That didn't stop me from launching into the "let's get to the doc" discussion though, when it became clear sophomore year that Jess and Richie were an item. But she just responded with the standard, "Oh, Mom."

"Oh, Mom, what?" I asked, putting the carton of milk down on the breakfast table.

"Nothing," she said, pushing it away and eating her blueberries plain. "I just think you've been watching too many MTV videos or something."

"What's that supposed to mean?"

"It means why do you assume that just because we are teenagers, Richie and I are doing it? We aren't. I'm not saying we won't ever, but if we do, I can make my own doctor appointments, and I can buy my own condoms."

I had to stop myself from saying, "Let him buy the condoms." It was a retro sentiment and I knew it. Relying on anyone but yourself to be in charge of your personal future was stupid—the existence of Jessica herself was pretty solid proof of that. So all I said was, "Well fine, Jessica," but it came out a little bitchier than I'd intended.

Jessica apparently heard that. She slammed her spoon down on the table and asked, "What's *that* about?"

"What's what about?"

"That ticked-off sound. God, Mom, what's with you? I'm not *lying*. Most moms would think it was awesome that their daughters were not sleeping with their boyfriends. That wasn't all that easy a decision for us to make, you know." And then getting up to rinse her dishes she hissed, "Well, yeah, I guess *you* do."

"Nice one, Jess." But then I dropped it. I did not want to get into some my-teen-morals-are-better-than-your-teen-morals thing. But the comment brought me face-to-face with something I hadn't ever even thought I could feel. And it was that on some hopelessly neurotic level, Jessica's decision not to sleep with Richie felt like a thumbs-down comment on my decision—if you can call it that—to have slept with her father. I really hated that.

So we never talked about it again—at least not until one Sunday morning about a year later when Jess was still asleep and I had run out of tampons. I picked up Jess's purse in the front hall to see if she had one zipped away in the inner lining and she did. She also had a three-pack of Trojan-Enz—an *open* three-pack of Trojan-Enz.

I was so good. I didn't say anything for a whole two hours. Which wasn't all that hard, because Jessica was still sleeping. But around noon, after she'd ambled into the kitchen where I was pretending to read the papers, I did say in this fake chatty voice, "I ran out of tampons this morning, so I borrowed one from your purse."

She looked up from pouring her coffee.

"Don't worry, I went to Walgreen's, got a box, and I replaced your purse one. It's right back in that little zipped side pocket—you know, the one with the condoms."

Jessica sat down and looked right at me—no guilt, no

shock, not even a sliver of discomfort. I could have killed her. She just said, "Oh."

" '*Oh*'? That's it?"

"That's what? What do you want me to say, Mom? You needed a tampon. You went in my purse. You found my condoms. '*Oh.*' Is there something else I should say?"

"I don't know about 'should,' Jessica," I said, taking a gulp of my lukewarm coffee. "It was just kind of a moment."

"Well, I suppose it was," she said and then she did one of those hair-tossing things girls practically major in in high school. "But then *moments* can happen when you start going through someone's purse, Mom. I mean I could make a moment out of it too. You've always told me not to go into your purse. So I'm a little pissed off that you think that rule doesn't hold for you too. So fine. You found out something that maybe you did or didn't want to know. But now you know. I don't really want to talk about it. If I'd wanted to, I would have in the first place."

She had me. She really did.

"Mom," she said, softening some, "I mean it. I'm seventeen and I'm allowed to have my own sex life. I'm smart, I'm responsible, and all you need to know is that Richie and I are fine."

And for the longest time I think they were. The two of them seemed very stable and loving. I even learned to deal with the extremely humbling fact that at least for the moment, my daughter had a hotter sex life, and a more caring, committed love life than I did.

But things between Jessica and Richie had gone consistently south ever since November, when she had gotten the softball scholarship to North Carolina. The second she signed on the dotted line, she began to mentally pack up and move to Chapel Hill. And while I was only somewhat bothered by it, Richie was absolutely devastated. He just couldn't grasp that Jessica had emotionally vacated the premises.

The problem was, Jessica had inherited my inability to bail out of a crummy relationship. Once Tony walked on me, I just didn't have the heart to do that to anyone, so I usually stuck around until the deal just curdled and died. In fact, I'd say that my track record at saying, "Here's your hat, there's the door" in my first ten years as a gay divorcee was somewhere around zero for thirteen. I dated drips until the drips figured out I was not being premenstrual, I was just being mean. And the reason I was mean was never because I was really mean, but because I was mad at myself for not being ballsy enough to say, "You know what, Ronnie, this is just not working out."

Four years ago however, when I actually was going out with a guy named Ronnie—this completely inappropriate twenty-two-year-old who was interning at the paper, and who provided me with some of the finer sexual memories of my life to date—I did manage to turn to him and say, "You know what, Ronnie, this is just not working out." It was an excellent moment. And ever since, which has been a grand total of twice, I have been able to utter it whenever necessary. No problem at all.

But Jess was having a hard time saying it to Richie, so

she had been walking around in full-blown pissiness for the past four months. And every night Richie came over for more sulking and abuse. I tried to get Jessie to talk about it, but she was shut down on the topic. So most nights I just retired after dinner to my bedroom, turned on the little TV that Dolores and Brian had bought me for Christmas, and vegged out.

Tonight I must have fallen asleep with it on, though, because when the phone rang, David Letterman was doing something upside down from the side of a building.

"Hello?" I said, reaching for the phone across the pile of clothes I'd planned to hang up before zoning out.

"Oh, shit, Lacy. I'm sorry, I guess I woke you. It's Charlie."

"Oh, hi. Where are you? You sound far."

"I am. I'm in Calgary. I'm really sorry to wake you."

"No, it's okay, I have to take my contacts out anyway."

"I didn't know you wore contacts."

"Yeah, for two years. I love them, but when I take them out I always feel like I'm turning into The Disposable Woman."

"Do you have the disposable kind?"

"No," I said, reaching for my clock to see the time. "That's what my uncle calls my Aunt Theresa, because first she takes out the contacts, then the teeth, and then this little hairpiece she wears 'cause she thinks her hair is too thin. I always wonder if I'm going to wind up like her, you know, going to bed with all my parts stacked up on the sink."

His laugh got crackled up with some long-distance

static. "Do you want to go back to sleep now? I can try and find you in the morning before I get on the plane."

"No, it's okay. Are you having a dating crisis? How're things with you and the vegetarian veterinarian?"

"Not that terrible if you overlook the fact that I'm allergic to cats and can only go forty-eight hours without eating some kind of meat. I don't want to talk about it. I need a sabbatical from all this. That's why I'm calling you."

"You want me to plan your sabbatical?" I asked, muting Dave on the TV.

"No. Just go with me on it. A friend of mine called me with two tickets for the Bulls/Knicks game on Sunday. I'm not usually off on Sundays and if I am, the last place I want to head is back to the United Center. But I haven't seen the Bulls play this year. And I know you love them. Do you want to go?"

"Are you kidding?"

"No, I'm inviting. Can you go?"

"God, I've only been to one Bulls game in my whole life. I'd love to go, really love to, but don't you think you should use these tickets for the doggie doc or for one of the other SWF-mom candidates?"

"Probably. But I don't want to. I'm looking for a break. Why don't you just come with me?"

"Really?"

"Really."

"God, I will. This is so cool. Thanks, Charlie."

"Great. I'll call you Sunday morning. The game is at twelve-thirty. You can give me directions to your place then."

"I could just meet you at the paper," I said, clicking the TV off for good. I was really excited.

"Why would you want to go to the paper on your day off? Don't be silly. I'll pick you up."

"Yeah, but if you pick me up, then it won't feel like a sabbatical from dating."

"Yes it will. Because I'll be picking *you* up, Lacy. And you and I don't date, remember?"

"Yeah."

"Yeah. Now go take your eyes out. I'll call you Sunday."

Lacy

FOUR DAYS LATER

From the very start, I loved every single minute of the game. The beginning is so cool—they black out the place, and these spotlights start twirling, and the announcer just bellows, ". . . and now . . . your World Champion CHIC-A-GO BULLS!" And then the whole crowd just slams to its feet pounding and roaring as each player runs out. By the time Jordan comes onto the floor, every inch of that room is pure raw screaming love.

The volume is so intense that when Charlie leaned down to whisper whatever it was he whispered, I couldn't hear a thing. I could only feel his lips graze my hair in an effort to be heard, and my whole inners came to a complete halt. He must have felt me stiffen too, because he squeezed my shoulder, smiled, and as the noise subsided he said, "Cool it, Lacy. I'm not moving in on you. It's an official un-date, remember?" And then after the tip-off, he left to bring us some hot dogs.

The Bulls and the Knicks both played great, and I could tell Charlie was kind of impressed that I actually *got* the subtleties of the game. I'm not one of those glamour chicks who thinks the whole of it is simply basket shooting. I'm not that great at football, but with basketball, I've sort of developed guy eyes. I mean, I can really see the switches on defense. I can even see a lot of the pick-and-rolls. So when the Bulls won by four in overtime, I was pretty emotionally fired up.

"Where did you learn about NBA basketball?" he asked, as we pushed our way out of the United Center and found ourselves in this bizarrely-warm-for-March afternoon. "Did Jessica teach you?"

"Nope, she knows baseball cold, but her boyfriend got us going on NBA basketball. I don't think he's going to make it through this season though, there are some big love problems going on in teen land lately."

"Love is tough," he said, opening the car door so I could fold myself into it. The car, a red Miata, had been a surprise. Someone as rumpled as Charlie just didn't seem like a sports-car kind of a guy. I always figured sports-car guys were preeners, you know, kind of blow-dryer guys.

Actually, as we drove east, he confirmed my instincts. "This isn't mine," he said, sort of apologizing for the smooth-guy accessory. "My Toyota has been in the shop for a week. This belongs to a buddy who is out of town this week with his family."

"A family man with a sports car?"

"A divorced guy with a sports car. He's taken his two kids to Disney World for spring break."

"Hmm." I smiled.

"What's the smile for?"

"Just the whole cliché of it."

"Disney World and spring break? Or Disney World and divorced guys?"

"Divorced guys and sports cars."

"Yeah. I suppose. Is that what your ex-husband has?"

"Are you kidding? My ex-husband was too cheap, *is* too cheap to buy a sports car. It's going to be one of the great moments of my life, when Jessica turns twenty-one and I am through playing games with that bozo for good." We were on Wabash and an El train rumbled by.

"You've been divorced from him for nearly sixteen years," he yelled above the din. "What kind of games are you still playing with him?"

"Money and cajoling games, but in four more years I will finally graduate from the Blow Job School of Divorce."

Charlie nearly rear-ended the car in front of us.

"The what?"

"The Blow Job School of Divorce. That's what my friend Steffi and I call the way we have to handle our ex-husbands in order to get them to be cooperative about stuff. You know like the three summers Jessica went to softball camp? That was something I couldn't have paid for unless Tony had helped out. I mean, even though morally he should have shared the costs, by decree he didn't have to. So, like on those years when he'd ask for her on Thanksgiving and then again on Christmas, even though I was supposed to have her one of those days, I'd say okay. I hated it. But it was like balancing one day for me against a whole month for her, and it was what I had to do to get what I wanted. That's why Steffi and I call it that, because even though you're divorced, you're still giving the guy blow jobs."

"Jesus, Lacy."

" 'Jesus,' what? What's the matter?"

"What's the matter is that kind of thing gives a really bad name to blow jobs."

I had to laugh. "Maybe we should have put 'good sense of humor' in your ad after all."

"No, you were right," he said as we passed the Art Institute. "The ones who said they had great senses of humor did not know the difference between being funny and being addicted to laughing. The vet is like that. I say something like, 'Do you want to go to dinner first and see the movie after?' and you'd think I was Groucho Marx."

"I think the chronic laughing thing comes from sitcoms. Because in sitcoms, no matter what anyone says, it's followed by a laugh track. I think people get nervous in real life when they don't hear a laugh track, so they think that they'd better provide it. It's like if they don't, then maybe it might not sound like they are having a good time, and the evening will get low ratings, and then they will be canceled."

He gave me a weird look. "Well, I don't know why it happens, but I sure as hell know that it does, and it's damned unnerving. Lacy, I don't want to talk about this. This is my dating sabbatical. Remember?"

"You're right, I'm sorry. We could do the weather or religion or something. God, look at the beach—it really *is* gorgeous today." We were on Lake Shore Drive across from Buckingham Fountain and you could see Grant Park was still jammed with people who had bought into the pretend spring day.

"I know. They said it was going to almost seventy. When do you have to be home? We could head up to North Avenue beach for a couple of minutes, if you've got some time."

"I've just got to be back for dinner," I said, unsure why being able to say that made me feel safer. I guess part of it had to do with Jess, and the fact that I still had her as an anchor, a kind of framework for my life. A year from now I wouldn't have that, and I think I was carrying that sense of that future formlessness around with me all the time. Charlie's offer to go to the beach was definitely nice, but unsettling. I liked Charlie, but he rattled me some.

For starters, he kept getting better and better looking the more I got to know him, which was a totally unfair thing. I'm not saying he did it on purpose, but he did it. And secondly, I was getting used to having him in my life. I loved talking to him whenever he called. He always made me laugh, and he was interesting, and challenging, and easy to goof around with. We had a game where we made up weird book titles—I was keeping the list—and so far we had forty-three. And thirdly—not that this was relevant—but Charlie had these great hands. I hate stubby hands or unexpressive hands, but Charlie had hands that looked like they *knew* a lot—a lot about protecting and a lot about pleasing. So for all those reasons going alone with him to the beach made me nervous. I'd never been alone with him with no people and just Nature.

But there we were ten minutes later, on a completely deserted slice of the North Avenue beach. Chicago is so cool. You have all these fancy gorgeous urban-looking apartment buildings on one side of Lake Shore Drive and across the street is this perfect resortlike wonderful beach. When I was a little girl, Dolores and the husband of the moment would take me up to the Evanston beach on Sundays and we would swim and grill sausages and peppers. The beach was always jammed and festive, and it made me feel like we'd left our real life behind and were on a small, hot, wonderful vacation. And then on Mondays, it would happen all over again, only this time it would be just me and Dolores. The shop would be closed, she'd make sandwiches out of the leftover sausage and peppers from the day before, and the beach would feel like it belonged to just the two of us. Dolores would bring the newest movie magazines from the shop, and we would spend hours poring over the love lives of all the people in *Photoplay* and *Modern Screen*. As far as we were concerned, you could never read enough tragic things about Elizabeth Taylor.

"Did you go to the beach a lot when you were little?" I asked Charlie, who had picked up a rock and was skipping it across the water.

"Not a lot," he said a bit wistfully. "Sophie was never too comfortable in a bathing suit. Sometimes I think my entire childhood would have been different if my mother hadn't had varicose veins."

We plopped down and he picked up a stick to doodle in the sand. "I think the first time I ever came to the beach," he mused, "was with Elise Marcus and her family. It was the day I fell out of love with her."

"How old were you?"

"Seven. So was she. Exactly. It was her seventh birthday party. And she'd invited a bunch of us to the Foster Avenue beach to swim and cook out. I was the designated boyfriend, though. Which seemed only fair since she and I had been playing a relatively hot version of doctor for about two months. Do you want the short or the long version of this? It's pretty traumatic."

"The short," I told him. For March it was hot, but still, I was wearing a leather miniskirt, which made sitting on the sand not all that simple to pull off. Charlie had made it easier by taking off his windbreaker and laying it down so I could stretch my legs out and wonder what he thought of them. God, it was so beautiful there—the lake was having one of those days when it thought it was an ocean—bunches of waves and drama. It was great to sit and just be with it all.

"Aren't you cold?" I asked him. He had on a light blue shirt under an olive-green sweater—his eyes almost matched the shirt today. He was wearing khakis too, which was sort of a date look if you ask me.

"Nope. I'm fine. So anyway Elise was the new girl in our class. And I think the reason she decided to let me play doctor with her was that she thought it was the fastest way to make friends."

"Was it?"

"I guess so. By the time her birthday party rolled around, she had six or seven of us there. I was the only one she played doctor with, but who knows? Even seven-year-old women can be tricky. Anyway, I thought that I was in love with her. Until that day."

"And then what happened?"

"What happened was when we were coming home in the car, she threw up all over me."

"Oh, God," I said, leaning back on my elbows and hoping my skirt would behave, "I hate these birthday party tragedies. Jessica threw up at her nine-year-old party and it was such a mess."

"Yeah, well, IT wasn't a mess. I was a mess. And mortified. Just like she was. But it was pretty clear that was the end."

"Charlie, you rat! She couldn't help that she was sick," I said, pushing him.

"I know that now," he said, as a guy ran by us with his chocolate Labrador. "I'd never bail out on someone for heaving now. I'm a very evolved guy. But when you are seven, you can't keep on loving a girl that everyone has seen throw up on you. No second grader has the moves to deal with that."

"Yeah, I suppose. Are you any better at breaking up now?"

We shook the sand from our backsides, and started to walk south. "You mean am I less abrupt?"

"Less abrupt would be a start."

"Well, I must be pretty good at it. I seem to have broken off with several women lately. I guess the biggest breakup should have been the one with my wife, but we were married such a short time. It was real clear to both of us that we had done a dumb thing. There was none of the heartache shit you usually associate with divorce. She just walked in from work one day and said, 'We need to talk. I've fallen in love with Bernie Grobstein.' "

"God, what did you say?"

"Well, I was definitely interested in how that could have taken place. But she was adamant about sparing me the details."

"Did you really want them?" I asked, watching him dragging the same stick along in the sand.

"Damn right. When your wife falls in love with a proctologist, if you don't have the details, you get to imagining terrible things."

"So are you still imagining them?"

"No. She finally told me. The accounting firm where she worked did this guy's books. That was how they met. Marcy was really a very nice lady, and a doctor who kept good records was perfect for her. I was too chaotic then. I was caught up in my work, busting my ass on every story, but always mind-fucking myself over whether the *Tribune* would beat me out. I made her crazy. And I felt shitty all the time for doing it to her. The proc doc made her happy, so in a sense, the divorce was a relief. I don't suppose yours was that way."

"Not even close," I answered. An elderly couple were walking toward us. Which of course was what I'd always figured Tony and I would be someday. I still hated talking about it. Nearly sixteen years later, and I could always touch back to the pain of that morning I woke up to find the note from Tony that said, "Sorry, babe, I just can't do it. The kid is great, you are great, but I've got to split." That was it. Nineteen years old with a twenty-month-old daughter and no high school diploma. Bye, babe. Thank God for Dolores. Dolores, who her whole life had shuttled husbands in and out the door, took one look at that note, said, "That son of a bitch," and called her regular lawyer right away to make sure Tony kept supporting Jess. Then she scooped up my shattered ego, punctured my justifiable terror, and showed me that, dammit, life goes on.

Dolores moved Jess and me into her place, made sure I graduated from secretarial school, and taught me the hugely important lesson that strength isn't rooted in clout, it's rooted in resiliency. Dolores is a complex woman—on one hand she is this hard-driving business-person, and on the other she is this total girl. She can spend forty minutes debating the merits of one nail polish color over the other. The bane of her existence has never been that her daughter was left to raise a child alone—no, it's her daughter's hair. Dolores, who has never committed to a single hairdo or a single color for more than three months at a time, is tormented by the fact that I refuse to cut or color my hair. She is always leaving notes for me, "The bob is back!" or "Short is in!" She has never accepted that wild and curly hair counts as a hairdo—not even after Julia Roberts made it okay.

I spared Charlie the unabridged edition of "The Story of My Divorce," and gave him the three-minute version. He listened intently and then he asked me point-blank why I wasn't seeing anyone now. I didn't know the answer to that exactly.

I think it's just that I do such a terrible job of picking guys. Tony taught me not to trust men, but my dating history has taught me not to trust me. Sometimes I think it could be genetic, even. I mean until Brian, Dolores was a pretty terrible chooser too. It was like both of us could step into a room filled with men, pick one out and go, "Hey! You. The one that's gonna break my heart. I think I love you." Maybe I'll acquire better selecting skills by the time I'm fifty, but in the meantime it just seems smarter to keep my distance.

There is this guy Randy I hang around with when I go country dancing on Tuesdays, and sometimes we make out, but the main attraction is that he is a fabulous two-stepper. He's cute and all, but we're just flirting with each other. In real life, I haven't been involved with anyone for more than a year, which probably explains why I've sublimated all my romance cravings into a couple of short stories. Even Jessica and Steffi didn't know about them. I am pretty sure they aren't terrible. In fact, I am thinking of sending one of them off to *Redbook*. The lead characters are named Jade and Richard—he used to be Ramon, but I decided that was too much.

"Where is he now?" asked Charlie as we passed a shuttered-down concession stand that was shaped like a landlocked boat.

"Who?"

"Mr. Gazzar. Rhymes with 'bizarre.' "

"Oak Park—until the wife throws him out."

"Why? Does he drink?"

"Nope, he fools around. Tony speaks two languages—fucking and English. And with Tony, English is his second language."

"What's he do?"

"Heating and refrigeration. You know what he got Jessica for her sixteenth birthday? A humidifier."

"What a guy. Does he spend much time with Jessica?"

"Holidays is about all, and maybe some ball games. He's kind of a miserly guy—miserly of spirit, miserly of money. He's not a—what's that Jewish word that starts with an 'm'? You know, that means like warm, but solid and huggy?"

"'M'? I don't know," he said, stopping in his tracks for a second to think about it.

"Sure you do. The one that means good guy, a real man."

"'M'? You mean *mensch*?"

"Yeah. Tony is definitely not one of the world's great *mensches*."

"Do you know anyone that is?"

I was surprised at the question. Because an obvious and true thing I could have said was, "You are." Only if I said that to him—unofficial date or not—I was scared that he might mistake it for some sort of green light. And then maybe he'd move in, and then I'd pull back, and then he'd get all ticked off/defensive/withdrawn—take your pick—so, it was just easier to say "not really."

It must have been almost six, because the sun was nearly gone, the sky had gone to purple, and the temperature had dropped enough to make hanging around the beach much longer seem stupid. "I really should get you back," said Charlie, turning his back on the Drake Hotel so we could head north again toward the car. The wind began to slice through me so I started skipping up the beach. "Hey, how come boys can't skip," I yelled from thirty yards away.

"We can skip," he yelled back. "We don't want to. It's a girl thing."

"Is not, Charlie. Boys don't skip 'cause they can't skip. I have never in my life seen a boy skip. Look I'm skipping backward," I taunted, "can you do that?"

"Are you daring me?"

"Definitely. I dare you to skip twenty feet forward, and ten feet backward."

"What do I get if I do it?"

"You get to take me home."

"What do I get if I don't do it?"

"You get a choice—you get to take me home, and I make fun of you, or you get to take me home, only you let me drive the car, and I'll be well behaved."

God, I loved driving the Miata. In my whole life I had never driven a sports car. "It's incredible! This feels as hot as it looks like it feels. You can't say that about much in this world."

"That doesn't speak too well of the men in your life, you know."

"Do I ever." And then, preferring to change the subject, I asked, "Hey, Charlie? Can I use the phone? It's just so cool sitting there. I just want to call Jess on it."

"Sure," he said, punching up my number. It made me feel weird that he had it memorized.

"Jess," I said into the speaker, "guess where I'm calling from . . ."

"Not a hospital I hope. 'Cause the manicotti will be perfect in twenty-five minutes and I'd hate you to miss the bubbly part."

I had no clue Jess was making manicotti tonight—Charlie's favorite. He'd told me that time in the restaurant. But if I invited him for manicotti, it was like the *mensch* thing—he could get the message all mixed up. On the other hand, he *had* just taken me to the Bulls, and Jessica always made enough of it for twenty. So if I invited him, what was so terrible?

Terrible was that Jessica really liked him—right off. From the minute we all sat down at the dining-room table, they talked softball, they talked colleges, they talked the pressure of competition, and the narrowness of the world of professional sports. I left the two of them at the table after I cleared and did the dishes, and they were still yammering away. It was pretty weird. Charlie seemed very at ease with Jess, almost as if the two of them were the real friends and I was the extra person.

"God, Mom, what a cool guy. For a grown-up and all, I mean," Jessica said when she came into the kitchen for the coffee mugs. "He's so funny. And sexy. I don't mean for me, but . . . What's the deal with you two?"

"The deal, Jess, is that this man is dying to have a baby with someone, so there is no deal. Because I am *not* dying to have a baby with someone. I already had one, remember? I like him well enough, and I'm helping him—mostly by listening to him—while he tries to hook up with the future mom of his baby."

"Mom, you make him sound so calculating," she said, filling the mugs with coffee.

"Calculating? This guy isn't calculating. He's just dying to get his new life started because he's running about twenty years late."

Charlie left about a half hour later. When I handed his jacket to him, I said, "I really liked today. Thanks a lot for taking me on your dating sabbatical. Did it help you feel more ready to plunge back in?"

"I don't know. Maybe I should revise the ad a bit. Go back to being more self-effacing. A new lead or something."

"Like what?"

"Like, 'So what if I can't skip backward . . .'" Then he held up his hand for a high five.

Okay, yeah . . . I was smiling when I closed the door.

Charlie

MAY

I know the poem says April is the cruelest month. But T. S. Eliot did not happen to be covering hockey. For those of us who have this particular gig, the killer month is May.

May is the month we're in the thick of the play-offs. Not only does that make my life completely unpredictable, it means I don't have enough of a real life to even be unpredicted. The pressure at play-off time is unfuckingbelievable. It's easily twice that of the regular season. And by May it already feels as though it has dragged on long enough. Truth is, by the middle of spring, every single writer on the hockey beat is secretly praying for his team to blow it and to be out of the running. No one said it was ethical; no one said it even felt good. But when you could be home for all of May and still collect the same paycheck you'd be collecting if you were busting your ass covering the play-offs . . . well, it made it real hard to be hungry for the championship.

The problem was, it was now May twenty-third, and it looked like the championship was precisely where the Blackhawks were headed. They had just set a league record for games won in a row and were major contenders for the Stanley Cup. To say that I was beat to shit did not do justice to the depths of exhaustion I felt. The forty-eight hours that I had back in town gave me about enough time to get one decent night's sleep and to take care of the four things I needed to take care of . . . my laundry, my dad's birthday present, my three paychecks that were waiting to be picked up at the paper, and my alleged love life.

Not necessarily in that order.

I have been seeing Jo Beth Lindbloom for over two months. When regular people see someone for over two months, it totals more than eight dates. It doesn't if you're on the hockey beat. Hockey games are played when working people are free to see them, so even when I'm in town that means I work when everyone else is off. It also means that my dream woman is destined to be a second shift woman—a nurse, a waitress, a cop, anyone who basically hasn't seen the *Today* show in years. Jo Beth fits the bill. Except she *does* see the show. That's because she works at NBC. She produces their local ten o'clock news. Jo Beth lives and breathes TV. She hangs around the studio until eleven-thirty or midnight every night. Which means if I'm in town, by the time I've finished filing, she is still wired and ready to go out.

In fact, logistically, it's great. Intellectually, romantically, and sexually, though, it leaves something to be desired.

I'm not saying Jo Beth isn't smart. She went to Brown and even though she is a TV person, she still reads. But I'm not sure she is smart at handling me. I admit I advertised, and I admit it was a very goal-oriented ad. A let's-hustle-and-get-this-family-going ad. But I get the feeling Jo Beth is too eager to close the deal.

And Jo Beth is attractive. She's a tall, leggy redhead with wide-set brown-black eyes and a great smile. Granted, her voice is a little nasal, and she has this habit of finishing people's sentences for them, but I am trying to keep an open mind.

And the sex is decent. Sex these days is complicated. There's the blood test discussion, the your-condom-or-mine discussion . . . It's nuts. It's like sex has these built-in commercial breaks all the time now, which is tough on a guy. Guys are used to clicking through the commercials. I do not have a lot of tolerance for the *interruptus* aspect of the event.

Plus, Jo Beth is one of those women who makes a ritual out of birth control. She likes to put the condom on the guy. I know that screwing was basically designed as a two-person activity, but shit! Rubbers are one part of sex that is not enhanced by participation. No doubt she read in some woman's magazine that co-opting the un-rolling process was perceived by guys to be some sort of aphrodisiac assist. I haven't figured out how to break the news. It's not.

Maybe that's because we've only slept together a couple of times. And while physically gratifying, those times were definitely short in the passion department. It could be because we're new to each other. But I'm wondering if the lack of heat is based less on unfamiliarity than on uncertainty about why the hell we're having sex in the first place. Of course we're having it because sex was what you do next after you've spent four or five pretty decent evenings together, and dry humping is ruining your underwear.

But the lack of intensity thing has been gnawing at me. I gotta believe she feels it too. I think we should talk about it. In a nice way, but real straight. I don't want to shelve it. I've spent too much of my life shelving shit, particularly with Janice. When you stash things away in favor of short-term tranquillity, you wind up being long-term pissed off. At least I do. This time I figured as long as I was trying to do something right, it would be a good idea to hash things out. So as soon as I put some laundry in, the plan was to call Jo Beth.

She beat me to it. I was in the middle of separating the grays that were always grays from the grays that used to be white when the bedroom phone rang.

"Charlie! You're back."

"Back and knee-deep in grubby socks and underwear. How are you doing?" I asked, sitting down next to the sock pile on the bed.

"Terrific! We had a twenty-one share last night."

It was sweeps for all the networks. Jo Beth, who was usually only frantic about ratings, was now completely consumed by them. This was not a big assist if we were going to pick up the lust percentages in our little duo, but then the Stanley Cup play-offs weren't exactly a help either.

"Is that good?" I asked, sitting down on the bed. "Did you beat out channels two and seven?"

"Yeah, for the past three nights. We're hoping the numbers will carry through all week. Your paper slammed us for our 'Housewife Hookers' series, but what else is new? It's sweeps, and sex sells."

"Don't worry. What the hell do our TV critics know? Watching TV all day annihilates a person's intelligence."

"Jesus, Charlie," she snarled, "why are you always so snotty about TV?"

"Jo Beth? I was just trying to make you feel better about the mope who's our TV critic. I wasn't attacking you."

"I know. I'm sorry. I'm running on too little sleep and too much adrenaline. Besides, I think I've missed you more than I like to admit."

Now I knew what I was supposed to do. I was supposed to say, "I've missed you too." And I had . . . in a vague unarticulated way. But unarticulated doesn't cut it when someone has just stuck her neck out. So I jumped in with a pretty sincere, "Me too."

It made her happy. And suddenly I was glad that I could make her happy and that I was going to see her in a few hours.

"What's your schedule today?" I asked. The cordless was fading in and out and I had to stand next to the window to get it to work. "Do you want to try and get away for an early dinner, or is it going to be easier for you if I just come by for you after the show?"

"Why don't we do both?"

"Great, if you've got the time. I've got a shopping problem though. I need to stop and pick up my dad's present at some point."

"Oh, listen, you don't. I remembered you'd said that you wanted to get that book about the Rockies for him, so I picked it up for you when I was at Barnes and Noble last Sunday."

What I said was, "Oh, God, Jo Beth, thanks." What I thought was, Oh, God, Jo Beth. I wish you hadn't done that. I knew that wasn't a gracious way to feel. I knew buying the book had been a thoughtful gesture. But still, it felt too something. Too pushy. Too domestic. I had already accepted that Jo Beth was a Filofax sort of a woman, and that she led a very organized life. But I was not ready to have her leap in and organize mine. She was so damn anal. I'd gotten my first dose of that the morning after we'd first spent the night at her place.

Jo Beth has a small duplex in a brownstone on North Dearborn. Unlike lots of women who crammed their homes with that dry smelly stuff in bowls that you get in soap shops, Jo Beth has a tailored, guy-friendly place. The couches are big and comfortable, you can put your feet up anywhere, and there are big TVs in all the rooms. That morning we had decided to go out and buy the food for brunch. When we came home to unload the groceries though, she opened the egg carton and started counting the eggs as she set them in the compartment.

"Jo Beth, why are you doing that?" I asked, coming over to hug her. "There are twelve slots in the egg carton and twelve places in the egg compartment."

"But you never know."

"Never know what?"

"You just never know, Charlie. It's always better to know."

Jo Beth needed to be sure of everything, to monitor everything. She was a walking mission control. I wanted to be grateful, but in truth, I wished like hell she hadn't gone shopping for Abe's birthday present. Particularly since I hadn't decided what I was going to get him, and even more particularly because I hadn't decided whether or not I was going to bring her to Abe's party.

The party was scheduled for six the next night. We were all meeting at Myron and Phil's steak joint up on Devon. Sophie and Abe, their best friends Hy and Marion Isaacs, Roger and Elaine and the two older kids, and me. Me, and all my fucked-up, conflicted feelings about bringing Jo Beth. It was a hard call. Sophie and Abe would plotz to see me walk in with a certifiable woman, considering I'd been such a solo act since Janice. They'd been crazy about Janice, and having her with me at family gatherings had always been easy. But the Jo Beth thing was different. Jo Beth and I were *getting* into it, but we weren't into it yet. It felt too early and too sticky to show up with her at a full-family gig. I did not need looks or questions or any of the bullshit—albeit loving bullshit—that would come down. My plan was to not say much to Jo Beth about the Abe-Fest.

"So what time is the big event tomorrow night?"

There went the best laid plans . . . "Uh, six or six-thirty, I'm not sure. It's way up north at Myron and Phil's. It would be a real haul for you to get there and back before the show," I said, doing my best to discourage her.

"Well, I suppose it would, but I would really love to meet everyone. I could run up on my dinner break and at least have a drink with you all. It's really up to you, Charlie, I wouldn't want to barge in or anything."

"No," I heard someone say, "it would be great if you could come."

In the end, when I told Sophie, she did a great job of not hyperventilating.

"You're bringing a TV producer?"

"Yeah, Mom, she does the ten o'clock news on channel five."

"Sara McCauly does the ten o'clock news on channel five. I see her every night. Does this girl work for her?"

"Not exactly."

"Is this girl her boss? You're going out with Sara McCauly's boss?"

"No, Mom, not exactly. I mean yes I am going out with her, but she's not exactly Sara McCauly's boss. But you'll like her. She's nice."

"It's not important if *I* like her, Chuckie. How do *you* like her?" Christ, where do moms learn to do that with pronouns?

"I like her fine. She wouldn't be showing up if I didn't like her. I just don't know her all that well. We've only been out eight or nine times."

"So?"

"So eight or nine times' worth is about how well I know her. But she's heard me talking about you and Dad, and she wanted to stop in and meet everyone. It's sweeps month, so she has to get right back to work though."

"A girl with a night-shift job, Chuckie, just like you always wanted. That's good. How did you meet this TV lady?"

"Her name is Jo Beth Lindbloom, Mom." Then saving her the trouble of asking, I added, "And yeah she's Jewish."

"Jewish. That's wonderful, Chuckie. How did you meet her?"

"A friend." I lied. I couldn't get into it. In all these months of Abe's recovery (and the guy hadn't looked this good in years), I had never found the opening for a straight discussion about this baby thing. Or the personals ad thing. Not that I had a long history of reporting in to my folks about all my life moves, but this one was pretty relevant. At some point it was something that I needed to let them in on. But I was holding back for the obvious reason. I was scared shitless that I could never pull it off, particularly in light of my current Jo Beth ambivalence.

Which only got worse when I saw Lacy that afternoon.

It took me fifteen minutes to unearth my checks from payroll, and then I headed up to the fourth floor, to deal with my mail. Lacy's department and my department had both moved back to our respective corners up there sometime in January, so there was no more casual running into each other. Not that Lacy and I were casual. We were *involved*. Not romantically (her choice, not necessarily mine), but involved in a way that felt a little edgier than just being friends. At least it felt like that to me.

It sure felt like that when I spotted her at her desk. It was the first time since the Bulls game we'd seen each other in person. Chicago had moved full throttle into spring, and somewhere along the way Lacy had picked up the beginnings of a tan. Knowing her, it could have been one of those bottle tans, but bottom line, she looked great. Particularly in the dress she was wearing. It was blue, but the key thing is it had no sleeves. I had never seen Lacy's arms before. They were gorgeous. Long, firm, graceful. I know guys come across as limited to tits and asses, but it's a mistake to underestimate our vulnerability to things like a bare arm or shoulder.

She was on the phone when I got to her desk and she signaled for me to wait a minute. It gave me time to pick up the pile of snapshots she must have just gotten of Jessica and some other incredible eighteen-year-olds in tight black prom dresses. "Charlie! You're back!" she said, standing up to not exactly hug me, but just to touch my arm. "I was wondering if you'd show up today. I couldn't tell from your story if the Hawks were back in town today or tomorrow."

"Since when are you reading my stories?" I pulled up a chair and we both sat back down. "You've never told me that."

"I don't tell you everything, you know. Like I didn't

tell you that for the next few days while Ruthie is out sick, I am writing her part of the column."

"Yeah? Are you pleased or are you pissed?"

"Both. I'm a woman."

"Like I didn't notice."

She grinned. Shit. It wasn't fair for her to look that good, for me to like her that much, and for her to be so damn off-limits. The more I got to know her, the more idiotic it seemed to me that she had put herself on the DL.

"Well, given that you've noticed that I seem to be a woman, I don't want to go coy on you, but could you do a man-chore for me?"

I leaned forward and said in my best Jack Nicholson imitation, "I've been wanting to do a man-chore for you for a long time, darlin'."

"Charlie, you are so lame at imitating a slime bag. It's just not in your genes."

"To the contrary, kid. It IS in my jeans."

"Stop it!" she snapped, green eyes flashing. "I don't like it when you're not you. I'm just asking for you to help me carry a computer out to my car. I drove Dolores's car in today, because the paper had a sale on our old computers and I bought one for Jessica to take to school. I'm parked about four blocks away. Do you think you could drop the Neanderthal routine for a minute and just give me a hand?"

She definitely didn't want to play. Fifteen minutes later, the boxed-up computer was in the trunk of her mom's Taurus. I felt like pretty schmucky for having bummed her out with my high testosterone routine, and I put my hand on her shoulder to apologize.

"Don't," she said, stepping away from my reach. "You don't have to apologize. I'm just a nervous wreck when I have to carry the column for a few days. I shouldn't have jumped on you like that. I just think sometimes we're so used to dealing with each other on the phone that we don't know how to deal with each other in person. Somehow on the phone, it's easier."

"Easier than what?" I asked as we headed back up Wabash.

"Easier than seeing each other live and in color— we're just not used to it. It's like we have a rhythm to our phone calls. It's always the end of the day, we're always completely unwired. It's just a real good time to connect. I like our phone calls."

"Me too," is all I said. I couldn't begin to tell her how much. How as often as I could, when I was on the road, I'd call Jo Beth first. Jo Beth wasn't big on long calls, so after we'd hang up, I'd settle into bed so my real last call of the night would be to Lacy. A couple of times we'd talked so long that one of us fell asleep while we were still connected. It felt good.

Not that seeing Jo Beth that night felt bad. She slept over at my place for the first time, and I've got to admit, being on my own turf made it better. The beer was mine, the pillows were mine, even the condoms were mine. This time I put them on solo. She was fine about it.

And when she showed up at Abe's party, she couldn't

have been more terrific. Granted, she was a little cling-ing and heavy into the hand-holding, but she was ner-vous, and I understood that. No problem.

What I had a problem with came later. When she met me at my place after the game the next night. It was nearly midnight, and she walked in holding a videocas-sette.

"Here," she said, handing it to me, "it came into the station the other day, and I thought at some point we could watch it."

"What is it?" I asked, kissing her.

She kicked her shoes off and collapsed on the couch. "It's this Wisconsin doctor who says he has had a ninety-eight percent success rate in helping his patients have a girl baby or a boy baby."

"I always heard those were the only two choices," I said, hanging her coat up in the closet, and wondering why the hell we were discussing this at nearly one in the morning.

"No, Charlie, what I mean is ninety-eight percent successful conceiving whichever one you choose. If you're dying for a girl or you're dying for a boy, he has a system that can make it happen. I thought we should look at it. We haven't really talked about this much, but I've always seen myself having a girl. For my whole life, I have always thought of myself having a daughter. And if that poses some sort of problem for you, it seems to me we at least should get some discussion going on it. Be-cause I am willing to consider having a boy, but at this point it's not my preference. And, before I forget . . ." Jo Beth reached her purse and hauled out the Filofax.

"My parents' anniversary is in five weeks. They really want to meet you. I thought I would make a reservation for four at Ambria on the twenty-first. Is that okay for you?"

I didn't know I had that much sweat in me.

Charlie

EARLY JUNE

"I thought you said you didn't give a damn who won, that all you wanted was for it to be over," Lacy said.

We were having tuna fish sandwiches down on the Wendella boat dock. We'd made a pact after the parking-lot conversation two weeks before. The deal was once the season was over, we'd try to get as comfortable with each other in person as we were with each other on the phone. My idea of course. But I didn't want to lose touch with Lacy. And I could see that happening once the season was over and I was no longer calling her from the road and once Jo Beth closed in for the shit-or-get-off-the-pot discussion. The latter being a dreaded inevitability.

Chicago was showing itself off to perfection that day. The river had gone aqua on us, sun silvered the buildings, and everybody seemed juiced about finally being sprung from the muck of winter. It was June 3, two days after the Blackhawks had been brutally trounced in the Stanley Cup finals. We had gone down in four straight games. It had been short and it had been ugly.

Lacy was right. I had said I didn't give a damn who won the play-offs. But when it was over, and I had to haul ass into that Blackhawk locker room where every square inch was reeking of heartbreak, I sure as hell did not feel that way. Those guys were grieving. And they had been my guys for the last eight months. No way could I not grieve with them.

Lacy understood that. She got the part of sports that was poetry and the part that was agony. Lacy was a terrific comprehender. Not only about sports, but about real life stuff. That was one of the reasons I wanted to stay connected. The other reasons—shit! what was the point? She refused to even consider the possibilities. Lacy had made it very clear these past eight months, she was hell-bent on going to college, hell-bent on retiring from daily parenting, and hell-bent on never ever acknowledging that the genuine warmth between us could convert to genuine heat.

"Hey, Charlie, what do you think of the look?" she said, pointing to this flowered dress that was sort of a cross between a clean-the-house dress and middle-of-summer dress. "Jessica gave it to me for Mother's Day. She said I have too many short black skirts and tank tops and that this dress is a compromise between her idea of fashion and mine. I personally think it's a whole lot closer to hers, but I didn't want to hurt her feelings, and anyway I wanted to try it out. It makes me feel different, sort of like Debbie Reynolds or something, like any minute I might get up and tap-dance."

"Give me a sixty-second warning if you do."

"Why? Are you going to run away?"

"No, I'm going to go over to the souvenir stand and buy a camera."

"Maybe you could just borrow one from one of the tourists getting off that boat." About sixty people were filing off the little Wendella cruiser that took them up the Chicago River and out onto Lake Michigan for ninety minutes of skyline gawking.

"What do you think," I asked, eyeballing the crowd, "are there more people from Wisconsin or from Japan?"

"It looks pretty evenly divided to me. Have you ever been a foreigner anywhere? I was in Mexico once, and I hated feeling so foreign, you know, where you can't read the signs, and you are always scared you're going to screw up."

"Mexico? Hell. That's how I feel right here in America in my eight-month role as The Relentless Dater. Unable to read the signs and scared shitless I'm going to blow it."

"Yeah? What's up? I know you're upset about the Blackhawks going down the tubes. Are you and the TV producer headed that way too?" .

"Not down the tubes so much as we've moved into an emergency holding pattern." Lacy had been getting regular bulletins from me all along on the Jo Beth situation. But the brutal truth was that I still had more fun talking to Lacy *about* Jo Beth than being *with* Jo Beth.

"Was there an emergency?"

"Yeah. The first emergency was the finals. I have no moves when games are being played back to back, and I'm filing four and five stories a night."

"What was the second?"

"The second emergency was having the finals be over. Because now I have to deal with Jo Beth."

Last week I'd told Lacy about prebought birthday presents, preconceived baby ideas, and premeditated egg-counting. "I've got a feeling that I am in way over my head with this woman. She could have me penciled in for a late summer wedding, only she just hasn't told me yet."

"Oh, come on," said Lacy. "She can't be that bad if you've spent this much time with her," Lacy said, pointing to my tooth to let me know I had some tuna stuck in there. "Don't you just hate that?"

"What?"

"When no one tells you about gunk stuck in your teeth. Do I have any? You'd tell me wouldn't you?"

"Sure." She bared her teeth. "Nope, no gunk."

"That's a thing that would have been cool to put in your ad."

"What?"

" 'Promise to tell you if spinach is hanging from your teeth.' That's a nice thing about being in a couple, you know? Having someone you can count on to tell you stuff like that, being able to fart in front of someone . . . No one ever talks about that—the farting thing—but it's a very important relationship milestone. Have you and the TV producer gotten past it yet"

"Christ, you are such a guy, Lacy. Jo Beth is an

accomplishment-oriented woman, but I'm sure she doesn't list farting as one of her great relationship milestones."

"Well, I do," she said, checking her watch because we'd already hung around for more than an hour. "Come on, I've got to get back. Are you coming back to the paper?"

"Nope," I said as we headed up the stairs to Michigan Avenue. "I'm going home. I've got piles of crap to deal with. I'll be doing expense reports until midnight."

"No big date with The Fartless Femme Fatale?"

"Jesus, Lacy."

"I'm sorry. But *you* seem so down on her . . ."

"I'm not sure if I'm down on her, or just down. It's pretty clear Jo Beth is not the solution. She's bright, she's into the baby-having plan, and she's very attractive. But put all that together and there still isn't a click. I may be forty-four, but I still feel I'm entitled to a click."

"A click?"

"Yeah. Some sense of heat. Something that makes a guy say, 'This woman is the greatest. I'm crazy for her. Turned on by her. I want to do the rest of my life with her.' That's what I want. Am I some kind of romantic dork to think that is possible?"

"I'm not exactly the right person to ask this sort of stuff, Charlie, you know?"

"Yeah, well all I know is that I am looking down the throat of June third, and I am no closer to pulling this off than when I started. An entire hockey season committed to dating and all I've come up with is a big long-distance bill—half of it to you—a good stash of unused condoms, and a video by some doc in Wisconsin on how you too can have a girl baby by simply fucking sideways on an ottoman for three days. I can't believe fatherhood is this tough. Every other schmuck in the world manages to pull it off."

"Every other schmuck in the world starts a little earlier and is free on Saturday nights. You've had some scheduling difficulties, that's all."

"Yeah, like this Saturday. This is the first whole weekend I've had free in eight months and the woman I'm seeing will be out in San Francisco for a TV convention," I said, draining my Coke can and taking it over to the sidewalk trash basket.

"Don't tell me you're sad about that, not after what you've been saying about her. What would you be doing anyway if Jo Beth were in town?"

"Probably breaking up," I announced, surprising even myself. "But at least we could have done it over a good steak dinner."

"Dinner before the Bulls game or dinner after? I've been a wreck with this series."

The series? Oh, yeah. Basketball. It takes me a couple of days after the play-offs to remember that hockey isn't the only sport consuming people's lives. But of course the entire town of Chicago was wired for another big NBA Championship. Part of it pissed me off, because while Hawks fans were even more intense than Bulls fans, they only numbered about twenty thousand for the whole city. Bulls fans were the *whole* city. "What time does the game start tonight?" I asked.

"Tonight and Friday, I think it's at eight. You aren't going then, huh?"

"Are you kidding? Tickets are impossible."

"Yeah, but you're a sports guy—don't you just kind of *get tickets*?"

"No, Lace, there are a lot of delusions about sports guys and what we supposedly get. You know, like *get* tickets, *get* laid. My friend Bobby is convinced that when you're out on the road, you can always get laid."

"Oh, come on, Charlie, are you about to tell me there is no sex on the road?"

"Not *no* sex, but it's not what people think."

"People don't even know what they think. I mean, I don't. I just assume there's a fair amount of sex in your world."

"What's a fair amount of sex? Ten times a season? Twenty times a season? Thirty?"

Shielding her incredible green eyes from the sun, Lacy pondered a second and then said, "I don't know— ten, maybe twenty?"

"Yeah, well in the past eight months that I was on the road, I had sex exactly twice."

"What do you count as sex?" she said.

"What kind of question is that?"

"Well there's getting laid, and there's getting blow jobs," she said.

"What do you mean?" I asked, incredulous that I was having this discussion on Michigan Avenue with hundreds of people walking by.

"I'm just asking, Charlie. Do you count getting a blow job as having sex?"

"Definitely. Don't you?"

"No. Guys count it, but we don't. It's one of those leftover rationalizations from high school. I mean blow jobs were what you'd do with a guy because you couldn't have actual sex, not if you were a 'nice' girl, anyway. So we don't count it."

"You're bullshitting me, right, Lacy?"

"No," she said, shaking her head so hard her curls bounced all around. "What I'm saying is, if some woman gave you a blow job, you might describe it to one of your friends as having sex, but she doesn't necessarily see it like that."

"I don't describe sex acts to my friends."

"Well, that's very reassuring to know, Charlie. Like the ad said, you really are a sensitive guy . . ."

I looked at her to see what the hell that was about. But she instantly put her hand on my arm and said, "I'm sorry, I don't know where that came from. I didn't get a lot of sleep last night, and I'm pretty ragged. I can't wait to take off this weekend." We were standing in front of the paper now.

"You're going to be gone too? Where are you headed?"

"Camping."

"Camping?"

"Yeah. Normally we'd leave on Friday, but we want to stay home and watch the Bulls. So Saturday morning Jessica and I are going on our annual un-Memorial Day camp-out. We go every year to the Indiana Dunes."

"Un-Memorial Day? What's the deal?"

"It's too packed on Memorial Day—even if the

weather is crummy, it's always jammed. So we wait a week for the maintenance crews to clear up the trash from all the Memorial Day creeps, and run out there before the full summer onslaught hits. We've been doing it for years, and I don't know, we just always have a great time."

"Camping?"

"Yeah. You already asked that—do you have a problem with camping?"

"Not at all. I love camping. I used to go with Janice and Tim. It's just hard to picture you camping."

"Why?"

"You don't seem the type."

"Listen, Charlie, just because a girl gets the occasional bikini wax, doesn't mean she isn't capable of camping."

"Yeah, I guess. Is it just you and Jessica?"

"Well usually. Only there's a girl from Japan, a foreign exchange student who Jess has become friends with and she's never been camping, so Jess asked her. I asked Steffi because she's never been camping either, but her grandmother broke her hip, and her mom lives out of town, so Steffi and her sister have to stay around and help her . . . but it'll be fine."

"Yeah, it should be great."

I must have said that more forlornly than I'd intended, because Lacy was quiet for about ten seconds and then she said, "Charlie? You could come instead. I mean you could if you want."

"Are you shitting me? Is that a real offer?"

"Yeah, I think so. You said you loved camping, and

the TV girlfriend is out of town, and—didn't you say once that you were pretty good at cooking?"

"You mean in my ad?"

"Yeah. And other times too, you've said that, right?"

"Right."

"Good. Then we'll all go camping and you get to be in charge of the food."

I gotta believe that good things always come to those who wait. Christ. The first weekend after a long hard season, and I get an offer to run off in the woods with three women.

To be their cook.

Lacy

THAT WEEKEND

The thing about being a mom is that when you go to bed you may look like you're sleeping, but you are really only lying down between kid emergencies. They may be eighteen years old, but you're still out of bed the second they go into the john and start throwing up.

It was three-twenty A.M. when I heard Jessica doing just that.

"What's the matter, hon?" I said, pushing on the bathroom door that she'd left ajar. The question did not require an answer—I could see what was the matter. The poor thing was kneeling on the floor and hugging the toilet bowl for dear life. Her head rested on the rim, her eyes were closed, and one of those burning after-you-barf tears was sliding down her cheek.

"Mom," she whimpered in a voice I hadn't heard since she was little, "I'm sick."

"Oh, hon, I can tell," I said, picking up on that old ooh-poor-baby voice I used when she was little—but she really was sick. In fact, once I located the thermometer behind some of our vintage wave-setting lotion, it became clear that Jessica was 100.5 degrees' worth of sick. I tucked her into her bed, but two hours later she was back in the bathroom hurling her little guts out.

Jess wasn't a kid who got sick a lot—which had been a big help to a single working mom over the years—but it meant I was not all that practiced at being Florence Nightingale. "Jess, let me get you something—aspirin or Tylenol . . ."

"Don't worry, Mom," she said, heading back to her room to crawl under the covers. "All I want to do is sleep. Wake me at nine, so I can pack up for the Dunes."

"The Dunes? We're not going to the Dunes, Jessica. You're sick. Go to sleep."

"Mo-om."

"Mom nothing. Just go to sleep. You can argue with me when you wake up—you're too weak to win now anyway, okay?" Then I leaned over to kiss her, and went back into my own room.

Shit, she had been so wired for the weekend. Her friend Kozuko had borrowed a sleeping bag, and Jess had been really psyched about showing her all the tent-setting-up and cooking-out stuff. Oh, God, cooking out. I remembered I had to call Charlie before he left to buy supplies. It didn't seem fair to call him much before seven, so I set the alarm, and in spite of the random stripes of daylight sneaking through my shutters, I tried to go back to sleep.

I wasn't that successful. Even before the alarm went off, I punched the button down and resigned myself to the fact that my day had apparently started a few hours ago. I staggered into the kitchen, brewed up some seriously leaded coffee, and waited to call Charlie. It was gorgeous out so I opened the back door and sat on the stoop with my Oprah coffee mug.

Ruthie had given me the mug. She and Adrienne were occasionally invited on the show as experts, and I guess Oprah gives the mugs to her guests as a post-show thank you. It was cool to have it, but it would have been a whole lot cooler if Ruthie and Adrienne had asked me to go to the studio with them and sit in the green room. Only they never did. The day they came back from the show when Ruthie handed the mug to me I felt like one of those kids who gets a "my parents went to Paris and all I got was this lousy T-shirt" shirt.

The backyard looked great—sun glinted off the dew on the lawn and the impatiens and begonias that Brian had come over to put in last weekend were already filling in. He was coming by later in fact to put in two more flats—this time he was trying lobelia. I think Brian loved being married to Dolores, but he sure did miss his garden. So every summer he came back to do the planting and tending—the deal was, we kept up the lawn and he did the flower beds. Every year he tried something different. Last year the yard was filled with reds and pinks, but this year he was into blues, and yellows, and whites.

At seven I went in to call Charlie, only he didn't

answer, and his machine didn't pick up either. Then I checked on Jess, and went in to shower. Since the jeans and T-shirt I'd planned to wear to the Dunes were on top of all the bags I'd packed up last night, I just put them on when I got out and went back to try Charlie. No answer again. I *was* able to get ahold of Kozuko though, who couldn't have been sweeter about our not being able to go.

"I'm really sorry, Kozuko, but Jessica is pretty sick."

"Is okay Miss Gay-sar. I will call later to see how is Jessica."

"That will be great, hon. We'll figure out another time to go camping this summer before you go back to Japan, okay?"

"Is very okay."

What was not very okay, however, was Charlie and his phone. He still wasn't answering when I called at nine. I wondered where the hell he'd been all morning.

"Hi, Mom," said Jess, padding into the living room in her gray terry-cloth robe. "Did you get back to sleep?"

"Oh, baby! Hi! How do you feel?"

"Crummy, but better," she said as I put my hand on her forehead and found that it was actually pretty cool. "Can I have some tea?"

"Are you sure you want something?"

"Yeah, it would taste good I think."

She followed me out to the kitchen and sat down listlessly at the table. As I put the water on to boil, a knock came on the back screen door. "Hey, you girls still home?"

It was Brian. He had set the lobelia flats down outside

along with a few bonus pots of yellow pansies, and he wanted to know if he could help us pack the car.

"We're not going," I said, "Jess is sick."

Then the front door rang and it was Charlie. I opened the door and repeated the same thing to him.

"We're not going? What's she got?"

"Stomach flu I guess. Mostly she had it last night—barfing and fever and stuff. She's a little better now. Come on in, I've still got some coffee."

Charlie followed me to the back of the house. And for the first time in ages there were two men in our kitchen. I don't know why I noticed that—I just did. Maybe what I was really noticing as I said, "Brian, this is Charlie; Charlie, this is Brian" was that these were two men from such different parts of my life. Anyway, once the intros were over and everyone said yes they wanted coffee, I motioned Charlie to sit down and asked, "Where were you all morning? I tried to call you."

He pushed his sunglasses up on top of his head. I was glad he didn't do backward baseball caps. Not that he wasn't good-looking enough to overcome the dorkiness of backward baseball caps, but Charlie was one of those guys who looked great unaccessorized. No Indiana Jones hat, no designer sunglasses, no chains, no rings, none of the stuff Tony and half the guys I'd gone out with thought made them Mr. Macho. "I was at the grocery store getting our food. Then I went over to the outdoor farmers' market to get two quarts of these strawberries. I'll leave them with you guys for your dinner tonight."

"What do you mean 'you guys'?" Jessica asked, setting

down her tea. "I know I can't go to the Dunes, but what about you two and Kozuko? You're going, aren't you?"

"Right, Jessica," I said. "I'm taking off for the Dunes, and leaving you here to throw up alone."

"Mom, I'm eighteen."

"You're eighteen and sick."

"She's eighteen," said Brian, reaching across his old kitchen table to take my hand, "and her grandmother and I are one phone call away, Lacy. Don't be silly. I'll be around until one or so doing the planting, and then I may stick around and watch the Sox. I was planning to anyway. If Jessica feels up to it, Dolores and I will fix some dinner here. If she can't stand the sight of food— or the sight of us—we'll fix her some soup and vanish. Either way, she'll be fine, and she can call us if she needs anything. We'll be home. What do you say, Jessica?"

Jessica undid her French braid and fluffed out her hair. "I say that if that makes Mom feel better, at least better enough to go anyway, then fine. It's stupid for the three of you not to go. Kozuko will be here at nine-thirty anyway."

"I already called Kozuko and told her we had canceled."

"You did? Well, I'll call her back and tell her you've uncanceled."

"Jess, don't do that. I don't know Kozuko that well— she's *your* friend. And you tell me she's shy to begin with so there's no way on earth that she is going to be up for going on a camping trip—which she's never done before—with someone that she's never met before. Come on, it's not fair to put her on the spot like that."

"Well, yeah, maybe you're right," she said, getting up to make a piece of toast. "But what's your excuse, you guys?"

Charlie looked at me like maybe he didn't want to have a vote on this topic. "Come on," she nudged. "Charlie's bought the food. You've packed the bags. The day looks incredible. And, look, Ma," she said, sticking her thumb in her little wiseass mouth, "there's even a baby-sitter willing to deal with me."

"I don't know, Jess." I felt monumentally conflicted. And Charlie was no help at all—he was just sitting there with his muscles and his tight navy T-shirt watching me squirm. "Charlie? What do you feel like doing?"

"Me?" he said, taking his cup over to the sink. "I'm pumped to go, Lacy. And until a few hours ago you were pumped to go too. Come on, let's do it. It's great out, we'll have a good time, and by three o'clock tomorrow afternoon you'll be back here sitting at your kitchen table."

I guess that's how I found myself sitting next to Charlie Feldman in the front seat of his Toyota with my pillow and toothbrush packed in the backseat. I was on my way to my first overnight with a guy in more years than I cared to remember.

"This is pretty weird, you know," I said as we crossed over the Skyway and hit the edges of Indiana.

"Yeah it is," he said, grinning—kind of like a Cheshire cat.

"Why are you looking so smug, Charlie?"

"I don't know. It was just funny to see you running out of excuses to be alone in the woods with me."

"I'm not afraid to be alone in the woods with you," I snapped.

"Good, Lace, 'cause I'm not afraid to be alone in the woods with you either."

It was very helpful having that little chat.

Lacy

THAT AFTERNOON

AND EVENING

Charlie had never been to the Dunes before, which was pretty amazing considering he was born and raised about fifty miles from them. The Indiana Dunes are a fab dose of Nature plunked between the rotting steel mills of Gary and the nuclear power plant near the Michigan border. There they stand—a fifteen-mile stretch of sand mini-mountains, probably the tallest hills within two hours of Chicago. On one side of the Dunes there are endless flat, wide Lake Michigan beaches and on the other side of the steep sand hills is a wonderful woods that make up a huge state park for campers.

"Our" campsite was located behind a clump of oak trees closest to trail number five over the dunes. I liked it back there because it was away from the main cluster of campers and RVs—it wasn't exactly isolated, but it was definitely antisocial.

Charlie and I pitched our tent in less than twenty minutes, fixed a quick couple of sandwiches for lunch, and then took off to see the beach. It was a fifteen-minute climb to get up the dunes. Actually, the way the sand disintegrates under your feet as you try to climb is pretty humiliating. Lots of times you practically have to scratch your way up on all fours. But eventually you get to the top. And then you can stretch out and roll down them sideways like a kid—I love that part. Today, when I landed on the flat damp sand, Charlie was still standing at the top looking amazed. "Come on down," I yelled. "Then we can go over and say hello to the lake."

"Hello?" he yelled, still from the top. "It's the same damn lake we see every day in Chicago."

"Yeah I know. But here it's a vacation lake—there it's just regular."

And then with no warning he came rolling down and landed about ten feet from me. Standing up to brush the sand from his hair and his shoulders, he laughed and said, "Jesus, that felt great."

People were clustered all up and down the beach—not mobs like there'd be in a few weeks—but we definitely didn't have the place to ourselves. After we got up to the water and said hello, I told Charlie we had to do the toe thing.

"What's that?" he asked, watching me roll up my jeans and take off my socks and shoes.

"It's a contest Jess and I always have. You put in your toes and see who can hold them in there the longest—the first one to pull out has to get up tomorrow and make breakfast." It was the first time I'd actually acknowledged out loud that Charlie and I were going to be waking up together the next morning.

"I thought I had KP duty regardless," Charlie said, pulling his shoes off. "But if sticking my feet in fifty-eight-degree water can get me out of it, what the hell?"

Now, guy feet are sort of an interesting topic. Not that I sit around with Steffi and talk about them or anything, but guy feet are *not* like girl feet. Girl feet can go from really ugly to really pretty—guy feet can go from really ugly to okay. I like guy bodies a lot. I like guy extremities a lot—hands being my particular favorites—but guy feet just never get any better than okay. Charlie's were nice and okay—and mine, well usually they were pretty good, only I still hadn't polished my toes yet, which was odd since it was already a week after Memorial Day. Actually, I was glad I hadn't—Charlie would have hated red toenails on a camp-out.

The water was amazingly warm. "Wanna go back and get our suits?" I asked.

"Are you nuts? This is fucking freezing," he said, laughing at me. Then he yanked his foot out. "You win."

"Good! I like my eggs sunny side up," I yelled after him as he headed up to his shoes.

He sort of bowed and said, "Yes, Ma'am." Then he gave me the finger.

We walked along the beach for about an hour before reclimbing the dunes to the woods side and taking the trail back to the campgrounds. The people closest to us must have taken off on a hike, because their Irish setter had settled herself in for a nap in a fat strip of sun just outside their tent. We got beers from the cooler, propped our heads against our rolled-up sleeping bags, and settled down in the wrap-around warmth of the afternoon to read. I was working on *The Joy Luck Club* but kept getting mixed up about which daughter belonged to which mother, and which mother belonged to which Chinese tragedy. Charlie's book turned out to be a collection of short stories.

"I didn't think guys liked short stories that much."

"Depends what guys you hang out with. I like reading them. I even like writing them."

"You do? I thought you only wrote news or sports. Have you ever had one published?"

"Three," he said, reaching for the pretzel bag.

"Charlie! How come you never told me this?"

"You never asked. I had one published in the *Sewanee Review* and two in *Playboy*."

"God, that is so cool. Can I read them?"

"Well sure. But I thought women didn't like to read *Playboy*."

"Depends which women you hang out with," I said, saluting him with my bottle. I decided that if I didn't ask him now, I never would. "Charlie? No one knows this, but I've been messing with some short stories too."

"No shit?" He put down his book and turned toward me. "That's great, Lace."

"Well, that's the thing, see, I don't know if they're any good or not. But I do have this one that . . . I don't know . . . would you be willing to look at it sometime?"

His eyes crinkled up when he smiled. "Sure I'll look

at it." I liked that he didn't ask me what my story was about. I wasn't ashamed of it or anything, I just thought it was better to let the story do its own telling.

At dusk, Charlie pulled on one of those heavy Irish fisherman sweaters and started messing with the fire. A little eight- or nine-year-old girl from the family camping next to us came over and asked if we had any ketchup they could borrow.

"Nope, sorry we don't," Charlie said. "We've got some Worcestershire sauce though."

The word "Worcestershire" must have scared her to death. She looked at Charlie like he was a serial killer, turned, and ran off. It was pretty funny. "Worcestershire?" I asked. "How come we have it anyway?"

"Because it's one of the ingredients in my secret marinade sauce, which I am about to prepare, once I get this fire going."

"And what's my job?" I asked, watching him poke the twigs and sticks we had gathered earlier.

"Your job is to admire my kick-ass cooking and to pick out the music. My tapes are in a plastic bag in the backseat," he said, pointing to the car.

I'd brought some tapes too, and a boom box. Not everybody approves of mixing electronics and camping, so I was glad Charlie wasn't one of those purist types. Not that I think it's cool to haul a portable satellite dish into the woods, but a little music never hurt anybody— even cowboys had guitars and harmonicas.

The amazing thing was, our musical tastes weren't all that far apart. Not that he was about to put up with Randy Travis, or I was willing to hack four hours of

Thelonious Monk—but we both liked the Eagles, and Bessie Smith, and Willie Nelson, and Leon Redbone. So I did okay on my job, and Charlie—well, he was fantastic with his.

"What exactly is this?" I asked an hour later, pointing to this big brown gob of stuff on top of the steaks. Charlie had set a huge plate in front of me and began to uncork a bottle of red wine.

"Mystery mushrooms."

"Come on, Charlie, what's in them?" I'd seen him open a bag and dump all this chopped stuff into a frying pan, but I had no clue what it was.

"Mystery ingredients," he said.

"You mean you're not going to tell?"

He picked up his cup of wine and clinked it against mine. "You've got to deal with mysteries every day, Lace. So what's one more?"

"What do you mean 'mysteries every day'?"

"I don't know—mysteries like why did the Bulls fall apart in overtime last night?"

"I don't even want to talk about it, I'm so upset." The Bulls had gone down in overtime 115 to 104 the night before and it had been heart-wrenching to watch.

"Or," he said, reaching for the salt, "all the regulation gender mysteries that happen all the time."

"What are gender mysteries?"

"It's the shit that women do that men don't get. Or that *we* do that *you* don't get. You know all those sentences that start, 'Why don't men?' or 'Why can't women?' "

I thought about it for a minute. "Like why don't men

wash their faces before they go to bed at night? They brush their teeth, but they don't wash their faces. I always wonder about that. Or beer—why if there are two guys and one last beer, why do guys flip for the beer? Why don't guys share it?"

"*That* is not a mystery. *That* is based on the fact that a beer is of a whole. It is an entity—both philosophically and physically. It is not divisible. Plus, a beer must be consumed in its original vessel. If you split it, one of you would have to drink it from a glass. That is a repugnant concept for a guy."

"I don't get it," I said, cutting into my steak.

"Well, it's not a mystery at all. Here's a mystery—why don't women get lint in their belly button when they wear T-shirts?"

"Why do guys roll down the window in a car and spit?"

"Why do women go to the bathroom in pairs?"

"Why *don't* guys go to the bathroom in pairs?"

"Why do women have to have the last word?"

"What's in the mushrooms?"

We burst out laughing. Charlie was really very darling.

"You know what I always wonder," he said, nodding toward the family whose campsite was about a hundred yards through the trees. "Look at that. Why do dads toss their kids in the air? And moms hug them close in? That's a mystery."

"God, I don't know. You're right though. Do you think it could be as simple as maybe dads try and give kids a sense of freedom and moms try and give them a sense of security?"

"You tell me. You're the mom. What do you think?" he asked, getting up to throw more wood in the fire, and to bring the wine bottle back over.

"I think I'm a bad person to ask," I said, letting him fill my cup again. "Because the one thing I found out is no matter how many Little League games I got hooked into—even as a coach which I did for two seasons—I just couldn't be a mom *and* a dad to Jessica. I could only be a mom. I think I was a good mom—maybe even a terrific one—but it would have been cool, fuller or something, if she'd had a daily dad in the picture too."

"What the fuck, Lacy?" Charlie set down his wine and leaned close to me. He'd gotten a lot of sun during the day, but his reaction to my remark made his face even more flushed. "Weren't you the one who told me last fall when this whole baby deal started that a kid doesn't necessarily need both parents? Didn't you lay some shit on me about how a person could do this alone?"

"Yeah, I did say that. But I didn't say it was the greatest way to bring up a kid. Look at those people way over there with the three kids," I said, pointing to the ketchup kid family. "I mean I know that just because they have a mommy and a daddy doesn't mean I have to sit here and envy them. One of them could be really jerky. I was just saying, Charlie, that when you wind up being the only parent you'd save a lot of time if you could just accept that that is what you are—instead of trying to be the phantom parent too."

Charlie was quiet. Maybe he didn't want to hear any more about parents and kids for a while. I wouldn't have wanted to if I'd been working my butt off to find someone to start a family with for nearly nine or ten months, and I was back at square one. Leaning against the log in his jeans and white sweater, with the firelight all glimmery on his face, I had to admit he looked definitely sexy. It's weird how sometimes quiet can be boring and sometimes quiet can be so sexy. And yeah, it helps to have great cheekbones and light blue eyes too. If we'd been other people it would have been a perfect time to lean over to kiss him. Instead, I leaned back to change the music, but he reached over and held on to my wrist.

"Don't change it, I like it. What is it?"

I smiled—it was one of my faves. "Mary Chapin Carpenter—do you know her?"

He shook his head.

"She's wonderful. She's won best female vocalist at the Country Music Awards and she . . ."

"Shhh," he said, putting his finger over my mouth for a second. It was so skin on skin. "This is great. What's it called?"

" 'Slow Country Dance.' " I could still feel where he'd touched my lips. "It's a waltz."

"I know it's a waltz." He took his hand off my wrist and absentmindedly pushed some of my hair back off my face. "Christ, I remember when Sophie stuck me in this brutal six-week crash course in dancing the summer between sixth and seventh grades. It was at the JCC. She told me there would be no party for my bar mitzvah unless I could dance with my grandmothers and not just push them around. Abe sucks at dancing, and I think she was worried it was genetic."

"Was it?"

"No, I'm actually a helluva dancer. Here," he said as he stood up and pulled me up with him, "we'll waltz."

There was nothing to do but dance. We were already standing there face-to-face in the middle of some wonderful music—music that wrapped its gauzy, heartachy, love-struck notes around us and glued us together with its graceful, wavy rhythms.

Oh, God, how can I explain it? How it was so hokey and so hot at the same time? Being under a big-moon sky with a man I knew so well but was scared to know any better, a man who was doing just what he said he would do—a great job of dancing. And a man who was also doing a couple of other things too, like smelling really good, and holding me really close, and—damn him—making me a little bit crazy.

Charlie didn't let me go when it was over—not that I tried to get away. The next song was slow too, but it wasn't a waltz. It was the kind where you pull the girl to you and you move around just a little while you breathe each other in, and fit your bodies tight together just to get an idea of what that feels like.

How it felt was incredibly good.

Charlie

THE NEXT MORNING

I was too fucking old to be going to bed with an unrelieved hard-on.

There wasn't a damn thing I could do to relieve it though, considering that the cause of that hard-on was dead to the world in a sleeping bag about seven feet away.

How the hell could she fall asleep?

Something had happened out there between Lacy and me. Not just from rubbing up against each other and calling it dancing. Not just from red wine buzzes either. But somewhere between leaving her kitchen in the morning and putting out the fire around midnight, Lacy had let me in. She was softer. Less adamant. I had to believe she was as stirred up by all this as I was.

God, I wanted her. I wanted to be in her, with her, around her. Yeah, maybe some of it was the firelight and

the booze, but it was a hell of a lot more than that. It was
Lacy. It was how her hair smelled. It was the slope of her
shoulders. It was the way her jeans pulled across her ass.
It was tits and eyes and teeth, and the fact that all of
them were Lacy's. And it was months of getting to know
a terrific woman. Jesus Christ, I was strung out.

And it was a pisser lying there next to her. Each time I
heard her breathe, my balls went a deeper shade of blue.
It was a long night.

But somewhere in the course of it, I must have fallen
asleep. For a couple hours anyway. Because when I
opened my eyes, Lacy's green sleeping bag was empty
and a solid hit of morning light was coming through the
tent's front flap. I went outside, but she wasn't nearby. I
took a leak, rinsed my mouth out with some flat Coke,
and ducked back into the tent to locate my watch. It was
only five-thirty. I had no idea where the hell she'd taken
off to.

My watch said six-fifteen when I heard her come in. I
had crawled back in my bag and was nearly asleep when
she tiptoed past my pillow. She set a wet bathing suit
and some shampoo down on the floor so I figured she'd
gone for a swim and then taken a hot shower. She had a
gray sweatsuit on and when she crouched down to reach
into her duffel, the bottoms pulled down and bared the
top curves of her ass. God, she was shaped gorgeous.

Then she sat down cross-legged to dry her hair. Her
face was tilted away from me toward the sun streaming
in through the flap. It was the first time I had ever seen
her with no makeup. No lipstick, no eye crap, nothing.
Nothing but golden skin, clear dark green eyes, and a

full almost pink mouth. I could feel myself getting hard all over again.

A few minutes later she got up and walked over to her purse. This time when she walked past my pillow it was impossible not to touch her. I reached out. My hand cupped her knee. "Lacy?"

She stopped midstep. "Hi," she said, tentatively.

"Hi."

I looked at her. And I told her as straight as I could. "Lacy? This is just too tough."

And that was it. I don't know if she dropped down to meet me, or I reached up to find her. All I know is that from that moment on it was wild. Suddenly she was in my arms and just as suddenly there were no clothes between us. No words either. It was skin and tongues and hands, and lips. It was shameless, hungry loving. It was devouring, and melting, and sucking, and groaning, and licking, and fucking, and naked raw amazement at the power of it all. Somewhere in there was a condom. Reaching over me at one point, she lunged for her purse and pulled out a beat-up foil packet.

Make that two beat-up foil packets. We were at it again within twenty minutes.

Not all of it was lust. There was too much tenderness in it for that. The second time anyway. The way her mouth grazed me as slowly and lovingly she moved down my belly until she took me in her mouth, the way her eyes shone when five minutes later she kissed her way back up again, and mounted herself proprietarily on top of me, the way she nestled back into the curve of my body when happy and exhausted we finally could do nothing more except lie there stunned and sated.

I pressed my lips into the damp curls at her neck and then turned her face back toward me, expecting to see the same smile that was on mine. Instead, a tear was sliding down her cheek.

"Lacy! What the hell? What is it, baby?" I started to wipe the tear away with my hand, but she flung it down and bolted upright, covering her breasts with the top of my sleeping bag.

"Oh, God, Charlie, we're fucked. That was so damn stupid. What the hell were we doing?" Her eyes were wide open and she looked terrified.

"Lacy," I said, sitting up and taking her arms in my hands, "we were doing what we wanted to do. You know we wanted to."

"I didn't want to." She pushed me away to pull on her sweatsuit while she ranted, "I didn't want to start in with you, Charlie. It's the last thing I ever wanted. It makes no sense. I hate that we let ourselves be so stupid. It's too confusing. I like you, Charlie. I loved fucking you. But I don't want to start with you. It would just be a mess—it already is. Oh, shit shit shit. Damn Jessica for getting sick."

And then she stormed outside.

By the time I grabbed my jeans and a shirt, she had begun packing up our things.

"Lacy, for Chrissakes. Let's fix some breakfast and talk about this."

"There's nothing to talk about," she said, dumping the melted ice out of the cooler. "We did it, we're not doing it again, it's over. Our lives have no business getting mixed up together. I don't want to get mixed up with you, Charlie."

"You're already mixed up with me," I said, easing the cooler out of her hands. She snapped her hands away from mine.

"No I'm not. I may be a little mixed up about you, right this minute. But I am not mixed up with you. I don't want to be and I won't be."

"Fine, Lacy," I said, moderately pissed about her plunge into all this bullshit and denial. "Fine. Don't be mixed up with me. Why don't you just fuck me from time to time in that nice unmixed up way you seem to be able to pull off?"

I thought she was going to slug me.

"You shithead," she said, turning and walking into the tent.

I followed her in. "Who's the shithead, Lacy? We just have this amazingly connected morning, which was based on this amazingly connected evening last night, which was based on months of solid friendship. And then you decide that you don't want to be mixed up with me. Just what the fuck do you want?"

"I want to go home. And I don't want to talk the whole way there."

She got what she wanted.

Lacy

I tried to act regular. "Hi, Steff, how's your grandma doing?"

Steffi was out on her sleeping porch that she used as her own private den because the rest of her house looked like a huge locker room. Not that she could help it—considering that four high school sophomores lived there—but whenever you walked in, you had to slog through mounds of damp socks, tennis shoes, and stuff.

Instead of spending most of her waking hours yelling about it, she just sectioned off her bedroom and the sleeping porch as the adults-only zone of the house. The porch was insulated and she'd painted it a glossy magenta, filled it with plants and rattan furniture, and put all these old Marilyn Monroe pictures on the walls. Steffi was hung up on Marilyn Monroe, which was pretty weird considering that she was only five when

MM checked out. Anyway, the magenta Marilyn shrine room was where I found her Sunday afternoon after I got home, dumped my stuff, and made sure that Jessica was feeling okay.

She was seated cross-legged on her green-and-white-checked couch in the midst of balancing her checkbook. "Hey, Lace, when did you get back?" she asked, clearing away some of the Sunday papers so I could sit on the rattan chair.

I was in no shape to sit. Leaning seemed okay though, so I slouched against the door frame with my arms crossed over my stomach. It was rumbling—I guess I'd forgotten to eat. "An hour ago." And then continuing my imitation of a normal person, I asked, "So is your grandmother doing better?"

"What's better when you've broken your leg and the doctor explains to you that it is going to take eight weeks to heal? God, is she pissed off about being in the world of the formerly young. My grandma does not deal at all well with the aging thing."

"Like we're going to? Please. We'll go kicking and screaming. We'll be bathing in Retin-A. How come you got out of hospital duty?"

"Denise is doing it. Big Sis finally found some time in her busy life as a Lake Forest matron-in-training to get her butt down here to the hospital. Anyway, I have this huge checkbook mess that I can't figure out. I either lost the kids' support check from Johnny last month or he is screwing me over yet another time with some of his bullshit cash flow acrobatics." She reached over to grab the bag of Fritos on the coffee table. "Want some?"

I didn't want anything except to get to the part where we talked about me. But I took a handful and said, "What kind of cash flow acrobatics?"

"Well, I think Johnny has got some money problems. Seems now that he's divorcing Mrs. Ranalli number two, he's a guy with two monthly payments."

There was some major laughing and screaming coming through the open window. Her two girls, who had been lying outside in their bikinis working on their tans, had apparently decided it was time for a garden hose fight. Some water shot up through the window.

"Cool it, you guys!" Steffi yelled out.

"Why is Johnny paying wife number two? They didn't have any kids together, and I thought she was this rabid feminist."

"Yeah she was. But she has apparently created a new category—feminists on alimony. Evidently it is possible in the state of Illinois for a woman to not shave under her arms for years and then decide that a guy should support her for life. It almost makes me feel sorry for Johnny, but she was always such a pain in the ass, I guess I'm not surprised. All I want is my check."

"All I want is for this morning to never have happened.. Steff, I just did a colossally dumb thing."

"What?"

So I told her. About the night before, and the dancing, and how funny Charlie was, and how he smelled so good, and how he felt even better, and how impossible it was to sleep, and how it got totally mixed up and hot and fucky in the morning, and how it scared me to death. There was so much power in it, power beyond just the chemistry, which was in and of itself so incredible. But it was the power of really connecting to Charlie—all the goodness in him, and tenderness in him. "God," I groaned, "this is such a mess."

"Hon," said Steff, going over to the window to make sure the water fight had ended, "don't string yourself out about this. It happened, it's over, it was a moment. You told him it was a mistake, didn't you? And you didn't mislead him. I'm sure you'll be able to refind your friendship."

"We can't refind it—I don't even know if I want to," I said, putting my hands over my eyes as if that would make the whole thing go away. "It's too complicated, too charged. I don't need that. I've loved talking to him over all these months, learning about him, and laughing with him, maybe even a little bit depending on his calls, though I'd never tell him that. And I guess I'll miss him. But it will just be simpler if we get out of each other's lives now."

Steffi walked over to me and put her arm around me. She smelled like Neutrogena. I wondered if I still smelled like Charlie. "Well, if that's what you think, then that's what you'll do. I don't necessarily think it's right, though. I think if you completely push this guy out of your life, you'll miss him more than you know. But far be it for me to try and change your mind. I've known you too long for that. But do me a favor, Lace, okay? Just don't beat yourself up about this. No regrets, okay? They're a waste. We're on the Edith Piaf track remember?" And then she started to sing "Je Ne Regrette Rien" in this jerky nasal bistro voice. It was impossible not to laugh.

"Lace," she said, hugging me hard, "I'm sorry you're so jangled. But your job is to look forward, okay? You've got to get Jessica off to school, get yourself enrolled at DePaul, and take one giant step toward your future."

My future, however, took a jagged turn south a month later. After all my plans and all my safe sex lectures, my period was three weeks late.

Charlie

JUNE 12

Jesus, what a week. For starters, I figured Lacy had more balls. I hadn't pictured her as a woman who didn't return phone calls. Chickenshits don't return phone calls. Bitches don't return phone calls. Lacy wasn't either of those. But evidently she had freaked.

I'd left messages on her machines at home and at the paper every day all week. Still, if she didn't want to talk to me, she didn't want to talk to me. Payday wasn't until Friday, so I didn't even have an excuse to run into her at the office until then.

In the meantime, Jo Beth had shown up on Wednesday. About four hours before she was scheduled to. She had taken an early flight and headed directly to my place. No message first. No phone call. I was out having an early dinner with some golf buddies while she was talking her way into my apartment via the doorman. The idea was to surprise me.

I hate surprises.

I hate acting too. But the choice was between acting as if I didn't hate the surprise or having a scene. I hate scenes even more.

The door opened before I got my key out of the lock. "Jo Beth. When did you get in?"

"Around six," she said, pulling me in and kissing me. "God, it's good to see you."

She looked great. Tan, scrubbed, and almost naked. "My suitcase didn't make the flight, so I took a bath and borrowed one of your T-shirts. I didn't think you'd mind."

I worked hard at a smile. "Did the meetings end early?"

"Nope," she said, running her hands up the front of my shirt. "I left early. I wanted to see my boyfriend."

I hung on to the smile, but it wasn't easy. "Want a beer?"

"I already had one. But why don't you grab one so we can sit down and catch up," she said, patting my couch. "I can't wait to tell you how the conference went."

For the next twenty minutes I heard plenty about the National News Conference and the connections she'd made with some suits from New York. "You know what, Charlie?" she said, putting her hand on mine. "I really think I've got a shot at something national, if they launch this new weekend news magazine next March."

"That's great, Jo Beth."

"Charlie!" she yelped, yanking her hand away.

"What?"

"How can you say that? If I go national, that means big problems for us."

"Shit, Jo Beth. I was just being glad for you."

"I suppose," she said, curling her feet up under her and hugging me hard. "So how are you? Did you have fun on your little camp-out with that friend from the paper and the two teenagers?"

"Yeah. I've never been to the Indiana Dunes before. It's a pretty remarkable spot."

"And?"

"And what?" I didn't see the point of getting into it. Jo Beth and I were destined to split anyway. Even before the Dunes. The Dunes only made that clearer.

I walked over to the window, and took a look twenty-two floors down. At eight-thirty there was still light enough to see that Lincoln Park was jammed with after-work joggers and bikers. The Drive ribboned north toward Evanston and a few boats were still out on the lake. "Listen," I said, sitting back down at the opposite end of the couch, "do you think we could talk?"

"That's why I'm here, Charlie. To talk, to fuck, and to just hang out with you. I've missed you." She stretched her long legs out and put them across my lap. It is very hard to break up with a woman when she has her legs over your dick.

"Yeah? How about another beer?" I asked, sliding out from under and heading into the kitchen. The phone rang while I was in there. It was Bobby calling to set up a golf date for Sunday.

When I came back into the living room, Jo Beth had

turned on the TV. "Just want to see what they are promo-ing for the ten o'clock news. Do you mind if I leave it on?"

"Nope. Even though it's probably the first time in history the guy wants to talk and the girl wants the tube on."

Jo Beth didn't smile at my lame humor attempt. But she turned the volume down a bit. "Well? What is it you want to talk about, Charlie?"

"It's tough to explain this, Jo Beth, but I think we have a style differential here."

"What the hell does that mean?"

"It means that you and I don't do things at the same speed. Or with the same set of expectations."

"And I repeat—what the hell does that mean?" This time she shut off the TV and tossed the remote on the table.

"It means your brain has sped things along to a different place from my brain."

"Charlie. Talk to me in English. I have very good listening skills." She got up and began to pace back and forth behind the couch.

"What I want to tell you, Jo Beth, is that we are not going to work."

She stopped moving. "Why not? I think we can work just fine."

"We aren't going to work because we already don't work."

"What specifically doesn't work for you? Be straight."

"Okay." As gently as I could, I said, "It does not work for me that you let yourself in here. It does not work for me that you bought my dad's birthday present. Or that you brought over a how-to-make-a-baby-girl video. It's too fast. And there are too many underlying assumptions. I think you are smart, and talented, and very attractive. I like you. But you are busting my ass. You've already got me signed, sealed, and delivered. And much as I'd like to, I can't get there."

Her eyes went to ice. And then she did the weirdest fucking thing I've ever seen. She walked over to the wall, and crashed her fist into it. Guys do that kind of shit. I never knew a woman could.

"Christ, Jo Beth, is your hand okay?" I said, charging over to see if she'd broken anything.

"Get away from me, asshole," she hissed. "Asshole who advertises in the goddamn newspaper. Asshole who takes six dates to figure out how to fuck a girl. Asshole who gets a whole lot more than he bargained for, but is too big an asshole to handle it. God, you are such a fucking asshole . . ."

Jesus Christ, I was dealing with Sybil. It scared the hell out of me. Jo Beth slammed into my bedroom, locked the door, and five minutes later she was dressed and out of the apartment. Gone.

I was rattled by Jo Beth's one-eighty for sure, but not nearly as rattled as I was by Lacy's response to me when I finally cornered her on Friday. It was high noon when I stood dead center in front of her desk. "We need to talk," was all I said.

"Charlie"—she swallowed hard—"I don't want to do this now. Not here."

I leaned across the desk, put my hand over hers, and

whispered, "It doesn't have to be here, but it does have to be now." I must not have whispered quietly enough. The woman just to the left stopped typing and looked over. "Come on, let's go down to the Wendella dock."

"I'll meet you there in ten minutes," she said, smiling at the girl to let her know I wasn't a rabid kidnapper.

"No you won't. You haven't returned one phone call. Let's just go now and get this over with."

It was an interminable four-minute walk out the back door of the building, down to lower Michigan, and over to the dock. When we got there, Lacy turned her back to the river, folded her arms over her waist, and asked, "What exactly do you want me to say, Charlie?"

"Lacy, I'm not the enemy here," I said, dying to touch her, but knowing she'd pull away. "It's just me. I miss you. I want us to talk about what happened. I want us to acknowledge that it was extraordinary. That maybe we've made a huge mistake not taking the possibilities between us seriously."

Her hands flew up over her ears. "Oh, please, Charlie, stop. Please, please. This is so hard to talk about with you. I don't want to hurt you, I don't want you to hurt me—"

"Hurt you?" I was stunned. "How can I hurt you?"

"Men hurt, Charlie."

"Jesus, Lacy—don't you think that's something of a gender-wide condemnation?"

"All I know," she said, almost rocking back and forth, "is that most of the men who were ever important to me have hurt. Tony walked out on me and that hurt. A dad and a couple of stepdads disappeared on me and that

hurt. I just haven't experienced a lot of constancy from
key people of your gender's persuasion."

"Yeah, well I'm not Tony, and I'm not your dad, and
I'm not your stepdad. I'd appreciate your not getting us
confused."

"I'm not confused. I know who you are."

"Yeah, who am I?"

"You are trouble for me, Charlie. At least the way we
were that morning, you are big trouble. I think we have
to just disengage. Right now."

"Are you kidding? Why?"

"Because we messed up, and we need space. That's
why. Why is this so hard for you to understand?"

"It's hard because I care about you, Lacy. And you
care about me. You know that."

She turned her back so I couldn't read anything on
her face, and said, "I care, but that is not the point. The
point is that I will not change my whole life plan for you.
I just cannot. I have had no life of my own, not ever. I
have no life that wasn't linked up to have-tos—have-to
please my mom; have-to please my husband; have-to be
strong for Jess . . . Do you know in my whole life I've
never once gone to the movies without having to tell
someone when I'd be home? First my mom, then the
baby-sitter, then Jess. There were no breaks. Not one
single movie! You've never had to call anyone in twenty-
five years! I just feel entitled to some time with no man-
dates and attachments. You are just the opposite—you
are looking for all kinds of attachments—wife attachment, baby attachment, the whole tangly complex

thing . . . I can't let myself be part of that. It has nothing to do with you. It has to do with timing."

"Then why does it feel like it has everything to do with me?" I said, turning her back around and looking into those green eyes. "Why does it feel so personally crappy?"

"It feels crappy for me too, you know," she said, turning her head away and biting down on her lip. "But we need to take a long sabbatical from each other. For at least the whole summer. I just know if we take the summer off, it will be better."

"Lacy, I don't want to do that. It will feel like too radical an amputation. Don't you think . . ."

"You just heard what I think, Charlie!" she snapped, pulling away from me. "And if you care about me at all, you'll just cooperate, okay?"

And then she raced past me, and ran up the curved cement stairs to the street level. Over and out.

I left the Wendella dock, headed over to Billy Goat's, and downed a couple beers. Man, there is something about having two women go off on you in the same week that makes a guy decide to back off and maybe just concentrate on golf. It's a much simpler way to feel shitty.

I spent the next month doing that. Playing golf badly. And missing Lacy even worse.

Lacy

MID-JULY

Obviously the first pregnancy test was wrong.

There was no way that I could be pregnant. I was too old, I'd used condoms, and the whole thing was just out of the question. That's why I took the test again—and one more time after that. And each time that little pink stripe showed up on the stick, I saw my whole future going down the toilet. I couldn't even cry.

I mean I had done this before, right? It was the original been there-done that—only the last time I knew what to do. The last time I was sixteen years old, so I married the guy and had the baby. The last time stupidity made sense—this time stupidity was only stupid. I was absolutely paralyzed.

So what I did not need when I was lying wide awake at midnight panicked about it all was Jessica, barging into my bedroom and waving a pink and blue Be Sure box in my face. "What is this, Mom?" She was screaming. "Is this yours? Is it?"

The hall light silhouetted her, but I didn't need to see her face to know that she'd come completely unglued. "Jessica! Where did you get that?" I snapped, sitting up in bed.

"You left it in the bathroom wastebasket! A pregnancy test! God, this is so horrible! How could you do this to me?"

"Do what to you?"

"You're pregnant, right?"

"I don't know," I lied.

"You don't know?" She flipped on the light. "Come on, Mom. You either are or you aren't!"

I could see she was not only furious, but she was crying. Damn! Damn, damn, damn. Damn her for finding out, and damn her for making it *her* tragedy. Eighteen years ago Dolores had done the same thing. When did I get to be pregnant, and have just *me* ripped up about it?

"Jessica, stop it!" I said and got out of the bed to go to her. She started to push me away, and then she heaved herself against me. Huge sobs hiccuped from her and I didn't let her go. "Oh, Mom, this is so gross! How could you do this?"

"Jessica, stop it! This is my problem—not yours."

"Yeah, but what are you going to do?"

"I don't know, Jess. I honestly don't know what I am going to do."

I didn't know one other thing too. I didn't know who the father of the baby was.

• • •

"You're kidding me," said Steffi, when I called her the next morning at seven and told her why I had to come over and talk.

"Kidding you about what? That I'm pregnant or that I don't know whose baby this is?"

"Both," she said. "Just come over. I'll put on some coffee, and we'll figure this out."

"Don't even say the word 'coffee' to me."

"I forgot. What sounds good to you?"

"Coke and Wonder bread."

I love Steffi. When I got there, the first thing she did was hand me a loaf of Wonder bread, and give me a huge, incredibly needed, girlfriends forever hug. Then finally, I started to cry.

"Damn, I hate when I cry. Give me some Kleenex."

She did, and we took the Wonder bread to the Monroe porch. "So," she said, settling into one corner of the couch while I took the other, "you have no clue what you want to do, right?"

"Right." I sniveled, and then blew my nose some more. "I've been up all night thinking about it. I mean you know that in spite of Dolores and all the church stuff from when I was a kid, I am definitely pro-choice. I just don't know if I am pro-choice only for other people or for me too—it's different. It's also different because maybe this is Charlie's baby."

"Tell me about the *maybe* part. About how it could NOT be Charlie's baby . . ."

"Well, I didn't get into this with you, because it was

such a nonevent and it got pushed out of my brain by the weekend with Charlie, but you know I go country dancing on Tuesdays?" I opened the bag of bread and pulled out a slice.

"Yeah . . ."

"Well, I've told you about this guy there—Randy— he's been flirting with me for months. We dance together a lot—and, you know, sometimes make out—and he's real young, and dear, but it's been all play. Anyway, that Tuesday before Charlie and I went camping, when Randy and I went outside to cool off, we started necking, and it was a warm night, and I was horny, and I'm not proud of this, but we wound up in his van. It didn't mean anything huge to either of us, not even enough to get embarrassed about afterward, except for when he had to wiggle up to the glove compartment and get a condom . . ."

"So you used a condom with him," said Steff, getting up to open the window wider. It was going to be an ungodly hot Chicago summer day.

"Yeah. But I did with Charlie too. Only with Charlie I used my own. I bet those condoms had been in my purse nearly a year."

"A year?"

"Probably. You know I haven't been in bed with anybody for a year. I'm sure that's why it finally happened with Randy. Charlie too. I don't know, once those hormonal floodgates kicked open . . . Shit! Do you believe a whole year of celibacy, and then in one week I have sex with two guys?"

"Well, at least you didn't break the twenty-four-hour sperm rule, Lace."

Steffi was referring to the cardinal rule she and I had made up years ago never to do it with two different guys within the same twenty-four-hour period. A rule which of late hasn't been much of a problem. But this was the worst problem ever.

"Oh, God," I wailed, "it's like being in some stupid Sandra Dee movie where you fuck someone once, and you're pregnant!"

"Once?"

"Okay, twice . . . Okay, three times, if you count both times with Charlie."

We sat without talking for a few minutes. The heat was unbearable—it had been all week. "So what are you going to do?"

"That's just it, Steff. I can't figure this out. I tried last night. Not just in my head, but on paper. I wrote it down. 'Number one—I do not want to have a baby.' But I got stuck at 'number two' because if I don't want to have a baby, I only have two choices—I can have an abortion, or I can go through with the pregnancy and give the baby up for adoption."

"Right." She got up to move the fan closer to us.

"But how can I do that if this baby is Charlie's? It's the one thing he has been hoping to have in his life . . ."

"Lacy," Steff said, pulling her hair up to get it off her neck. "What do you owe Charlie?"

"It's not a question of owe. It's how I feel. He's my friend. I know I've been a creep about cutting things off, but he really is my friend. He's sweet and I like him, and what if this is really his baby?"

"What if it isn't? Listen, Lacy, you can't decide anything until you talk to him about all this."

"Are you nuts?" I sat forward and pulled my T-shirt away from my back. "He'll go crazy if he finds out it might be his baby. And even crazier if he finds out it might not be. Then he'll make me crazy because he's going to want to believe that it IS his baby, no matter what. I'm telling you, Charlie will nag me and nag me not just to have the baby, but to be its mother. And I cannot do that—it's too permanent. I mean I'm not about to do what Tony did and only go with the starter kit version of parenthood. Charlie has got to be willing to be the one parent for life . . ."

"Charlie can't make any decisions, Lacy, until you tell him what's going on."

"Oh, please, I don't want to. But I know I can't *not* tell him either."

"And what about the cowboy, Lace? Are you going to tell him too?"

I hadn't gotten to that one yet. Oh, God, what a mess—I couldn't stand it. It was the most abnormal situation I'd ever been in. But I behaved perfectly normally. I walked into the bathroom and threw up.

Charlie

A WEEK LATER

Man, I've had some brutal conversations, but nothing like the one in Grant Park with Lacy. No way was I prepared for what came down that afternoon. Granted, her message on the machine wasn't exactly breezy: "Charlie, we need to meet. It's too complicated to do on the phone." But even so, when I heard her voice on the machine, I was glad. Schmuck that I am, I figured she was calling because she'd missed me as much as I'd missed her.

That was before I heard her say the word "pregnant," when we sat at Buckingham Fountain.

As a kid I'd always loved it when Sophie and Abe took us there to play. Roger and I would bring our boats to race in the big calm pool that surrounded the four mammoth tiers with all those jets of spewing water. Night was the best, though. Lights shifted colors on the liquid arcs, and we would run around the perimeter leaping and yelping, pretending we were flying fish.

I'd been sitting on the fountain's edge a couple of minutes when I saw Lacy striding toward me. Her hair was pulled back in a ponytail and, because of that and the little white Keds she wore with her miniskirt, she looked maybe nineteen. Nineteen and tense. She was wearing big black shades. The kind the Kennedys wore to funerals. There was no smile on her face, either.

"Hi," I said, trying to sound casual. "How're you doing?" I patted the ledge on the fountain, for her to sit next to me. She stood.

"I'm doing just great. I'm pregnant."

" 'Pregnant'?" I repeated like an asshole.

"You heard me, Charlie."

"No shit? Christ, Lacy. That is . . . unbelievable." I stood up to pull her close in.

She pulled away from me. "Don't!"

"Don't what? Don't have a reaction? For Chrissakes, Lacy, you're pregnant! That is amazing! You know I'm dying for a kid. This is great!"

She looked at me as if I were insane. Then she bolted away from the fountain's rim, and spun around to face me. "Charlie! You are such a jerk! This is not great—this is terrible!"

She was yelling. Loud. Heads turned, hot dogs were put down, a few kids even stopped screaming. I grabbed her elbow and said, "Let's get out of here." I was pissed and confused. I sure as hell did not want to be someone's lunchtime entertainment. I steered her toward the Petrillo Band Shell. Not too many people were on the grass over there. We angled toward one of the trees up on a knoll and I motioned for her to sit.

"I can't—this skirt is too short."

"Yeah right," I said, leaning against the tree trunk. "God forbid a guy should see your underpants while you're telling him he got you pregnant . . ."

She whirled around to face me. "That's the other thing, Charlie. I'm not even sure if it's *you* that got me pregnant."

It took me about a minute. Then it kicked in. "I'm going to try and be one hell of a good guy here, Lacy. But what the fuck are you saying? Are you saying that this *could* be my kid, or it *could* maybe be some other guy's? Are you saying that you fucked two guys in the same week?"

She didn't say anything. The shades were on top of her head now, and the green eyes looked right back at me. Unapologetic as all hell.

"Nice, Lacy, nice."

Then she exploded. She yanked her shades off her head and the eyes blazed. "Where the hell do you get off? What about you and the TV chick? You were fucking her, Charlie! You and I weren't an item—we weren't even dating! I was free to fuck anyone I wanted! Anyone!"

"So," I said, grabbing her arm, "was it anyone? Or was it someone whose name you might even know?"

"Of course it was someone I know—for a lot longer than you," she said, jerking her arm away. "It's that guy I've been dancing with for two years at that country-western bar—not that it's any of your business. We just got stupid one night."

" 'Stupid'? Is that how you always describe your sexual encounters, Lacy? Isn't that what you said after we fucked? The *second* time I mean."

"You bastard."

"I'm hardly the bastard in this group. You're the one currently housing the bastard. Have you told the dancing cowboy the good news yet?"

"Charlie, stop it! Just stop it!" She put her hands over her ears. Anyone else would have started to cry. I wouldn't have blamed them. I was acting like a real prick. Lacy took a couple of deep breaths, put her hands down at her sides, and said softly, "I'm just trying to figure out what to do, Charlie."

"I know," I said quietly. "Christ. I'm sorry. This is just such a major dose of information."

Four teenage girls paraded by us in oversize shirts that said "Smashing Pumpkins." One of them carried a boom box with music blasting out of it. Lacy waited until they had passed before saying anything. The pain in her voice was real. "I didn't even know if I should tell you—I knew it would make you crazy. I know how much you want a kid. But that's the thing, Charlie, there are two out of three chances that this baby is yours."

"Oh, great . . . you only fucked him once? What about the condoms? *We* used condoms."

"I know, I always use condoms. So much for condoms," she sighed. "Listen, we've got to do something— what do you want to do?"

"What do I want to do?" I thought a minute. "Well,

number one, I want to make sure the baby is mine. Number two, I want you to have the baby. And number three. I want you to raise it with me. That's what I want."

"No way," she said, shaking her head. "Tops—absolute tops—you only get number two."

"Two? How can you go for number two if you don't go for number one? You can't have this baby without knowing whose it is!"

"Yes, I can."

"Why? How hard is it to take some sort of DNA test?"

"I don't know. Maybe not hard at all. But DNA is not the point."

"Finding out who the father is, isn't something of a point?"

"No, it isn't. Deciding whether or not I'm going to have this baby is the point. It's a life-and-death decision. And I'm not going to make it based on whose little sperm swam up there first—that just makes it more complicated."

"But, Lacy, it wouldn't be complicated. It's so simple. Just go and get tested!"

"You're not hearing me, Charlie."

Maybe she was right. This was so much to digest. I sat down with my back against the tree and stared at my hands. They were shaking. "I don't get it. Are you saying you're thinking of having this baby even if it isn't mine? Even if it's his? Are you making the same offer to the cowboy?"

"Can you stop? Can you stop with all this 'his' and 'mine'? I'm not even telling him. I'm just telling you—you're the one that wants a kid."

"Yeah, but, Lacy, I want my own kid."

"Listen to yourself." Taking my hand and placing it over her stomach, she said, "This is a baby here, Charlie. Most likely it's *your* baby. There's a sixty-six percent chance that it is your baby. But there's a hundred percent chance that it's a baby you could love and be a father to."

Then she took my hand off and let it go. "But it's an either/or choice for both of us. You either want to raise this baby, or you don't. If you do, then I will go ahead and have it. If you don't, then I have to decide whether I'll have the baby and give it up for adoption, or I won't have the baby at all. But I can't make my decision until you make yours."

I shook my head. It wasn't a no. It was an acknowledgment of the enormity of this whole proposal.

Lacy's voice softened. "Charlie, don't you get it? DNA isn't the answer. The answer is in you—in your heart. Not in some test tube. Parenting has nothing to do with biology."

"Yeah?" I said, getting up. "Tell that to the courts. They still come down pretty heavy in favor of bloodlines. Remember what happened with Baby Jessica and Baby Richard? Biology counted plenty."

"Well maybe it does in a court. But in real life, once you fall for a kid, that's *your* kid. I'm telling you, it's about connection—about bonds, not about biology. But if you think that you can't love the baby without a certificate of genetic authenticity, then tell me."

I didn't say anything. Neither did she for a minute. She opened her purse, pulled out a stick of gum, offered me a piece, and for a few minutes we just leaned against the green iron railing chewing.

"So if I don't take this baby, you're saying you'd consider an abortion?"

"I don't know," she said, staring straight ahead. "It's a huge decision. I don't go to church anymore or anything, but I just don't know how I feel about all that. I do know showing up for work every day and at college at night would be a lot easier—physically and emotionally—if I'm not pregnant."

"Yeah, probably."

"No, *definitely*." She put her glasses back on and smoothed out her skirt. "So let's do this. You think about whether or not you want this baby. Because if you do, we have to go to a lawyer and draft an agreement that says you will raise the kid yourself and that you won't ever take me to court for abandoning it. It will be just like you have contracted me to have this baby for you."

"For Chrissakes, Lacy. You've been watching too much bad TV. Where the hell did you come up with that?"

"Just now—in my head."

"So you're saying you would legally commit to going through this pregnancy for me?"

"Who said it was for *you*? God, Charlie. This doesn't revolve just around you! I don't want to be pregnant. I hate this! But if you want the baby, at least if I go through with it, there'll be this truly wonderful result—you'll be a dad."

"Christ."

"Yeah," she said, shifting her purse to her other

shoulder preparing to head back to the office. "It's a lot to decide. But the thing is, we don't have much time on this. You've got to let me know by Monday. I mean if you decide you don't want the baby, I need to make some decisions too. So I'll talk to you Monday, okay?"

"Okay," I said, watching her turn to leave. "Lacy?"

"Yeah?"

"I didn't ask if you were feeling sick or anything. How do you feel?"

She almost smiled. "Just great, Charlie. Just great."

She walked over to Michigan Avenue and got on the bus going north. A skywriting plane looped over my head and slowly began to scrawl its message against the dusty blue backdrop. I wondered, if I closed my eyes and counted to a thousand, if maybe when I looked up, there'd be a message for me. Some sign. I began to count. By the time I looked up, the first word had already faded. But I could read the second one.

It said "chicken."

Charlie

THAT WEEKEND

For a skinny state, Indiana has a lot of America jammed into it.

You can't see much of it from the Indiana Toll Road. It's all to the south. But you know you are in heartland territory. It's not only that this is Dan Quayle country, or that the license plates say AMBER WAVES OF GRAIN. But you're driving through a state that has two big-ten schools plus Notre Dame. A state that cares more about high school basketball than anyplace in the country. A state that claims to have the largest RV dealership in the country. And a state that hosts the Indy 500, where you can see more SHOW US YOUR TITS bumperstickers than anywhere in the country.

I'd been on the road about four hours and had maybe another hour to go until I hit the outskirts of Columbus, Ohio. I was on my way to see Andy Freeman. He and I had roomed together for two years at Michigan. I was tight with Andy, but in a different way from with Bobby. Partly because we didn't live in the same town and partly because we had fewer intersecting passions. Andy was a classics professor at Ohio State. When you're chasing hockey puck chasers for a living, it's not that easy to grab hold of your buddy's theories about Aeschylus. Not that I talked a lot of root canal with Bobby, but he and I shared a common interest in sports, jazz, and the general world of business. Andy was different. He operated in the rarefied world of academia. There was nothing mainstream about him. He hated TV, had no time for sports, he was a very NPR guy. But he was never an asshole about it. I liked him. I liked his mind, his values, and the way he had raised his daughter. And we always could talk.

Andy generally kept the real world out. Except in one arena. Parenthood. He had let plenty of real world in about ten years ago when the first wife walked out on him and Molly, their four-year-old daughter. From then on, Andy took on the whole shot himself. Granted, he had remarried two years ago, but this was a guy who'd done nearly a decade as a solo dad. He was the guy I needed to talk with this weekend.

I think I would have gone to see him even if Bobby hadn't been in Europe. Sherry had the family scheduled for something like seventeen cities in twenty-five days. It was mind-blowing to think that by the time Bobby got back, all this would be decided. I would either be on my way to being a father of a kid that was mine—or *maybe* mine—or Lacy would be making the impossible decision between abortion and adoption. Christ.

Andy's house was about ten minutes from the Ohio State campus. Three summers ago when I'd been there, his place had the regular lived-in look that a guy-only joint would have. Not dirty or anything. Just frayed, and crammed with more stacks of newspapers than a wife would go for. But as I parked, I could see that the new wife either owned a toolbox, or she'd busted Andy's ass and gotten him to pay attention to things like porch swings and fences that worked. Flower pots up the stairs were also a pretty good sign that a woman was living on the premises now. I'd met Liesel once before. She was lanky, German, and crazy for Andy. I liked her.

They both came to the screen door when I rang.

"Mr. Feldman, I presume." Andy grinned, opened up the door, and threw his arms around me. Christ, he was such a professor prototype. The glasses, the spindly legs sticking out of his shorts, the little paunch, and the pipe he'd begun affecting our senior year. But he looked good. Happy. Life with this Liesel was not hurting him one bit.

"Come on in, Sharly," she said with a dusty accent. "Your vroom is in the back. Ve get you settled, and then maybe a nice cold beer on the back porch?"

Andy must have told her I'd come to hash out some major shit. Because she brought out the beers, put in ten minutes with us, and then left us alone to talk.

I told him everything. The waiting room, the dad longings, the hookup with Lacy, all the dating, the way things kept looping back to Lacy, the Jo Beth deal, the Dunes, and now this piece of maybe-it's-your-kid, maybe-it-isn't news. Plus the ball-busting options I had to choose from.

"I'm fucked no matter what," I said. "The thought of this kid being scraped or suctioned away kills me. The thought of having someone else raise this kid kills me. And the thought of raising a kid alone—a kid who might not even be mine—that kills me the most. But I also know I am forty-fucking-four years old. And this is my chance to change everything. Everything."

"Hmm," said Andy, lighting up. "It's most definitely a lot to consider. But remember, if you say okay to taking this baby, *everything* in your life will change. I'm speaking not only of your logistical life, but your emotional life as well."

"Change for better, or for worse?"

"For both in a sense. Obviously there's considerably more better in it, or people wouldn't continue to compound their situations by having more children."

"You want more kids?"

"Liesel can't have them." He sucked on the pipe for a minute. "And no, I'm not sure that I do. The energy drain, the vulnerability . . . Molly has been a joy. But frankly, I'm not sure I would be interested in complicating our lives with another child—even now with a partner to share in all of it."

I chewed on what he'd just said. Then, pointing to two pairs of rollerblades leaning against the steps, I asked, "Does Liesel rollerblade with Molly?"

"What makes you ask that?"

"The two pairs."

He smiled. "No. Both those sets of rollerblades are

Molly's. The first pair we bought in January. On sale—for a mere hundred and thirty dollars. She outgrew them. We bought a new pair last month. I don't believe they were any cheaper."

"Is that part of it? The money? Another kid would cost a shitload of money, right?"

"Charlie," he said, looking at me as if I were a kid in one of his classes who couldn't grasp the concept, "you are egregiously off the mark. Money is the least of it. And I am not rich. The issue is skin. The French have a saying 'bien dans sa peau.' It means at ease in one's own skin. Plain and simple, the minute you have a child, when it comes to that child, you not only are no longer at ease in your own skin, you no longer have any skin on. You are a raw exposed mass of potential pain. You are heartbreak waiting to happen. Every time that child gets on the school bus, and goes off into the world of possible hurts, you are poised to hemorrhage. If I sound melodramatic, I apologize. But I don't know any other way to explain the exposure to anguish that a child puts right in the center of your being. I teach the philosophers, and poetry, and Greek drama, right? The great tragedies. And I will match the torment of Odysseus cast out to sea for forty years—I will match that any day to having Molly come home one afternoon in the fifth grade saying no one would eat with her or talk to her and she didn't know why. She was just shut out. It lasted for five weeks. Five interminable weeks."

"Was that when you got the ulcer?"

"No. I waited until the other kids were talking to her again. That's another thing about being a parent. You have to schedule your sick days for when your child can handle it. Want another beer?"

I passed. But I followed him back into the kitchen so he could grab one. The kitchen had changed more than any room in the house since my last visit. Liesel liked to cook so that was the room she'd made hers first. The old linoleum had been ripped up and the wood floors underneath had been stained dark. New counters had been put in, the walls had been painted white, and over the sink there was a greenhouse thing with all these plants growing. It almost could have been Bobby's house.

The refrigerator door was familiar though. It was papered with stuff from, by, and about Molly. Photos, notes from teachers, an essay of hers in *The Columbus Dispatch* about how important it is for teenagers to connect with older people. She ran a volunteer program at a local nursing home.

"I'm sorry you missed Molly this trip," said Andy. "She's got another week to go working out on a Hopi Indian reservation. Her letters are remarkable. If you have time, I can show you a couple. Last week was her birthday and the family she's been living with asked her what she wanted for her birthday dinner. She didn't mean to hurt their feelings, but before she could stop herself she'd said 'pizza.' It was a genuine moment of anthropological truth."

"She was always a great kid, Andy. You did good by her."

He was quiet a minute. "I did. I'm doing even better for her now. Partly because Liesel's being here has enabled me to be more balanced about everything. I'm still

ready to bleed at any given moment, and I still cherish
Molly in the same way. But I find that the cherishing is
less focused on only one entity. I think that is the inherent danger of being a single father. Mother too, no
doubt. You imbue that child with far too much responsi-
bility for your own emotional equilibrium. It's better for
you and for your child when you have an emotional
investment in someone else too."

"Yeah. Well that doesn't seem to be an option for me.
Lacy has made it damn clear that the second the kid
takes its first breath, she is history."

Andy unlocked the dishwasher and started to empty
it. "Perhaps. But believe me, that does not mean that
other women aren't going to cross your path once it's
you and the baby."

"Right, I'm sure there will be millions. There were
for you, right, Freeman? That's why you wound up raising Molly by yourself for eight years. Too many offers
and you couldn't decide."

Andy picked up a towel to dry off some of the still
damp wineglasses. "In truth, Charlie, being a single
man with a child has a rather remarkable effect on
women. And I'm not convinced it's because they see you
as some sort of domestic oaf. On the contrary. I think
when women see that a man is capable of being a good
nurturer, they are inspired—freed up perhaps—to nur-
ture him. They aren't afraid of him the way they are of
some men."

"What kind of men do you think women are afraid
of?"

"The ones they perceive as pathetic or needy. All

those books that have come out on that Oprah woman's show tell them to steer clear of men who are looking for mothers. I don't disagree with that. But when women see a man who is doing a good job of parenting on his own, then they are considerably less leery of his potential neediness. Though believe me, capable as I was, I was terribly needy."

"What was the main thing you needed?"

"The main thing?" He set his beer on the edge of the sink. "I don't think there was a main thing. In the beginning I needed to heal from the pain of Linda's walking out. Once I got past that, what I needed was respite. When there is no backup, no one to hand off duties to, it is very depleting."

"What about confidence? Or did you already have that because you'd had some experience of being a dad with a partner?"

"No. I think confidence is illusory. You can be confident that what you're doing feels right for you, but how a child ultimately turns out is too much in the hands of the gods for any mortal to walk around feeling supremely confident. Unless of course he's an arrogant, stupid mortal, like most of us."

"But you were okay on your own, right?" He wasn't telling me what I wanted to hear at all.

"Okay? Of course I was okay. But the fact is, I have done it both ways—parenting on my own and parenting with a partner. And I would be lying to you if I didn't say that this way is better. But I think the reason for that is that Liesel and I are solid. She has an extraordinary capacity to infuse any situation with calm. And she is able to simply be there for me. I am not saying that partnering in and of itself is better—I'm very sure it wasn't better with Linda—there was too much tension between us—but partnership with the right person most definitely makes it better."

"But the doing it on your own? It's do-able, right?"

"Do-able, but constant. And assuredly not easy. It's also not something that anyone else can tell you to do or not do. It has to be your decision."

I knew he was right.

That night they took me with them to some outdoor theater. The night was hot and muggy. We lathered ourselves with repellent and Liesel packed up a thermos of gin and tonics, and some cold broiled chicken with a couple of salads. It wasn't the kind of evening I usually had, but it turned out okay. The show was *Stop the World, I Want to Get Off.* It sure as hell was the way I felt. Too much was happening too fast.

We sat on a blanket on the grass. There must have been five or six hundred people already sitting in the theater. We'd put some sweaters on our seats, but it was hot as hell in there and the show wasn't going to begin for another fifteen minutes. A few kids were running around catching fireflies while their parents packed up the dinner stuff. I still had some gin and tonic left, but wasn't much interested in finishing it.

Liesel began packing up our silverware. She was a tall, blonde woman, with a serious face and large strong hands. She used them to touch Andy all the time. Sometimes on his arm, or around his waist. Once she even leaned over to wipe some mayo off his mouth with her napkin. Normally that kind of shit makes me uncomfortable, but she did it all in a nice way. Not possessive, or flirtatious.

"Andy tolt me about za big decision you must make, Sharly," she said. "I hope you don't mind. But ve tell each ozer most zings."

"I don't mind, Liesel. You guys are married. That's what married people do, right?"

"Some," said Andy. "If they're married to a good person for them to be married to." This time it was he who touched her arm. "Liesel thinks I might have scared you off though, on the subject of single parenting."

"Yeah? How so, Liesel?"

"Vell, it just seems zat Andy sometimes underrates how goot, how very gifted even, he vas wit Molly, all by himself." She smiled and I could see the blue eyes behind her glasses grow very contemplative. "I tsink this voman vit your baby does not vant to do a stupet tsing. She knows vat it takes to be only one parent. She must know you can do it, Sharly. Ozerwise, she vould not tell you about the baby."

"Yeah, maybe." I shrugged. Liesel taught sociology at Ohio State. Not that that exactly made her the end-all expert on shit like this, but it counted for more than if she'd been in retail.

Rain started to plunk down in big, flat drops, so we headed in under the tent. But an hour later, the stage lights blew out, and since the production was okay at best, we decided to split at intermission.

"How about a movie?" Andy asked. "It's only nine-thirty. Or maybe we could head over to Germantown. There's a great place to go and hear some jazz there."

"In Ohio?" I asked. For years Andy and I'd had a running gag on how I was the one who was now leading this big-city life and he was out in the sticks. Andy was from the West Side of Manhattan and had laid it on pretty thick about the Midwest when we were in Ann Arbor.

We wound up going home early like a bunch of old farts, but the next morning the three of us got up early to play four sets of hard sweaty tennis. Liesel beat the pants off us both. Some rich friends of theirs in Bexley had a pool party going on that afternoon. I wanted to beg off, but Liesel and Andy insisted that I go because Sam Kantrel, an old buddy from Michigan, was supposed to show up. I hadn't seen Sam in ten years. He was a doc, divorced with three kids. Two of them were with him at the party.

"Christ, it is good to see you," I said to him when he walked over from the far end of the pool. He looked great. Maybe twenty pounds lighter than the last time I'd seen him, and clearly working out.

"You too, old man," he said, throwing an arm across my shoulder. Then a wail rose from the shallow end, and he turned. "Allison, leave Mark alone or you're out of the pool." A nine- or ten-year-old blonde in the water seemed to be jumping on the back of her brother every time he attempted a dead man's float. Sam didn't scream the warning to her. He didn't hiss it either. He just said it to her, real straight. Even so, the kid blew him off, and hammered the little boy again. So Sam did just what he said he'd do. He hauled the kid out of the water, wrapped her kicking and screaming in a towel, and carried her to a chair at the far end of the yard. A brief discussion ensued.

About five minutes later he was back and sat down next to me on the edge of the pool. "The whole trick is follow-through. That, and a standing appointment on Fridays at the kiddie shrink," he said with a grin.

The afternoon passed quickly. Somehow I managed to hang out with a bunch of people and pretend nothing major was going on in my life. Andy didn't say anything further to me about the real issue until around six that evening when I pulled out of their driveway.

He tossed my tennis racket in the backseat and said, "I know I said I wouldn't weigh in on this, but I've known you a long time. I know you are a man of integrity and diligence. You are also a man of great heart. I'm not telling you what to do. I am telling you, you would make an extraordinary parent."

Ten years before, I would have been so mired in my own macho bullshit that I'd have been embarrassed. I'd have figured guys didn't talk to guys like that. But at forty-four I knew different. Sometimes guys did. I was glad.

I drove home in the worst fucking thunderstorm I'd ever been in.

Lacy

THAT WEEKEND

These are the things you get to stop when you are pregnant: You get to stop drinking beer, you get to stop buying new size-nine clothes, and you get to stop having a relatively great relationship with your eighteen-year-old daughter.

Jess was still completely furious with me. She just couldn't believe that I had gone out and done the very thing that she and all her girlfriends had spent the past four or five years assiduously avoiding. I remember when she was in ninth grade she carried around a hand-drawn card that said "Official Member of GWGKUAS!" I asked her what it meant, but she wouldn't tell me. Later on I found out it stood for—"Girls Who Get Knocked Up Are Stupid!" Obviously a mom who had once gotten herself knocked up would have very mixed feelings about figuring out that particular acronym. But a mom who had twice gotten herself knocked up . . . well, *hell*, this time I had more important things to worry about.

And anyway, I couldn't blame Jessie for her rage and exasperation. I felt the same way—incredibly ticked at myself. All weekend I'd been having second thoughts about having let Charlie in on it; about how nuts that was. I mean, why did he get a vote? What was I doing turning my decisions—about my body and my future— over to a guy? A sportswriter, no less. If this whole scenario had shown up in a letter to the Advice Ladies, I'd have put it in the "hopeless" file. That's where we toss the letters from those people who you know no matter what advice you give them, they'll figure out a new way to screw things up. People like me.

Sunday night around eleven Jess and I nearly came to blows. I was standing out on the back porch wishing I still smoked. The TV from the porch next door had finally clicked off, and the night was so hot and still that you could hear the wheezing of the bus over on Halsted Street. Clouds made it pretty hard to spot the moon, so it was extra dark. Jess had alternated all day between ignoring me and swooping down on me to ask what I was planning to do. This time she followed me outside, and I lost it. "Jess, leave me alone. I do not know yet. When I do, I promise you'll be the first to know."

"Yeah?" she sneered. She wore an olive tank top, khaki shorts, and a turned-around Sox hat. "Well what about the nameless dad? Or doesn't he get to be as lucky as my dad was? You know, doesn't this dad get to marry you and then leave you and all?"

I spun on her. "Back off, Jess! Stop being such a bitch! What I do has nothing to do with you! Nothing! I'm still your mom, and you're still my kid, but in four weeks—no matter what I do about this situation—you are off to Chapel Hill to be the best version of you that you can be. I screwed up—I admit it. But I'll figure this out. I always have and I always will. If you are pissed and embarrassed, then fine, I accept that. Just stop breathing it in my face twenty-four hours a day, okay?"

"I don't know if I can," she said, her lower lip trembling just a little.

"You can because I need you to." I reached out to touch her arm. I thought she'd pull it back, but this time she gave me a break. She didn't move until I took my hand away, and then she turned to go back inside. The screen door slammed. I had to remind myself she always did that—it only *felt* like punctuation.

I was sound asleep when the phone rang.

"Lacy? Today is Monday."

"Who is this?" I asked. It was after midnight.

"It's Charlie. I'm stuck in a rainstorm on the Indiana Toll Road."

"Charlie, why are you calling so late?"

"It's Monday. You said to call you on Monday with what I decided."

I didn't say anything. The moment felt a bit more like *Wheel of Fortune* than I liked.

"Lacy?"

"Yeah, Charlie. I'm here."

"I want you to have the baby. I'd like you to take a DNA test though, but I want you to have the baby. I'll raise the baby no matter what."

I wish I hadn't started to cry. But I stuck to my guns too. "No DNA test, Charlie. I've got to believe you'll either love this baby because you've decided it's your baby, or you don't get this baby."

It was his turn to not say anything right away. "Okay. No harm in asking though, right?"

"I suppose." I turned on the lamp. There was too much reality going on to do this in the dark.

"Maybe no harm in asking this either. I'm going to offer you one last chance to be part of the kid's life. Why can't we do this together? Lacy, we could do this so right."

"Right? There's nothing right about it. This is the least right thing I've ever done in my life."

"What about when you were pregnant with Jessica? Didn't that feel like this? And look how great she turned out. Lacy, you are a sensational mother."

"Charlie, when I got pregnant with Jess, I was scared to death, but I also didn't have a choice. You come from my family and you get pregnant, you marry the father. And anyway, at the time, I was insanely in love with the father—or thought I was anyway."

"You were sixteen. That's when people are insanely in love. Have you ever tried being just deeply in love? Who's to say you couldn't work your way to being deeply in love with me."

"Charlie, I just can't do what you want. I have to do what I *need* to do. I just have to."

He was quiet for a minute. Then through the static on the line he asked, "So what do we do now?"

"I think we don't tell anybody about this. Because I'm not sure what we are doing is legal. You know, my having the baby but not wanting to be the legal mother. We have a lot of stuff to figure out—between us and with a lawyer. Do you know any lawyers?"

"Only my divorce lawyer. What about you?"

"Same. He's my will lawyer too. But he's also my mom's lawyer. I don't want to go to him. I'm not sure I want Dolores in on any of this, and if I don't tell her, it might make him feel compromised. Maybe what I'll do is go into the computer tomorrow and pull up some stories on adoption law. There may be a name we can use."

"What's adoption got to do with this? Are you telling me I'm going to have to adopt my own kid?"

"Charlie, I don't think we should be having this discussion when you're in a pay phone and I don't have my lenses in. I think we should talk tomorrow after work."

"Do you want to have dinner at my place?"

"No, Charlie, I don't. I just want us to figure out the details for pulling this off—get them down on paper, live through them, and get to the other side of them. So we can both get on with our lives."

"Right." He sighed.

"Great. So I'll talk to you tomorrow, okay?"

"Okay."

"And, Charlie?"

"Yeah?"

"You get to pay for the lawyer."

Charlie

A Week Later

The lawyer's name was Lipman, of Feinstein, Lipman, and Nudel. Not a firm name that inspired shitloads of confidence.

The offices were more encouraging. At least they had carpeting. My divorce lawyer's had linoleum floors. In my twenties, I thought linoleum meant he had integrity. In my forties, I knew it meant he wasn't making any dough. Lipman et al. were entitled to carpeting. They charged a hundred and fifty an hour.

"How much?" I asked Lacy when she called to tell me she'd made an appointment with him.

"One hundred fifty an hour. That's why I think we should go to the meeting all prepared. I don't want to waste a lot of time. So let's both spend this week making up our lists of what we want written into the agreement."

"Lacy, I don't want anything written into the agreement. *You* want this agreement. I just want to be the kid's father when it's born. Which reminds me, how do you feel?"

"Fine. Which reminds me, you've got to pay my doctor bills too. Anything that isn't covered by insurance. Okay?"

"Yeah, I guess. I hadn't thought about it."

"See? That's what I mean. There's a lot to consider when it comes to all this. I'm just suggesting that before we sit down with this lawyer, you take some time to think about all the contingencies."

I didn't need to. Lacy had thought of enough contingencies for both of us. When we sat down at the conference table in Lipman's office on Friday afternoon, she spread out five sheets of yellow legal paper.

"My list," she said, nodding apologetically at Lipman. He was a thin, bald guy in his fifties who blinked when he finished every sentence. Hard to figure out how a guy with a tic could be good in court, but hell, Harry Caray was a broadcasting legend and he sounded like he was talking through soup. Lipman's office overlooked LaSalle Street, and thirty-two floors up gave you a great view of the city.

"It's almost a straight shot from here to Wrigley," he said, noticing where my eyes had gone. "I try to get to some of the three o'clock games, but on a day like today, when they start at one, I just look out in the direction of the field and figure the view isn't much worse than a bad seat in the bleachers."

Lacy didn't smile. She was a Sox fan. Plus, she was in full biz mode today. White blouse, gray suit, some pearls in her ears. She'd been watching too many *L.A. Law* reruns.

"Uh, do you think we can get this started," she said, "I'm on my lunch hour."

"Surely." Lipman sat down in a big gray leather chair across from the window. "I'm not quite sure I understood everything you said on the phone, Ms. Gazzar, so why don't you explain."

"Right," said Lacy, putting down her pencil. "It *is* kind of out of the ordinary, but here's the situation. I'm pregnant. Mr. Feldman wants to be the father of this baby. In fact, he *is* the father of this baby—at least we think he is. It could be someone else's, but that's not important."

Lipman held up his palm. "Actually it could be very important, Ms. Gazzar."

"Well it's not," she snapped. "Because the other guy doesn't know, he doesn't care, and no one can force me to take any tests to find out. Right, Mr. Lipman?"

"Well, no one but the other man, were he to make a claim on the baby, Ms. Gazzar."

"Well he's not. He's out of the picture. In fact, he moved to Kansas City last week."

I looked at Lacy. I knew damn well that piece of fiction was just to get the lawyer off her ass.

"So anyway," she continued, waving her hand toward me, "Mr. Feldman here is the person who will be raising this baby. I, however, will not. By mutual agreement, I will have this baby, but I am *not* going to be part of this baby's life. I will sign any document you draw up saying that I renounce all parental claims."

Lipman tapped his pen against the edge of the chair. "Of course I can draw up a document," he said, "though with what is going on today in terms of biological parents reclaiming their children, I'm not convinced that it would hold up in court. And frankly, Mr. Feldman, you need to know that."

"Know what?"

"That there is a risk. At a later date, Ms. Gazzar could reverse her decision and make a claim regardless of the document I draw up."

Lacy jumped up. "Mr. Lipman! You don't know me. I am a very definite sort of a person. So don't you worry about me changing my mind. In fact, I would like you to arrange when the time comes to have my name removed from the baby's birth certificate."

Lipman did a few of his blinks. "That is not only an unorthodox request, Ms. Gazzar," he said, "but no hospital would take your name off a birth certificate. It would be completely illegal. In Illinois, the only way a woman can be severed from her legal connection as a child's mother is if the court declares her unfit, or if the child is put up for adoption. But even in the case of an adoption, the mother's name is on the original birth certificate. It is simply kept in a closed file. What is your reasoning for such a request?"

"My reasoning is that I am more than happy to have Charlie—Mr. Feldman—raise this baby. But if something happens to him—Mr. Feldman, not the baby—I don't want to be responsible—legally or emotionally—for this child."

Lipman was quiet. I was quieter. There was something about hearing all of this in the harsh light of day, high above LaSalle Street, that put a different spin on it. Or at least on Lacy. She must have felt it too, because her next words were, "Mr. Lipman, look. I know what I just said sounds heartless, even unmaternal maybe, but I have an eighteen-year-old daughter that I raised by myself. I've done a great job with her. I'm crazy about her. But in three weeks she is leaving for college, and I'm finally going to college too. So, I am not about to begin the cycle all over. I am here with Mr. Feldman because he wants this baby and is willing to raise it on his own. And all I am trying to do is work out an agreement between us that will set up the best way we can do this."

Lipman pushed back from the table and went over to the water pitcher at his desk. "Mr. Feldman, do you want to say anything?"

"Can I have some water?"

"Of course." He poured a glass of water and brought it to the table. "First of all, let me tell you that while I think it was wise of you to come in here, the fact is that any agreement you make between you will not necessarily stand up in court. It can't hurt to make the agreement, Ms. Gazzar, because should Mr. Feldman change his mind about your involvement with this child, should he want you involved or responsible for the child, he would have to go to the trouble of striking down the agreement in court. But as the law now stands, he could probably succeed."

"He could?"

"Yes."

Lacy's forehead furrowed. She sat down again in her

chair, folded her arms, and looked me dead in the eye. "Charlie? Are you gonna fuck me over?"

"That's not the plan, Lacy."

"Fine," she said, turning back to Lipman. "Well, call me stupid, but I believe him. Only I still think we need to get as much of this on paper as possible. Do you want to help us, Mr. Lipman, or are we maybe in the wrong office for a hundred and fifty dollars an hour?"

Lipman smiled. "I like you, Ms. Gazzar. You're in the right office. Why don't you start with your notes and I'll start drafting an agreement?"

Fifty minutes later a draft was done. Lipman said it was the most bizarre agreement he'd ever been privy to. In it, I agreed to never contact Lacy regarding either fiscal or emotional responsibilities for the kid. I agreed to pay any uncovered prenatal and delivery bills for her. I agreed to pay them in cash. I agreed to tell no one that Lacy was the one having this baby other than Andy who already knew. The story, as far as anyone was concerned, was that I was going to raise my own kid, and that the mom was someone I'd met on the road. Anyone pressing me for more details than that—and this included Sophie and Abe and even Bobby—got nothing. They were allowed to think I was crazy. They were allowed to think I was lying. They were allowed to think anything, other than that it might be my baby with Lacy. Pulling that part off was going to be tough but not impossible. People were used to my being vague. And few of my friends had ever met or heard much about Lacy.

Lacy wasn't allowed to tell anybody I was the father either except her best friend who already knew and Jessica. Where it got dicey was at the paper. Lacy could blow people off about who the dad was, but she sure as hell couldn't blow them off about the fact that she was pregnant. The plan was she would go through the pregnancy and tell people she was giving the baby up for adoption. Which would work out fine, except that I couldn't suddenly show up as the father of a kid. So I would have to quit my job. She'd saved that bombshell for the last ten minutes of our meeting in Lipman's office.

"Are you out of your fucking mind?" I yelled at her. "What the hell am I supposed to do for a living?"

"You're supposed to figure something out, Charlie. You can't raise a baby anyway if you're on the road eight months a year. Write novel! Get a real job! Figure something out. If that isn't part of the contract, we aren't doing this!"

"You're busting my ass, Lacy. You can't tell me what to do with my life!"

"Oh, no? Well you seem to be telling me what to do with the next nine months of mine!"

"That's different!"

"How?"

Lipman sat moving his head as if he were watching a tennis match.

"Lacy, I have been a sportswriter half my life. It's my job."

"Charlie, I have been a mother half my life. It's my job. Guess what? This is the year we are both changing jobs."

"I don't know, Lacy."

"Charlie, one of us has to leave the paper. You don't have a lot of friends there, I do. You don't need the health insurance right now, I do. And besides, you've got to find something that keeps you home more."

It wasn't that I hadn't figured this out before. And it wasn't that I hadn't put out some feelers from time to time whenever I was feeling burned out on the beat. Three years ago the *Minneapolis Tribune* had made me an offer to come up and cover pro football—arguably the cushiest beat of all. One game a week, six or seven plane rides a season, and the shortest season of any professional sport. But in the end, I couldn't see living in a place that had even shittier weather than Chicago. Then three months ago another guy had called to feel me out about an all-sports radio station that might start up in town. I was pretty lukewarm. I didn't mind computers, but I wasn't sure microphones didn't scare the hell out of me. He wanted me to audition, but I let the ball drop. Maybe that was because I *thought* I wanted to change jobs more than I wanted to change jobs. And now I had Lacy on my case telling me I *had* to change jobs.

"This is a deal point, Charlie," she said, folding her hands in front of her on the table. "So, do we have a deal?"

I watched my entire life pass in front of me. "Deal," I said.

Lacy

August

It's not that Dolores is melodramatic or anything, but it would have been nice if she hadn't started to faint when I told her I was pregnant.

"How could this happen twice?" she wailed, collapsing against me. I'd gone over to see her after dinner when I knew Brian would be at his Elks meeting. The bigger the audience, the higher the drama with Dolores, and I wanted to minimize the theatrics. I got her down in a chair and went to the tap to get her some water.

"Turn up the air-conditioning," she said, closing her eyes and fanning herself. "Don't I ever get any peace? What are we going to do?"

"Ma, *we* aren't going to do anything. *I* am going to have a baby."

"This is too much for a mother my age," she said, shaking her head. This month she was a brunette with lots of sprayed-in waves. "*Dio mio*, how can you do this to me all over again?"

I walked over to the credenza that was covered with pictures of Jess—I knew what I wanted to say, but I needed to get my delivery right. "Mom, *I* am the one this has happened to—not *you*. Why is everyone in the family making this their tragedy? You and Jessica are not the ones who are almost forty and pregnant!"

Dolores did not like being talked to like that. She sat silently for a few moments. Then looking at her coral nails as if they were the most important item in the room, she breathed in deeply and asked, "And when, might I ask, is this blessed event?"

"March."

"And who, if it's not too much trouble, is the father?"

"It doesn't matter."

"*Mama mia!*" She put her hand to her forehead and shook her head with despair. Then she went into the bathroom and took some Tylenol. I stayed another half hour trying to explain without being completely capable of explaining. But in the end she preferred to be inconsolable.

"Fine," she said, turning her face away from me when I tried to kiss her good-bye. "It's your life to ruin."

"Ruin how, Ma? I'll have the baby, give it up for adoption, and then get on with my life. My life may slow down for a while, and it'll be awkward explaining the pregnancy over and over, but then by March it will all be done, and I'll be right back on track."

She looked at me with red-rimmed eyes. "There

won't be a day in your life you won't wonder about that baby, Lacy Luccione Gazzar. Not a day."

That kind of talk was not helpful for me at all. I'm not saying I blame Dolores for flipping out. It's just that nothing short of waking up and finding out that my pregnancy was a dream would have assuaged her. And the worst part was that she and Jess were both so insufferably self-righteous about it all. At a certain point it would have been nice if they could have gotten past that, and we could have proceeded with getting Jessica off to college—a process that promised to be wrenching enough. But now with the pregnancy thing mixed into it, the whole month was just hell.

August was made up of these things: my throwing up; Jessica and Richie breaking up; Jessica and Richie going back together; Jessica and Richie breaking up again; my getting daily calls from Charlie to see how I felt; my mother never calling up to see how I felt, but only to see if Jessica wanted to eat at her house since I couldn't stand the smell of food at ours; my yelling; Jessica yelling; Dolores yelling; my crying; Jessica crying; Dolores crying. Oh, yeah, and the air conditioner breaking for good.

Not to mention having to go through the whole "this is what I can tell you, this is what I can't" thing all over again at the office a few weeks later with Ruthie. She at least had the good grace not to faint.

"I'm not sure I understand what you're saying, Lacy," she said, getting up to close the door. Her office was small and homey—lots of framed posters from art exhibits she went to, pictures from some of her trips, and a real person table lamp instead of the office kind. She even brought in a rug from her house to set over the regulation gray carpeting that ran through the whole floor. "Maternity leave? Are you telling me you're pregnant?"

"Yeah." I sighed. "I am."

"Well, that's something of a surprise," she said, unsure whether to smile or commiserate, particularly since I was giving her no signals. "Do you mind if I ask, if it surprised you too?"

"I don't mind. Yes it did. But I'm not keeping the baby, I'm giving it up for adoption."

I watched Ruth trying to digest it all and trying to pick out which questions she could ask from all the questions she *wanted* to ask. Because thank God, there are still some you just can't—like "How the hell did it happen?"

"So. Does the father know?"

"Yes he does. He's fine with it."

"I see," she said, fiddling with a button on her blue silk shirt—Ruth always wore blue. Of course I had no idea how Charlie *really* felt about any of it. I knew that he was going through some real changes though—not just job things, but he was even talking about moving out of the high-rise too. But I didn't ask a lot of questions. Partly because I didn't want to know all these getting-ready-for-the-baby details, but mostly because I was such a wreck about Jessica's leaving for school. And *that* was not exactly going smoothly at all.

I don't know if it was the mutual separation anxiety, the baby thing, or what, but we argued over everything. Should she buy a phone here? Should she wait and get one there? Should she take her old quilt? Should she just get a new one? Should we ship her things ahead? Should we try and jam it all into the car? Everything was an issue.

Two nights before she was supposed to leave for good we were standing in the middle of the new towels and sheets we had bought at Bed, Bath, & Beyond that afternoon, arguing over whether or not to wash it all first, when the phone rang. Jess grabbed it.

"Oh. Hi, Dad."

I continued ripping off the price tags when I heard her say, "Yeah, I think I told her—I can't remember. No, but I will. Now, I promise. I'm sure it's fine. Okay. Bye."

"What's fine?" I asked. It was hard to imagine anything being fine where Tony was involved.

"Dad wants to come along with us when we drive out to school."

I stopped stacking washcloths. "He does?"

"Yeah. Is that okay with you?"

What an incredible question. For months we had this whole trip to school set up. Brian was loaning us his station wagon and the plan was to take the long scenic route to Chapel Hill. First we were going to drive to Columbus, get up the next morning and cross the Ohio River into West Virginia. From there we would head to Charleston, West Virginia, pass some of the coal-mining towns, go through the Blue Ridge Mountains, cross Virginia, and then get into North Carolina where we would hit Winston-Salem, then Greensboro and Durham and straight into Chapel Hill. All of that would probably take two days. And two days was a whole lot longer than I wanted to be in a moving vehicle with Tony Gazzar.

"All of a sudden your father wants to come with us?"

"Yeah. He said starting college is a big moment in my academic career and he really wanted to be there."

"The only two times he's been involved in your academic career was sixth-grade science fair, because I was home with the stomach flu, and graduation!"

"I can't help it, Mom. He asked to go," she snapped back.

"Well when did all this take place?" I asked, stepping over some of the cardboard boxes to grab another roll of packing tape.

"Last week, when I had dinner with Dad for his birthday."

"Why didn't you tell me about it before, Jessica? Why two nights before we leave?"

"I don't know. I thought I did tell you. Or maybe I repressed it because I knew you'd freak. I didn't even know how I felt about it myself."

"Yeah? Well I know how I do. I feel your father has no business showing up at sayonara time. I know he's your dad, and I know he's paying for half your allowance while you're in school, but I don't see why he gets to make this grandstand appearance in the final act of your childhood."

"For God's sake, Mom, don't make more of it than it is. He wants to be there. I don't mind. In fact it might be kind of cool to have two parents around for that orientation meeting. I've heard some kids *like* having two parents."

That was Jessica's specialty lately—the covert bitchy remark. That remark was not about how deprived *she'd* been all those years—she knew perfectly well that she and I had been fine. That remark was about *this* baby—because not only was Jessica mad at me for being pregnant, she was even madder at me for not sticking around to raise it. Of course it made no sense, but it was pretty obvious that she hated the baby and overidentified with the baby at the same time—just to keep things nice and complicated.

Things got a lot less complicated travel-wise the night before we were to take off. The phone rang around seven and I heard Jessica say, "No, Daddy, it's okay. I understand. I really do . . ."

It was Tony, bailing out of course. God, what a dick. I mean it was definitely a better deal for me, but Jess had really counted on showing up in Chapel Hill as a three-some.

"Oh, well," she sighed, "I guess if I don't have to sit in the backseat, now there will be room to bring my stuffed gorilla."

I loved her so damn much.

It's the funniest thing—you can check out any highway in late August and you will see thousands of parents driving east in station wagons crammed with one fresh-man and hundreds of dollars' worth of shampoo, razors, and dental floss. You will also see thousands of parents driving west in station wagons crammed with one fresh-man and thousands of dollars' worth of shampoo, razors, and dental floss. Somehow, even though all of us are convinced there are campuses at the other end, I guess we aren't all that sure there are drugstores.

We sure saw some gorgeous countryside on our trip. Lush rolling hills, funny battered old motels, a wonderful vegetable stand in a place called Fancy Gap, North Carolina, that sold something called sourwood honey. I bought a jar for each of us—it was a weird reminder that from now on, Jess and I would be having breakfast in two separate places.

We pulled into the Chapel Hill Best Western University Inn around nine-thirty the night before dorm day. We got our key, hauled our overnight bags up the stairs to room 28, and flopped down on the aqua queen-size bed. The radio was playing elevator music.

I turned it off and said, "D-day kicks in at nine A.M. sharp, hon. What time do you want to set the alarm for?"

Jessica started clicking through the channels until she got to MTV—*Real World* was on, and she was addicted. It was a series of half-hour shows following six or eight kids, who were subsidized by MTV and living in some fancy apartment for the summer. She'd seen every episode, every year, bunches of times, but getting lost in their lives seemed infinitely preferable to focusing on hers—particularly since it was about to radically change in less than twelve hours.

"Jess? What time tomorrow?"

"Oh. Sorry. I dunno—maybe eight."

"Does that give you time to shower?"

"I suppose. We're only going to get all sweaty moving into the dorm anyway."

No doubt she was right. Even at nine-thirty at night, Chapel Hill was cooking in eighty-seven-degree heat. "Aren't the dorms air-conditioned?" I asked.

"Mom, I don't know. I visited here in November, remember? I'm just planning on sweating tomorrow."

I flopped down on my side of the bed. There were two foil-wrapped mints on the nightstand. I love motels. I love that all the rooms are the same, and no one expects you to say how pretty they are, and that even though motels advertise that they are there to welcome you, they are really always waiting for you to pay up and leave. Plus, they usually have pretty good vending machines.

"Want to eat something?" I asked Jess.

"Like what?"

"I don't know. Nachos. Ice cream. When we passed that Howard Johnson's a ways back it made me start thinking of clam rolls. Maybe we could find some seafood place."

"I don't feel like getting in the car again, Mom. You can go if you want. I'm fine here."

"Jess," I said, watching her sit there in her jeans, picking at her feet and acting as if it were a perfectly normal night. "I'm not about to go out and leave you here by yourself—this is our last night together!"

"Mom, when are you going to stop doing that?" She got up and went to her purse to pull out her brush, and began pulling it through her hair.

"Doing what?"

"All that 'this is your last' stuff. You've been doing it all year. In September when senior year began, you said,

'This is your last first day of school.' When teacher conferences came, you said, 'This is the last time I will ever ask a teacher how you are doing.' At Christmas you said, 'This is your last Christmas when you will really, really live here.' I mean all this marking off the milestone stuff is sort of creepy. It's not like I'm about to die or something." She stalked into the bathroom for some water.

What did she know? Not about dying, but about how forever it seems when you have a kid, how endless and tedious it is, and then *shazam!* it's over. For years you are on this hamster wheel of birthday parties, and lost tennis shoes, and school permission slips, and none of it seems like it will ever diminish, much less disappear. Then it does. And one day the drawers get cleaned out, and the quilt gets stripped off, and the kid is on her way to a new area code with her own cash card. And it's not that you're not happy for her, but suddenly you're a 312 mom with a 919 daughter and there is no way on God's green earth you are going to have a single clue how late she is coming home at night.

I definitely was *not* going out by myself for clam rolls tonight.

Instead, I took a shower, steamed some of the road grit off me, and threw on some boxers and a Travis Tritt T-shirt. Jess was on the phone when I came out and she was crying. Not huge gulping sobs—just the same two rivulets of tears she'd cried all summer every time she talked to Richie. He'd told her to call collect whenever she wanted, and I suppose the night before starting college was as good a time as any to dip back into a nice familiar angst. I went back into the bathroom and plucked my eyebrows while the two of them tormented each other another ten minutes.

This time when I came out of the john, Jess wasn't crying—she was chewing on her thumbnail and lying there with Phyllis, the huge, old stuffed gorilla Dolores had given her on her tenth birthday.

"Actually, I sort of like it that Phyllis is going to college with you," I said, reaching into my duffel for a package and getting up on the bed too. "That way, I don't feel so stupid giving you this."

She looked at the flat, small package and said, "Is this a book?"

"Open it and see."

She pulled the purple tissue paper back in seconds and, grinning in spite of herself, squealed, "*Madeline*! Mom! My favorite. What happened to my old one?"

"I couldn't find it. I looked. So I got us a new one instead. I mean I know it's not for *us*—it's for you—except for tonight. Tonight, I want to read it to you like we used to do. I know it's stupid and sentimental, and I know that things between us lately have gotten screwed up, but, Jess, I really want to do this."

She was great—she didn't balk at all. She didn't make any snotty comments about how if I really liked *Madeline* so much, I could read it to the next baby. She just got up from the bed, pulled her T-shirt out of her duffel, and said, "Okay, but let me brush my teeth first."

I was sitting up under the covers when she came back and crawled into her side. I didn't put my arm around her or anything, but we scooched together so we could both see the pictures and I began reading aloud to her.

" 'In an old house in Paris, all covered with vines, lived twelve little girls, in two straight lines . . .' "

Approximately twenty-four hours later I was back in the same room, on the same side of the bed, only this time I was alone. Jess lived somewhere else now. That morning we had moved her into room 516 in Morrison Hall and from that moment on, even when she slept in her own room at home, she'd just be visiting. The thing was— and I both loved and hated to admit it—she was just so damn ready, so incredibly poised for flight. When I was in the sixth grade studying Greece and Rome, I had to do a report on the statue *The Winged Victory of Samothrace*. Well, that was how Jessica had looked when she'd said good night to me at the dorm elevator—like a *Winged Victory of Samothrace*. In Nikes.

That would have been a wonderful image to carry all the way home. But it got erased the next morning when we were leaving the orientation meetings. Colleges do that—hold a big meeting to tell the parents a little about the school and a lot about backing off from your child and letting go. It was nice to be in an auditorium with so many people going through the same stuff.

The car was parked under a row of oak trees down by the gym, and Jessica was walking me there to say good-bye.

"Mom, thanks a lot for driving me and everything. I really appreciate it."

"Well sure, babe, I wouldn't have missed it for anything." I put my arm around her shoulder. She let me keep it there, but I could tell it made her a bit uncomfortable. When we got to the car, I opened the door, tossed my purse in, and turned to face her for the big moment. I hadn't really given much thought to what I wanted to say. It didn't matter—she had.

"Mom?" she said, looking somewhere over my shoulder. "I don't know exactly how to put this, but I need to say it to you. I love you a lot, and I'm going to miss you something terrible. But Parents' Weekend is the last weekend in October, and if you're going to start to be all pregnant-looking by then, I've been thinking that maybe it just isn't that good an idea for you to come, you know?"

I'd been planning to cry anyway, I just hadn't planned on being destroyed.

"Mom? I'm sorry!" she said, when she saw me put my fist to my mouth. "I just felt I had to say it now—in person—before you started making plans to come here. I don't mean it meanly!"

I couldn't talk for a minute. I was still reeling from the pain. I leaned against the fender and tried hard to think of the right thing to say to her. Sometimes the right thing and the true thing aren't even in the same language. The right thing was to grab her to me and say, "I know, baby, I know this has been hard for you." And that was what I did.

But the true thing was a line I remembered from some article I read. It said, "Why is it all the sad songs are about romance, when it's really only family that breaks your heart?"

Charlie

September

When it came to the deal I'd made with Lacy, it was one thing to shake on it, it was another to sign it. Writing my name on that paper freaked the hell out of me. What kind of schmuck says yes to a woman who tells him he has to pay all her bills, change his job, lie to his kid, lie to his friends, and lie to his parents?

I don't know how Lacy explained being pregnant to her family, but it sure as hell couldn't have gone any worse than the night I dropped the bomb at Sophie and Abe's.

"What do you mean you're leaving the paper?" Sophie asked, stopping midserve with the brisket plate. It was Labor Day weekend, not your basic brisket occasion, but Sophie had always made a great one. I figured I might as well have a great meal in my belly when I broke the news about my impending fatherhood.

Sophie and Abe lived in an apartment on Sheridan Road in that strip that always felt like Miami Beach North. High-rise after high-rise with names like The Doral and Seaview Towers. They lived on the twelfth floor of The Tidewater.

"I didn't say I was leaving, Mom. I said I was *thinking* of leaving." I took the platter out of her hand and put a second helping on my plate. A *Sixty Minutes* rerun was on the TV in the living room, and Abe had gone in to watch Mike Wallace sandbag some car dealer from Florida. I didn't mind. It had always been easier to start these conversations with only one of them at a time.

"Thinking of leaving to do *what*? You're forty-five now, Chuckie—what does a forty-five-year-old sportswriter do but write more sports?" And then before I could answer, she slammed down her fork and said, "Oh, my God, you're not moving are you? You're not going to another newspaper in another city are you? Is it Miami?"

"Mom, I'm not moving. In fact, that's the whole point. I want to stay put. I'm tired of busting my ass on the road for most of the year. Sports is a great beat if you want free miles. But it sucks if you want a life."

"Oh, please, Chuckie, you've been saying that for years. And you've never talked about leaving before. Is it that news girl that we met? Is something going on that she wants you around more?"

I scraped my chair back from the dining-room table. I'd been doing that for thirty years whenever Sophie or Abe shoved one of those inquiring-minds-want-to-know queries in my face. Whether it was prom dates, job prospects, love interests—it didn't matter. I was never comfortable with the fact that parents craved details about their kids in a way that kids never craved details about their parents. I'm not talking about sex. No one wants to think about their parents fucking. Parents don't want to think about their kids fucking, either. I'm talking about the minutiae of daily life. My mom would have loved it if I'd called her every night and told her what I ate for dinner. Not that asking me about Jo Beth was unreasonable, but it did get to me. It was also a leading indicator that I hadn't said a word about my personal life to my mother in a long time.

"Jo Beth and I stopped seeing each other in June, Mom. I guess I didn't tell you. Sorry. But leaving the paper has nothing to do with anyone other than me. And where I am in my life. And where I want to go next."

"Which is where, Chuckie?"

Abe walked back in. He was in white pants and a pastel golf shirt. I've never understood why guys who dress perfectly normal their whole lives decide the day they turn sixty-five that it's a good idea to wear ice cream outfits. Sitting down and reaching for a peach, he asked, "What are you two talking about?"

"Chuckie is thinking of leaving the paper," said Sophie. "Not to move out of town and not because of a girl."

"So, why?" asked Abe. "Are you having one of those mid-life crises that we never heard of until we were too old to have one?"

Where did I start? I'd never told my folks about the waiting room and about realizing how much I wanted kids. I also hadn't told them a thing about what the hell I'd really been up to all year with the mom search. So, considering that in about half a year they were going to have a new grandchild, it was time to bring them up to speed.

"I am six months away from being a father."

You want to talk silence? You've never heard that kind of silence. These people were screamers. Silence from screamers rips your ears out.

Abe recovered first. "What the hell are you talking about?"

And so it began. I handed them their first installment of truth-laced lies. The woman on the road fable, woven in with all my real and true daddy cravings. Ten minutes into it Sophie began to cry.

"I just don't understand," she said, using her napkin to wipe her eyes. "Why won't this woman marry you? Things were never like this when we were young! It's unnatural, Chuckie, to abandon your child. What's wrong with her?"

"Nothing is wrong with her, Mom. It's just that we don't love each other, and she has this invalid mother that she cares for, and for her it wouldn't work out."

" 'Wouldn't *work out*'? Who makes up these phrases?" she railed. "Things can't *work out*, unless you *work them out*, Chuckie. I didn't think it would work out to have you and Roger eighteen months apart and your father only making peanuts and us in a one-bedroom on Ashland Avenue and you with the almost crossed eye that needed an operation. But they worked out. We lived through them, and we made them work out. We didn't say to someone, here, take the new baby, we'll be too crowded and too poor, and it just won't work out."

"Mom, what you said and felt was what you said and felt. This woman is different. Arguing about it doesn't make her any less different. This is the deal. I know it's unusual. I know you didn't expect it, and that at first, it's got to be upsetting. But it is my life. It might not be what you want, but this is what I want. I want a kid. I want one bad. And now the great thing is, it's going to happen. Listen, I'm scared. I'd be lying if I said otherwise. But I'm going to do it."

Abe set his peach down. "I think this is the most cockamamy idea you've ever had, Charlie. How the hell are you going to raise a kid by yourself? You don't know shit from Shinola about kids!"

"Abe!" Sophie slammed her hand down on the table. She hated when he talked like me.

"What? He doesn't!" he said dismissively. And then turning back to me, he said, "And how the hell are you going to support yourself if you aren't writing about the Hawks for the paper? Are you going into real estate? Or plumbing? Or maybe a nice job in insurance?"

"Radio."

"Radio, Chuckie?" said Sophie. "You're going to be a disc jockey? Or a baseball game announcer? What kind of radio?"

"Sports talk radio, Mom. There's a station that started here a couple years ago that's doing pretty good, so some people who just bought an FM station are changing the format and launching another one in six weeks. They call it Sports Central. It's going to be on every day for fourteen hours a day in the beginning, and then maybe it'll go longer. They have to see. This format is all over the country. The owners think with five pro teams here, Chicago can probably support at least two stations. I think they're right. This could be real big."

"I never heard anything so ridiculous," she snapped. "Who'd listen?"

Abe and I looked at each other. "Guys, Mom. Thousands of guys."

Sophie got up to reset the air conditioner. She did this at least four times an hour. "Is that what you're going to do all day? Sit in front of a microphone all by yourself and talk to grown men about sports?"

"I'm not going to be by myself. All the shows are going to be done with partners. That's how they're setting the station up. That way if the phones get quiet, there's always someone to talk to."

"Two people talking about sports all day," she said, shaking her head. "Have you hired your partner yet?"

"Mom, I don't hire. *I'm* not even officially hired. They'll let me know for sure in about ten days. I think I've got the job, but it's not a lock. I sure as hell haven't quit the paper yet. That would be a dumbass move."

"Unlike raising a kid by yourself," Abe said. "For Chrissakes, Charlie, what the hell are you thinking?"

And on it went . . .

Two weeks later the station honcho called me in to say I had the job. As soon as he said it, I clutched. It was one thing to write on deadline. It was another to talk on demand. From three in the afternoon to seven at night. Four straight hours a day. I wasn't sure I could talk four straight hours even if I were delirious. So I was freaked about that, and even more freaked about the partner that the program director John Radley gave me. It was a woman.

"Yeah, Charlie," he said, "we decided on Bonnie Ginetti. We thought the chemistry between the two of you worked pretty good at the audition."

There was major street drilling happening right outside John's office window, so it was hard to hear. I leaned forward. "Bonnie Ginetti? Christ, John, she's great. I like her a lot. But isn't it a helluva risk to put on a woman? I thought you said a woman in sports talk was a real long shot."

"It still is," he said, leaning back in his chair and crossing his legs on top of the metal desk. He was in jeans and a sweater. Like newspapers, radio was another tie-free zone. "But we think you and Bonnie will beat the odds, maybe even be a major breakthrough."

"Yeah, but I sure hate my survival in this job to hang on the listeners' gut-level prejudice that women don't know squat about sports."

"Listen, Charlie, wanna know something?" he asked, scratching his belly. "There are more guys who don't know jack shit about sports than there are women. Or maybe it's just that the women keep their mouths shut, but the guys can't. They need to talk. That's why we're in business. But we're also in business to attract advertisers. I think with Bonnie, we can cut through the stereotype that women don't know anything about sports.

She's got a great reputation in this town. Believe me, if we can pull in some women listeners, that means big bucks for the advertising guys. Two years from now we could be sitting pretty."

"I just want to make sure I'm here in two years, you know?" I shook my head to the pack of gum he pushed across the desk. "Kicking off a whole new career at my age is pretty heavy, but when you combine that with having a kid show up in my life come next February . . . well shit, John, all of a sudden I'm pretty clutched about job security." I'd told John back when I'd auditioned that some time in March I'd be a single dad. I felt I had to tell him, so he didn't schedule my on-air time real early when it would be hell to line up some day care. He didn't grill me about the details, but then, that's the beauty of guys.

"Charlie, let me do the sweating about the station, okay?" He smiled and handed me an envelope. "Take this to your lawyer. It's a twenty-four-month deal that I bet we'll be renewing for twice as many bucks in two years. And don't worry. Bonnie isn't going to screw up. She's just as concerned about keeping bread on the table as you are. She's a single parent too."

"No shit? I didn't know that."

"Yeah. Meantime, I want the two of you to get to know each other some. Give her a call, and go to lunch with her sometime this week, okay? On us. And then plan to both be in on Thursday at ten. We're huddling with all the talent that morning for a couple of hours."

• • •

Bonnie Ginetti had doe-brown eyes, and shiny, straight brown hair. She didn't waste a lot of time pushing it behind her ears or handling it the way most women did. I liked that. I wondered how old she was. Thirty? Thirty-five? It was fucking impossible to tell these days. Women looked so damn good. She did. She had on a black sleeveless top and some white jeans. She looked like she worked out. Her arms were tan and strong-looking. Pretty.

"How long were you with the *Daily Herald*?" I asked. We were in the Blue Crab Lounge, which was part of Shaw's Crab House and the place was, as usual, jammed and noisy.

"Eight years." The *Daily Herald* was a bright, healthy paper out in Arlington Heights that gave all the in-town dailies a run for their money. Bonnie had covered the Cubs for a long time.

"But I have a three-year-old son," she said, squeezing two chunks of lemon together over her crab cakes. "And when my husband had a heart attack and died two years ago, it was obvious that I had to get off the road. He was an architect so he'd been the one at home most of the time. Anyway, the editors wouldn't give me a column, which would have been a perfect solution, so my mom moved in to help. When I heard about this job, I jumped. I'm really excited about it, aren't you?"

"Excited? Yeah. Also scared shitless, I think. Your husband died two years ago? Jesus, that must have been hell with a kid."

"It was. But sometimes I think having Greg actually

helped. I could focus on him, and still delight in him. He's a great kid." She grinned. "Wanna see his picture?"

"Sure," I said, realizing that I was only months away from pulling out pictures of my own kid. Her son was a chunky, black-eyed redhead. "Looks like you've got your hands full."

"I do."

I took a hit of my beer and said, "I don't know if John mentioned this to you, but I'm going to be a single dad myself."

The brown eyes widened. "You are? What do you mean? Are you getting divorced? I thought you weren't married."

I plunged in. Gave her the whole story about wanting a kid and the mom being a woman I'd gotten involved with on the road, but she had an invalid mom, etc. etc. etc. She looked at me kind of strangely, but she bought the story. And unlike Sophie, she spared me the third degree. Then again, Bonnie hadn't been waiting forty-five years for me to show up with a wife. But I felt shitty. I liked her, and it made me a little crazy to start our relationship with a lie.

Like I had a choice.

"What's her name?" Lacy asked when I called a few nights later to tell her about the new broadcast career.

"Bonnie Ginetti. She's with the *Daily Herald*. She's good."

"Did you try out with her?"

"Audition, Lacy. This is big-time show biz."

"Are you going to start calling me honeybabysweetie-cookie?"

It was the first time Lacy had even attempted to joke around with me in months. "Not likely. I am going to get on your case though about not calling me after your last doctor's appointment. I thought that was part of the deal. That you were going to keep me up to speed."

"Charlie, I'm not going to call you every time I put on a pound. It's stupid and boring."

"Is that all that she checks now—weight? Are you taking vitamins? Did you stop drinking beer? I'd like to know some of this stuff, Lacy." I looked at my bedroom clock, it was nearly midnight. "What are you doing up this late anyway?"

"Charlie. *You* called *me*. Remember?"

"Oh. Yeah." It was late. John had kept Bonnie and me in his office until after seven and then wanted us to go out to dinner after that. Truth was, by the time I'd listened to his schemes and to his take on where the station would be going, I was pumped. Getting into sports radio in a town like Chicago might just turn out to be a really smart career move.

"So, Charlie, when are you going to tell your editor?"

"Sometime this week. If you want, I'll stop by your desk after it's done."

"No, I don't think it's a good idea for us to be seen hanging around together at the paper. I don't want people adding two and two—my being pregnant, your leaving, and then their hearing that you've got this baby . . ."

"Christ, how the hell am I going to pull this off, Lacy? Starting a new job and then six months later I'm calling in to say, 'I might be a little late today, the kid has the trots.'"

She laughed. Not mean. Sweet. So sweet I wanted to be in the same room with her. "Charlie," she said, "you're going to be fine. You'll have to get a day-care person for when you're at work anyway. So whether the kid is sick or not, someone will be there. And you're luckier than most single working parents—you're free in the morning to take your kid to the pediatrician."

"Pediatrician? Oh, man, how am I going to do all this? I read these damn having-a-baby books and they scare the hell out of me. It sounds hard enough when there are two parents."

The laugh was even softer this time. It made me want to lie down with the owner of the laugh. "Charlie, I promise you will be able to handle it all on your own. Millions of mothers do it all the time. Dads do too. I did it for years and it was fine."

She got quiet and then she said, "I guess the only time it hurt was Mother's Day morning—well, in your case, it'll be Father's Day morning—before they are big enough to bring you breakfast themselves. My first Mother's Day, Tony did that, and it was such a sweet acknowledgment of the three of us being all woven together. Of course he walked out permanently two weeks later. And it was five more years until Jess was old enough to bring in the Mother's Day breakfast on her own."

"What could she make you when she was five?"

"Burnt toast, and cereal with orange juice on it because we'd run out of milk."

"What did you do?"

"It was Mother's Day. I ate every last bite."

Lacy

END OF SEPTEMBER

I had a new girlfriend. Her name was Josie and I met her the first night of my Critical Social Issues class at DePaul.

It must have been eighty-five degrees that night in room 306 of SAC—Schmitt Academic Center. I grabbed a seat as close as I could to the windows, but there wasn't much going on in the way of a breeze. About twenty people were in the class, maybe two-thirds were women, most everybody was at least twenty-five, and a couple of people were probably closer to sixty. The teacher, Mr. Reiser, looked about my age, but he was bald, sweating like crazy, and seemed a little nervous. I wondered what he did during the day—if he had another job too.

It was like that at DePaul extension—everyone did something else nine to five. Full-time students jammed the university all day, but by the time the evening students started filtering in, the whole place changed—it was definitely a campus of grown-ups. That was clear the first time I went into Stewart Student Center, and I passed a woman on the pay phone calling to check in with her sitter. The Ivy League this was not.

I didn't care—it still felt collegiate to me. DePaul may have been stuck in the middle of the north side of the city, but with those cool buildings in the quad, and the grass, and benches and statues . . . well, I loved being there. It felt like all kinds of new and good things could happen.

Every week, before class, I'd grab something to eat at Stewart. It wasn't exactly the way I'd pictured a student center at college—given that it had a whole room full of pool tables and video games—but still, it had some comfortable chairs for studying, a cash station that for some reason was never crowded, and endless bulletin boards filled with all sorts of notices about "looking for rides" and "tutoring available" and intramural sports things.

My favorite bulletin board, though, was called the Opinion Wall, where people could say anything that was on their minds. The only rule was that they had to sign their names to their opinions. It was sort of like Bitching Central—people griped about everything from the tuna sandwiches in a dining hall to the lack of moral fiber in the student government.

One night I spent about fifteen minutes reading the notices. One of them said, "Pay phone service in the library sucks—why the hell don't they put more pay phones in the library?" Then someone else stuck a notice over that saying, "Pay phones? What about books in the libary?" And then over that someone said, "Books? What about dictionaries in the library, so assholes like you can learn to spell?" I laughed out loud. I loved how removed from the real world college was, and I loved that belated though it was, I was finally getting a crack at it. It was weird that it was happening the same time Jess was getting a crack at it too. Weird and sad—Jess and I had been having a horrible time communicating since she'd left—she was never in her room when I called, and if I found her, she was always in a hurry. I understood, but still . . .

I guess missing college when I was her age was another reason I was so psyched about it now. There wasn't one part of it I didn't just adore—sitting in class two nights a week, coming home and not vegging out in front of the TV, but actually studying, and taking notes, and even writing a couple of papers—all of it felt great.

And if I did it too late to be allowed to wear sorority pins and go to basketball games when Ray Meyer was coaching the Blue Demons, then so what? I'd finally gotten there, and it was mine for the grabbing. I felt really lucky. Yeah, I was pregnant, and yeah, my daughter was far away, and yeah, she and I were still on shaky emotional ground, but given all that, each time I headed up to the campus on the El after work, I was a pretty happy person.

"What are you smiling about?" asked Josie one night when we ran into each other before class in Stewart. I was at a table, scribbling some stuff on a napkin. Most of the tables around us were jammed with full-time students. We didn't have the kids in our classes, but at least we could eat with them.

"I was messing around—trying to come up with an opinion for the Opinion Wall. It looks like a cool place to vent." I moved my books to make room for her.

Josie was gorgeous. She was an extremely regal-looking African-American, with mocha-colored skin, cheekbones for days, slanted slate-colored eyes, and the longest most expressive hands I had ever seen. She'd done some modeling for the Saks Fifth Avenue catalog, some backup singing for a group named "Hard On," and was now selling jewelry at Neiman Marcus on Michigan Avenue. But she was bound and determined to get her degree and go into social work

"We've still got twenty-five minutes before class, don't we?" she asked, sliding into the plastic chair. She was wearing this black jersey tank dress—real clingy—she looked like a Supreme without the hair.

"Yeah."

"How're you doing?"

"Terrific, except I'm a little nervous," I said. "Do you think he'll give last week's tests back?"

"He might as well. I'm wearing black, so if I get an F, I'll have a good outfit on for killing myself."

"I've always felt all-white goes better with suicide."

Josie and I had bonded on the first night when Mr. Reiser had asked each person in the class to stand up and tell her age, marital status, if she had any kids, and what her favorite rock group was. Josie was eight years younger than me, married, and had no kids, but the one thing we did have in common was "10,000 Maniacs"—

we both loved them. It was enough to start a conversation. We exchanged home phone numbers that night after class, but neither of us had made the first call yet.

"You hungry?" she asked.

"I'm always hungry—I'm almost four months pregnant." I pulled my big red cotton sweater tight behind my back. "It doesn't show that much in this."

"Holy shit," she gasped, knocking my purse off the table and then reaching to pick it up. "Pregnant? First night of school you said you had a daughter in college. You didn't say anything about pregnant."

"I didn't?" I smiled. "Let's get some dinner, and I'll tell you about it. I'm famished."

We walked back into the Marketplace, and got in line for some relatively decent lasagna and one of those institutional salads with all the vegetables decorating the top and then after two bites it's nothing but iceberg lettuce. When we got back to the table, Josie unfolded her napkin, put one of her gorgeously long hands on my arm and said, "Listen, we have a choice here you know. I mean if you don't want to, you don't have to tell me anything about the pregnancy deal. I know from class you're thirty-five, not married, and your daughter is eighteen. Call me wacky, but that makes me think this baby wasn't planned. So I can make some chitchat inquiries, skirting the issue and being very polite, or we can break through the crap. I can ask impolite questions, and we can be girlfriends."

"Those are the choices, huh?"

"Yup"—she grinned—"that's it, babe—good manners or good friends. Which do you want?"

I had to laugh. Some people might have found Josie to be a lot, but I liked that about her. I'd never gotten really close with anyone from the paper—I had friends, but no one I was really tight with. Between Dolores and Jess and Steffi, my life had always seemed full of enough great women. But now Jess was *gone* and upset with me, Dolores was *in town* and upset with me, and Steffi wasn't upset with me, but she was pretty hassled these days trying to get four kids through their college applications and all. So I definitely was open to getting out in the world and hooking up with new people.

"Well, I'm pretty polite all day at work, so why don't we pass on the manners thing, okay? What do you want to ask?"

"Only the obvious—why the hell are you starting all over again with another kid?"

"I'm not," I told her. "I'm giving the baby up for adoption."

"Oh," she said, setting down her fork. "Does the dad know?" She had the same look on her face that Ruthie had gotten when I told her about the adoption part. It was a look that said, on one hand adoption is such a practical solution, dear, but on the other . . . isn't it a bit aberrant?

"Explain something to me, okay?" Josie pushed her lasagna around on her plate. "Why would you keep your baby when you were a kid, and completely dense about being a mom, and now, when you have a decent job and know everything there is to know about the gig, why would you give your baby up for adoption? I'm not saying this judgmentally, I'm just curious. Consider it the aspiring social worker in me."

A bunch of kids at the next table started horsing around—shooting straw wrappers at each other. One bounced off Josie's shoulder and she threw them a killer look.

"Well, I guess the answer to your question is in your question," I said, taking a gulp of Coke though I knew it should have been milk. "The reason I am giving the baby up for adoption is because I *do* know, and *do* understand what being a mom is. At sixteen, I had no clue—not about its intensity or the complete hold it has on your time and energy and heart. See, Josie, the thing is, if I kept this baby, I'd repeat the whole cycle again. And where does that leave me? I never got to be young, or to study for a purpose, or to work at something I was really psyched about. I want to do that now. And anyway, I know when this baby is adopted, that it is going to be really, really loved. I couldn't do this, if I wasn't sure of that."

And I was sure of it. Charlie and I may have still tangled on the phone a lot—he could be so exasperating with all his questions about my health, and could he come with me to the doctor—but it also became clearer to me what a fabulous father he was going to be. Charlie just wanted this baby so much. Not only had he bought all those books and videos, but three weeks ago he began taking a class at the hospital for expectant fathers so he could sit around with other guys and air their fatherhood heebie-jeebies. Basically I thought it was a good idea, but sometimes he was a little overinvested in it. Not to mention, it *was* a little bit early—I mean most of the guys had wives who were a lot closer to delivery than I was. But Charlie didn't care—he said he'd probably take it twice.

"But isn't detaching yourself from this baby a hard thing to do?" Josie stopped for a moment and looked down into her plate. "I had a miscarriage after sixteen weeks once, and I was a mess about it for months."

The clock tower struck seven o'clock—we were late.

"Yeah, it is hard," I said quietly as we picked up our trays and carried them over to be wiped down and stacked. "But I've got to do it, anyway. Come on, guys do it all the time. I don't mean just assholes that walk out on their kids. What about all those guys jerking off in sperm banks? They deliver, and then *they* walk. I know being a sperm donor is not the same as carrying a baby inside you for nine months, but who says guys have a monopoly on biological detachment? No, it is *not* easy. There are some nights—and you're the only person I've said this to except my best friend Steffi—that I have a lot of doubts about pulling this off. But I *have* to get to the next part of my life—otherwise I'll just be in the middle of a rerun."

We pushed our way through the door into the fall night. Leaves were blowing around and it was already dark. "And like I said, the person that is going to get this baby—the people I mean—well, this baby is going to be adored. That is for sure."

"Do you know who it is?" she asked, scrambling up the stairs of SAC. "Did they tell you?"

"Yeah, I know who it is."

"Who is it?" Josie asked relentlessly, like a kid trying to find out about Santa Claus.

"Someone real nice," I said. "Who's wanted a baby for years. Trust me, this is going to be one cherished little kid."

Mr. Reiser didn't even look up when we slid in late—he was handing back our tests. When he gave me mine, I nearly flipped—I got an A! It was an incredible feeling, just incredible! And it lasted the whole way home.

I could hear the phone ringing when I got to the house but the porch light had burned out, so I couldn't get my key in the door fast enough to get inside and beat the answering machine.

"Hey, Lacy, how ya doing?" Charlie said when I picked up.

"Okay, Charlie. Actually really good! I got an A on my first test tonight!"

"That's great. Way to go."

"Thanks," I said, collapsing on the couch and putting my feet up. They were starting to swell sometimes. "What's up? You were saying something on the machine about your fathers' group meeting?"

"Yeah. One of the guys was telling us about this system he and his wife are doing where you let the baby be born into water or something. Have you heard of that?"

"Yeah. It's always sounded kind of creepy to me. But I've never been a great swimmer. Anyway, I already told you, I want to do Lamaze again. It's not perfect, but I don't like the idea of drugs. Even when I'm not pregnant I don't take Tylenol when I have headaches."

"Man, I saw a guy pop three of them tonight in front

of the whole class. He had just gone into a complete meltdown."

"Why?" I kicked off my flats and started rubbing my feet. My ankles looked like they belonged to Shelley Winters. "Was he freaking out about impending fatherhood or something?"

"Nope, that wasn't it. He was freaking out because he is a guilt-ridden mess. He's gotten himself involved in this big-time affair, even though his wife is about to deliver in two months."

"Jesus," I said, trying to imagine why anyone would confess that to a doctor and a bunch of strangers. "That's disgusting!"

"Actually, the doc says that isn't all that unusual. He says that guys panic right before a baby is born sometimes. That they fantasize about other women and some even act on it."

"What?" I yelled. "Are you kidding? That's despicable. I'd be really furious if you did that right now."

"Did what?"

"Started messing around with someone."

The phone was silent. "Wait a minute," Charlie said in a real quiet voice. "Are you saying that if I was seeing someone now that you would be pissed?"

"Of course." I pulled the afghan up over my lap.

"Christ, Lacy! Did I miss an installment here? Are you and I some kind of item? Are you and I having hot sex these days?"

"That's not the point," I said, unable to believe how dense he was being.

"Then what is the point?"

"The point is, Charlie, that it's just out-and-out bad manners for you to be messing around with someone else while I am being road-mapped by varicose veins because of this baby."

"Bad manners! Are you for real? Are you saying that *my* sex life is supposed to be contingent on *your* circulation?"

"If you want to put it that way, Charlie—yeah."

"Unbelievable."

We didn't hang up on great terms that night. I tried to go to bed concentrating on how great it felt to get the A on my test—but it didn't work. In fact, after about ten minutes of just lying there in the dark, with my hands over my grapefruit-size belly, I started to cry. I don't know if it was because of Charlie's colossal insensitivity, or because of the pregnancy discussion with Josie, or if it was just hormones. Sometimes things just get to you, I guess.

Lacy

October—November

When Parents' Weekend finally arrived, I was nowhere near Chapel Hill—I was in Chicago pretending it didn't matter that Dolores was the one who got to go see Jessica. Of course there was a good reason for it—Dolores was the one who met Jessica's dress code: No Maternity Clothes Allowed.

I'd hit Dan Howard's Maternity Factory a few weeks before to buy the six gargantuan outfits that would accompany me through my next four months. Maternity clothes had improved immensely in the eighteen years since I'd shopped for them. The old ones made you look like a ruffled lamp shade—these were sportier. Now you looked like a tailored lamp shade.

Not going to see Jess at school hurt a lot, so Steff spent the whole weekend trying to distract me. Saturday we drove up to Kenosha to hit the mall outlets for some early Christmas shopping. I'd never bought a Christmas present before December tenth in my life, but Steff was hell-bent on getting me out of the house. I'd just had a midterm, and it was the first Saturday in weeks I didn't have to study.

That night we rented two Tom Berenger movies and had Chinese at my house—which, I had to admit, really had felt completely like *my* house for the past two months. All the radios were set on my stations, the car keys were always where I'd left them, and pregnant or not, I didn't have to put on a good show and eat vegetables *every* night. That part of Jess's being gone, I loved. But I missed her bad. And our phone calls were like some stupid yo-yo—sometimes she pulled me in tight and talked and talked, and other times she kept me dangling way out there. I didn't know how much of it came with the lurches of being a normal freshman or how much came from having a mom who was single and pregnant.

"Do you want another Sharp's?" I asked Steff when the first Tom Berenger movie was over.

"Nope," she said, "I prefer my beer with a hit of alcohol in it." She got up to eject the tape from the VCR.

"Yeah," I said, putting another pillow behind my back. "There are parts of being pregnant these days that are such a drag. Not only is it harder because I'm older—did I show you I might be getting this one huge varicose vein, it is so gross—but it's harder because of all this stuff coming down now—no beer . . . no coffee . . ."

"No husband."

"Very funny. Since when did you and I have such high opinions of husbands—either personal or conceptual?"

She popped in the next movie, but didn't hit the start button. "I don't have anything against husbands as a category. Husbands can be very lovely to have around. Some of my best boyfriends have been husbands."

We laughed. Steff had been involved with a married man once. She didn't get all tormented over him or want him to leave his wife or anything—she just thoroughly enjoyed it. It was low maintenance, great sex, and daily phone calls. It had lasted almost three years, and she'd been the one to break it off because she met the next guy, who was nice and wifeless—availability on Saturday nights can be a big plus.

"I guess none of my best boyfriends have been husbands."

"What have they been?"

"I haven't had my best boyfriend yet. But when I do have him, I think I know what he *will* be," I said, pulling the afghan back over my feet and crossing my arms over my stomach.

"What?"

"He'll be a girlfriend with a dick. He'll be a guy who I'll be able to talk to the same way I can talk to you. And when we get done talking, then we'll fuck each other's brains out. I think that's the big mistake we all make. We all think we are looking for boyfriends, but what we really want is a girlfriend with a dick—someone we can connect with—not someone we have to be a certain way for."

"How's Charlie doing?"

I glared at her. "Why did you ask that? He hardly qualifies as a girlfriend with a dick."

"He qualifies for half of it," she smirked, patting my belly.

"Cut it out, Steff!" I pushed her hand away. "Someone did that to me in the supermarket yesterday. Why is it that complete strangers feel entitled to do that? Just walk up to you and put their hand on your stomach?"

"I don't know," she said, hitting the start button on the VCR. "No one did it to me. With four of them in there, I was so huge I think people just wanted to get out of my way before I exploded on them."

The next day the plan was to drive up to Evanston to go to open houses for rich people. Once or twice a year Steff and I liked to go into these houses for sale that we could never afford—it was always a lot of fun. We had never been able to figure out the difference between a five-hundred-thousand-dollar home and a six-hundred-thousand-dollar one. They all had lots of bedrooms and bathrooms and extra-new kitchens, so it must have been some hidden thing that rich people could see but we couldn't. We'd hear these people saying things like "I didn't like the traffic pattern" or "Don't you think the upstairs is a bit tight?"—but we never could see it exactly. The houses all looked pretty swell to us.

We drove up Sheridan Road with the smooth aqua lake on our right and one mansion after another lining both sides of the road. It was a perfect Sunday for poking around in a world we had no business being in. The air was crisp and silver-yellow. We passed bunches of rich guys in plaid shirts doing some sort of token raking of the leaves that had fallen since Friday when the lawn service probably had been there. Our first stop was a house in southeast Evanston listed for $979,000. I read the ad again to Steffi:

"FALL IN LOVE WITH this vintage eight-bedroom, five-bath Colonial, located just three blocks from the lake. Entertain easily in the elegant living room enhanced by a gracious marble fireplace and bay windows. The comfortable family room is off the gourmet kitchen and overlooks the deep backyard and gazebo. Enjoy lazy summer afternoons on the wonderful wrap-around porch while reminiscing of a different era."

"What era do you think they mean?" Steff asked as we pulled up in front of it.

"Probably the era where there used to be slaves. How else would you keep an eight-bedroom house clean? Let's go in."

We went up the red brick walk and passed a young blond couple—maybe a little younger than us—on their way out. They had very serious looks on their faces and very expensive-looking casual clothes on—you could tell because the clothes were beige—rich people wear a lot of beige.

"God," I whispered to Steffi when we passed them, "do you think they've got the money to buy a place like this? They don't look old enough to shop at The Gap."

"Who knows," she said as we stepped into an entrance hall that could have been in a church. It was two stories high and there was a big curvy staircase behind it—the kind that movie stars walked down in the movies Dolores liked to watch—Myrna Loy and people like that. The floor was dark wood and it had one of those rugs with hunters on it like you see when you go to the Art Institute on a field trip. It didn't look like the people who lived there worried much about maxing out on their Visa.

The real estate greeting lady barely smiled at us—I don't think we fooled her much into thinking we were real buyers. But Steff and I were used to that when we walked through these places. Lots of times, we'd say something like, "And when would they want to close?" We'd heard someone say that once, and it sounded pretty serious.

The best part of the FALL IN LOVE WITH house though was the master bedroom. It had windows on three sides and this huge fireplace and all these bookshelves and a window seat. It was a perfect room.

"Wasn't that a cool four-poster bed in there?" Steffi asked when we headed back to the car. "I've always wanted to do it in a bed like that with a big canopy, haven't you?"

I didn't answer. Random "doing it" was not a topic I was too fired up about of late. Our next stop was in North Evanston—a Victorian on the lake. "*MUST BE SEEN TO BE BELIEVED*" was the headline.

"So, you never answered last night—how is Charlie?" Steffi asked as we continued up Sheridan through Northwestern's campus. Lots of students were walking along the pathways, and it made me sad all over again about not being with Jess for Parents' Weekend.

"He's okay I guess. He's making me a little nervous though."

"Why? Is he hovering?"

"Definitely—he is so into this whole baby thing. I mean, I insisted on the job change—I'll cop to that. But he's moved out of his high-rise to this house off of Irving Park because he didn't want to 'raise the baby in an apartment.' And he sold his Toyota for a used Volvo station wagon because *Consumers Digest* says 'it's the safest there is.'"

"I think that's all sweet, Lace. Don't you?"

"Yeah, it's sweet. He's also joined this expectant fathers group to discuss all that will-I-be-a-good-dad stuff."

"So, is it definite that Charlie is going to be with you in the labor room?" We had just pulled up in front of a pale yellow Victorian home with turrets and gables and big pots of yellow and purple mums lining the walk—one million two hundred thousand dollars—even out of our imaginary league.

"We still have to work out the details. I don't know where I'm at with it. I mean I think he's entitled, and I know he wants to, but I'm just scared it might make him see us as this *couple* or something. And then when the baby is born, as this *family* or something. I mean the way I remember it, baby having *is* kind of a powerful moment. Last week he was wondering if it might be a good idea to consider an at-home birth! Please. A placenta in my living room? I don't think so."

"Where'd he come up with that?"

"This stupid group he goes to."

"Why do you think it's stupid?" she asked, taking the key out of the ignition and dropping it in her purse. The house had big swooping white curtains showing on all the windows in the front, and the porch still had dark green wicker furniture on it even though it was almost Halloween.

"It's okay I guess. But they talk so personally. I am not that happy to have my mood swings or my newly improved huge breasts be the topic of discussion with six guys I don't even know."

"Since when is Charlie seeing your breasts? You're not sleeping with Charlie." We got out of the car and headed up the walk.

"I know. But he better not be fucking anybody else right now either." Then I told her about the fight I'd had with Charlie about his messing around with other women while I'm pregnant.

"You're waaaay out of line, Lace. You have no claims on him," she said as we walked into another hotel-size front hall. "You blew off any you might have had when you signed yourself out of the kid's life."

"Dammit, Steffi!" I stomped my foot—always an attractive gesture—"I haven't signed myself out until after the kid is born! Right now, in case you didn't notice, I am very much involved with this kid—it's battering my belly eighty-seven times a day now. And all I was saying is that I'd appreciate a bit of restraint when it comes to fucking other women while I am walking around looking like a melted candle."

The melted candle part was not just my imagination

either. That week, I had crossed from the baggy sweater and safety pins over the zipper zone into the "And Baby Makes Two," mix-and-match, maternity ensemble zone. It was not an unnoticed fashion statement when I showed up at work that first morning.

Until then, Ruthie was the only one at the paper who knew, so as soon as my coat was off, I began getting stares. Of course, Martina Simmons, our notoriously bitchy society columnist, was the first to come up to me and actually ask. Martina had probably spoken to me a grand total of six times in the ten years she'd been there, but she beelined over to me that morning, sat down at my desk, and pushing her surgically reanchored face very close to mine, whispered, "Well, dear, was it planned or was it an accident?" I've always known that good breeding had nothing to do with good manners, but that question was absolutely over the top. I mean it wasn't like I thought the day was going to be easy, and it wasn't like I thought nobody was going to ask stuff, but I sure thought the questions would be more subtle than that.

"An accident," I said, turning away from her so that my swivel chair bumped into her hand and coffee flew all over her extremely expensive beige pants. I swear I didn't do it on purpose—but it was kind of a great little moment. Accident-wise.

The rest of the people in the newsroom were a lot easier to deal with. Celeste, my friend from the business page, came by a little later and after telling me she'd been wondering anyway about my weight gain, just wanted me to know that she hoped I was happy about this and that she had a lot of cute maternity clothes if I wanted to borrow them. Andy, a fortyish guy who works city side and who I think is still not completely in touch with his inner gayness, saw me at the Xerox machine later in the morning. "Lacy, hey, you're pregnant!"

"Hey, Andy," I said with a smile, "great deductive skills—no wonder you're such an ace investigative reporter." He blushed for a minute, but I didn't want him to think I was being sarcastic. I liked Andy, and even though he had no clue how much this baby was messing up my life, I could tell he was actually happy for me.

It was a complicated couple of weeks, while one by one the people who needed to acknowledge my pregnancy figured out a way to do it. And it reminded me of something Dolores had said a long time ago about when my daddy died. She said that each time someone came to her during those first few months, to acknowledge Daddy's death, it was like he died all over again. Each time they said, "Oh, I was so sorry to hear . . ." it made the profundity of his death rehit her.

That's what this felt like. Just when I thought I had integrated the full fact of this pregnancy, someone would come up to me and say something, and the hugeness of what had happened resonated through me. I didn't talk about it—not even to Steffi—but there was no way to pretend I had zero connection to the living person inside of me. I mean she/he would kick and tug and punch and do all the things I was so anxious about when it was Jessica in there, but I just couldn't risk getting excited about it now. It was like I was hoping to pull off this complete disconnect from every awesome, thrilling moment the two of us were having.

Sometimes at night, though, I'd put my hands on my belly and talk to the baby. I'd talk about how I hoped she/he would always be happy, and how she/he was so lucky to have a father like Charlie, and how I hoped that if, God forbid, she/he would ever find out what our true story was, that she/he wouldn't hate me forever. One night I even thought about writing a short story some-day, about what had happened, about how she/he would always wonder about the mom who disappeared from her/his life, and that she/he would start seeing a shrink, and of course the shrink would be me—the social worker mom, and how I'd have to decide whether or not to tell her/him.

Oh, God, the magnitude of this thing . . . I mean, I know people at the paper meant well, and I know my pregnancy was un-ignorable, but still . . . going through the whole fiction of giving the baby up for some random adoption felt very weird, when the only reason I was really having this baby was so someone they all knew—Charlie Feldman—could finally say to himself, "From now on, I am not just a son."

"You look great," said Charlie a few weeks later when I opened the door one Sunday morning. He was right—I was blimping out, but my color had been terrific lately even with no makeup on—I was saving a fortune in blush.

"Thanks. What's that?" I pointed to the big box in his hands, and motioned for him to come in out of the rain.

"You'll see," he said, taking off his jacket. He was wearing the same green sweater he'd worn that time we'd gone to the beach after the Bulls game. There was a little hole halfway down over his stomach. I touched it.

"Yeah I know. I'm going to get it fixed." He sat down and began to open the box. "Now don't blow up, Lacy. I ordered this from a catalog, and I think we should try it."

"What is it?" I said, staring at this megaphone thing with a long cord attached to a smaller megaphone.

"It's called a Preg-a phone. You just put it up on your belly like this," he said, setting the big megaphone end on my stomach and talking into the smaller end. "It's so you can talk to the kid all the time and tell it stuff."

"Charlie," I asked, amazed at the depth of his new-dad dopiness, "what did you pay for this?"

"Why? What does it matter?"

"It doesn't matter, but this kid hears stuff without phoning it in. That's what all the books say, anyway."

"What books are you reading?"

"I'm not reading any. You're the one reading parent-ing books. I just know that they say kids are familiar with their parents' voices by the time they are born."

"But I'm not around all that much for the kid to know me."

"You phone in almost every day, Charlie."

"Yeah, but I talk to you. Not the kid."

"You want me to hold the phone to my stomach when you call? That's crazy. I already turn your radio show on when I get home."

"You do?"

"Sometimes," I said. "You want some tea?" I asked, going into the kitchen to turn off the teapot. "I still can't handle coffee."

Charlie followed me in. "You hear the show? Why didn't you tell me before?"

"Because I didn't know if it would make you nervous to know I was listening."

"It makes me nervous to know anybody is listening," he said, getting the milk out of the refrigerator to put in his tea. "What do you think?"

"I think for sports radio—which I personally think is a dumb idea—you're pretty interesting."

"What's dumb about sports radio?"

"I don't know. I mean you might as well have outfit radio, or cooking radio—it just seems so narrow. But it's pretty weird to hear someone I know in real life talking on the radio—with your voice coming out of this box, like a famous person or an authority or something."

"I'm not famous, and the thing about sports radio is that *everybody* thinks they're an authority."

"Yeah, but you sound pretty smart. I thought the day last week when Reinsdorf exploded at the press conference you and Bonnie were really good. Actually that was the first night I turned you on, and I liked the way you handled the callers. People were really going crazy but you guys were very level and actually pretty funny."

We were sitting at the kitchen table. The sun had finally come out some, which was nice, only you could see all the dust everywhere. With Jess gone, I'd gotten even more casual about housework. She was staying in

North Carolina with a friend for Thanksgiving, but I was definitely planning to do a major scrub down before she came home for Christmas. I was anxious to see her, even though I was pretty nervous about how she was going to act when she saw how huge I was. The baby wasn't just a comma with a long tail now.

"So, really, how are you feeling?" Charlie asked.

I smiled. "Fine, Charlie. You ask me that every day and I always tell you fine."

"Yeah," he said, holding his teacup between his hands but not drinking it at all. "I guess I do. But I worry."

"Why? I *am* fine."

"I know," he said, trying to meet my smile, "but I still worry."

"About what?"

Charlie scratched his head, and leaned back in his chair. His eyes were fastened on something far away, and he said, "I worry about dying, Lacy."

"I'm not going to die."

"I'm not worried about *you* dying. I'm not even worried about the baby dying. Mostly I'm worried about *me* dying."

"Dying? You're not going to die, Charlie."

"Lacy, I could die. I could walk right out of this house and get hit by a car. Then what?"

"Let me explain something, Charlie. Dying is not an option for you. I don't need to be extremely pregnant with the baby you want and then have you die on me."

"But what if I do?"

"I'll kill you if you die, that's what!" I slapped my

hand down on the table. "Listen, you are not going to die! You'll be fine if you just look both ways before crossing for the next eighteen years."

"No, I'm serious. If something happens to me, what's going to happen to this kid?"

I pushed back from the table and slammed my cup into the sink. "Don't do this to me, Charlie! Don't bait me and try to make me say that I will take care of this kid. I'm not going to."

"Why do you keep referring to it as this kid? Why don't you just get the damn amniocentesis so at least we can know what sex this kid is?"

"Because I don't want to think about this baby in boy or girl terms! It's too personal! You'd understand that if you weren't so busy planning on being dead—which is not going to happen. But if it does, then it will give your brother a golden opportunity to be a parent again. He's had plenty of practice, right?"

"Practice does not make perfect, Lacy. My brother's kids are moderately fucked-up."

"You think your kid won't be fucked-up? Everyone's kids are fucked-up."

"Yeah, but I want my kid fucked-up *my* way—not Roger's way."

I laughed. I knew just where he was coming from.

I was less sure where he was coming from about ten minutes later, after we had gone back in the living room and I'd convinced him to return the Preg-a-phone. As he was boxing it up, he turned to me and said, "Lacy?"

"Yeah?"

"I want to see you naked."

My hand went to my heart. "What?"

"I know that sounds twisted. But the thing is, I've never seen a pregnant woman without her clothes on. And who knows if I ever will? I only know that growing inside you is this person that I am going to spend my whole life loving. I know I'd feel more hooked to this person if I could see what you looked like while he was growing inside of you. Does that make sense?"

The weird thing was, it did. And even though I felt a little odd just standing up from the couch and peeling off my clothes, I also felt okay about it. I made no excuses for having breasts that rested on my belly or for having a belly that was bisected by that funny brown line, or for any part of me that was distended or engorged or anything. Lately, I liked how I looked pregnant. Some women didn't, but I did. And Charlie? Well, Charlie was pretty awestruck. I took his hand and moved it all over me so he could feel where the baby's head was and foot was and how it is impossible to figure out where a baby ends and a mother begins—how it's all of one, and how all the slopes and curves on a woman that have always seemed to be there for gawking and for grabbing are really for a purpose. Charlie moved his hands gently, and respectfully, and with wonderment. And when he was all done exploring, he put one of those hands against my cheek.

His whole face was a smile. "Thank you, Lacy."

Charlie

DECEMBER

"For Chrissakes, Lacy, why are you being such a class-A bitch about the Lamaze thing? It's almost Christmas. The baby is due in less than twelve weeks. You still haven't signed up for a Lamaze class. So big deal . . . I signed us up for one. I wanted to guarantee us a place. How can you be pissed about that?"

It was nine-thirty on a Thursday night. I'd just gotten home from the station, and I called Lacy. These days Lacy and I were back to doing only phone. That last time at her house when she'd let me see her and touch her had jangled me. Her too, I think. It was pretty strong stuff. Plus, it was not much of an assist if I was going to get used to the fact that this was going to be *my* baby, not *our* baby. The Lamaze classes were the one part she was willing to let me in on. But she sure as hell was taking her sweet time nailing down a specific class time to begin.

"I don't need you swooping in and organizing my life, Charlie. I *told* you, I'd take care of the Lamaze thing. I just haven't gotten around to it yet. I'm busy, you know?"

I sat down on my living-room couch. The new house was great, but it still didn't feel like a home. The things I'd brought from the old place didn't fill it up. Even with the books unpacked and my pictures on the walls, I came up short on the homey look. I was also short on temper that night. The first ratings book was going to close in a few weeks, and the general manager at the station had been riding our asses. I had no patience with Lacy and her Lamaze delay bullshit.

"Come on, Lacy. We're just going to do it, okay? I've signed us up for a class that meets way out west at LaGrange Memorial Hospital. Nobody knows us there. Listen, this is going to be *my* kid, and I want to be there when he or she is born—for you, for the kid, and for me."

"Oh, shit! Shit! Shit! Shit!" she wailed. "T-shirt time strikes again."

"What the hell are you talking about?"

"I'm talking about how it always seems that every relationship should come equipped with two T-shirts— one that says 'guilt,' and the other that says 'resentment.' Because even if you compromise, deep down it *always* boils down to those two things."

"You've lost me, Lacy."

"Well, suppose a wife has a great job offer out of town

but her husband doesn't want to leave his job, so they stay. Then he wears the 'guilt' one, and she wears the 'resentment' one. But if he says, 'Okay fine, I don't want to move, but we'll move,' then he gets the 'resentment' one and she gets the 'guilt' one. It's the same for us. If I say 'no,' and renege on going with you to Lamaze, I get the 'guilt' shirt. But if I say 'yes,' I get the 'resentment' one. See?"

The woman was exhausting. "Lacy, do me a favor. Put on whatever T-shirt you want. Just be ready at seven o'clock January tenth. I'll pick you up for our first class. I'll work it out for Bonnie to go solo on the last hour of our shift." I hung up the phone, opened a beer, and fell asleep before it was half gone.

Getting the Lamaze class nailed down was a big help. Because I had a shitload of other stuff to deal with. Both logistical and emotional.

Tops on the logistical list was a baby nurse. After a couple of weeks of digging and interviewing, I came up with a woman who had a completely atypical m.o. She wasn't sixty; she didn't have white hair; and her first name wasn't Mrs. She was a thirty-two-year-old brunette named Sarah whose twin sister was a pediatrician. A baby nurse with a pediatrician twin was one hell of a twofer. It also didn't hurt that Sarah had a terrific smile and one of those molasses accents that Southerners have. Turns out she was from South Carolina. The pediatrician sister's references checked out too, and since her office was only five blocks away, that worked out great.

As to the rest of the logistical stuff, I carried an old reporter's notebook and every time I thought of something, I logged it. "Get car seat." "Check with Lacy re: poss. need for donor blood." "Have Roger measure space between slats on his old crib." "Think of name— Max? Joe? Zoe?"

The problem was, the main things I thought about, I couldn't write down. It was all the mind shit. How do you itemize the feelings you have when you unpack one of your moving boxes and come across all these old pictures of yourself as a kid . . . Sophie and I coming home from the hospital; Sophie cradling me in her arms while I suck on my bottle; Abe and Sophie each holding one of my hands while I practice walking; Roger showing up a couple years later and me standing next to Sophie while she makes sure I don't kill him. Piles of standard family pictures that I would never shoot with my kid. There'd be no mom bringing him home or feeding him, or being on the other side of him when he took his first step. There'd just be him and me, and who the hell would shoot the photos of us together?

Because that was the other batch of pictures . . . Abe and me. Abe at my birthday parties, Abe at my bar mitzvah, Abe at my scout induction. Not only was there a mom there to take them, but almost every one of them was Abe with me at some special event. When Roger and I were little, dads weren't around much. They worked hard and they weren't a part of your regular life. They were special. They were brought in for the occasion—sometimes it was a celebration, sometimes it was for dispensing discipline, sometimes it was just dinner.

Still, you cleaned up so when Dad showed up at dinner you were presentable. I didn't want my kid to feel that way about me. I wanted to be the most regular thing in this kid's life. No awe, no terror, just Dad. The way kids feel about their moms. I wanted to be essential to my kid on a daily basis. But I had a real dose of performance anxiety about pulling it off.

"Everybody feels that way," Bobby told me one Sunday as he carried in a stroller and some other stuff that he and Sherry had dug out of their basement. He'd been great during all of this, but Sherry had apparently gone apeshit when he told her. She thought raising the baby alone was the stupidest life move she had ever heard of. But then Sherry held the world title when it came to conventionality. Plus, she never had a particularly high opinion of me anyway. I was good enough to fix up with some of her divorced friends whose kids already had dads, but she was placing no bets on me as a future dad raising a kid solo. I didn't take her vote of no-confidence personally. Other than both loving Bobby, we didn't have a whole lot in common.

"Christ," I said, grateful for the donation, "babies need more equipment than a linebacker." We hauled in three additional cartons and brought them upstairs to the kid's room.

"Royal blue and white?" he asked, looking around at my paint job.

"Yeah. Cubs colors. I figured that way, whether it was a boy or a girl, it made sense."

He laughed. "What are those Hefty bags filled with over there?"

"More kid gear. Bonnie had a basement full of stuff that she's donated to the cause—mobiles, a playpen, sheets. I'm going over there again to get a changing table. I couldn't fit it all in the car last night. Want to see the rest of the house?"

"Sure. What do you mean 'last night'?"

I took him down the hall to my room. "It still needs to be painted, but it's a decent enough size and I think I can get this old fireplace working."

He nodded and looked around the mustard-colored room. "You didn't answer my question, Chas. What do you mean 'last night'? You see this woman every day at the station, and now you're seeing her on Saturday nights?"

I couldn't believe Bobby was still monitoring my goddamn social life. Like I had one. "No big deal," I said as we walked out on the back porch and I showed him the great oak in the yard that sold me on the house. "I drove down to her place in Beverly last night to pick up all this stuff. Then I hung around some, and we wound up ordering in some ribs. She has a three-year-old kid. Cute little guy."

We grabbed a couple of beers from the icebox, and went into the living room to watch the Bears.

"You watch a lot of sports with the kids?" I asked as Green Bay got another first down.

"Weekends, some. During the week Sherry has all these no-TV rules. And other than the Bulls, my kids would rather watch MTV than sports. I must've done something wrong."

"Christ!" I yelled. "Did you see that?" The Bears

linebacker had intercepted a Green Bay pass on the fourteen-yard line, lateraled it to the cornerback, and he took it eighty yards into the end zone.

"Unfuckingbelievable!"

"Incredible defensive touchdown!"

We watched the reruns a few times, and then Bobby said, "Why'd you ask about my kids and TV?"

"Just wondering. I spend a lot of time wondering how this is going to play out. You know, actual kid, sitting on actual couch in actual future."

"Don't think too much about it, Chas. Just let it happen. That's the best you can do."

"Yeah, but the thing is," I said, hitting the mute button for the duration of Coke and car commercials, "I've never taken care of anyone before except myself, and I did a pretty half-assed job of that. I'm scared shitless."

"It all works out. You go in blind, but after a couple of years . . ."

"Yeah?"

"After a couple of years, you're still blind. Only you're used to it," Bobby said.

"Thanks, pal. What about labor?" I'd told Bobby that "the woman on the road" had consented to having the baby here in Chicago so I could be part of the birth. Man, I *hated* all this lying. "Even with the Lamaze class, what if I choke in the labor room and wind up acting like Ricky Ricardo?"

Bobby laughed and pulled off a slice of the cold Malnatti's pizza I'd brought out. It was left over from Friday night. "Yeah, labor's a bitch. Mostly because you have so few moves. She's hurting like hell, and you can't help. So you say dumbfuck stuff like 'you're doing great' and all she wants is to either have it be over or kill you—whichever she can pull off first. But that's the thing, Charlie. Then it *is* over. And it's great. Seeing this kid come out and having it be this living, breathing reality that is the next generation of you . . . It's mind-blowing!"

"Yeah," I said, keeping the mute on even though the ball was back in play, "this generation stuff hits me even now. Big-time. I feel as if I'm leaving my regular category and getting pushed up one level, you know? Now I'm a father. Abe's a grandfather. I know he's one already, but this time he's one in my column. It's like we all move one notch closer to . . . something. Our own mortality maybe."

"Yeah," said Bobby distractedly, as we watched the Bears score another defensive touchdown.

December felt different this year. For one thing, it was the last time I would be at Toys "R" Us just because of Roger's kids. Next year, not only would I be there loading up for my kid, but Roger and Elaine would be shopping for my kid too. Amazing.

Christmas week I decided to stop by Lacy's. I knew Jessica was back in town and that they were riding each other hard, but I wanted to drop off one of those pillows pregnant women use to try to get comfortable when they sleep. Bonnie told me about them. They're called body pillows and they are about five feet long. She said women liked to lie sideways with them, hugging them to their body, flinging their leg over them, or lying with their back against them. She said hers had helped a lot. I knew Lacy wouldn't let me get her a real Christmas present, but I figured this thing would be hard for her to resist. She hadn't gone through the sardines and grape jelly phase, but insomnia had hit her big-time.

Jessica opened the door. She looked like hell. Tired, hair in big roller things, and some kind of sack dress on with combat boots. She didn't smile. She didn't say hello. She only said, "Mom isn't home."

Jessica and I had not seen each other since this whole thing had happened. I knew Lacy had told her that I was the baby's father and that I was taking the kid, but we'd only talked about Jessica's reaction to Lacy. Not her reaction to me. Evidently, there was room for two on Jessica's shit list.

"Hey, Jessica, how're you doing?" I asked lamely, wondering just how stupid I must have looked standing on her porch with a giant pillow. "So where did she take off to?"

"Who knows?" she said, not stepping back to let me in, and folding her arms over her stomach. "She stormed out of here. We're not doing that great at communicating these days."

"Yeah, these are pretty tense times," I said, wishing I were anywhere but face-to-face with the daughter of a woman I'd got pregnant.

Then Jessica did what every guy dreads a woman will do. She began to bawl. Throwing herself against me and nearly blinding me with one of those rollers, she sobbed, "Oh, Charlie, I'm being such a total asshole with her, but I can't help it. I hate seeing her like this . . . how could she have been so stupid?"

"*She?* I was there, Jessica," I said, rummaging through my pocket for a handkerchief to hand her and guiding her inside. "This wasn't something your mom engineered. And stupid has nothing to do with it. Your mom was having safe sex."

"Stop!" she said, clamping her hands over her ears. "I don't want to hear what kind of sex my mother was having. Mothers shouldn't be having sex anyway. That's gross."

"I was only saying, she's not a hypocrite—preaching one thing and doing another. And I'm also saying if you're reaching for adjectives, *stupid* isn't the one. *Generous* is maybe. *Nuts* is for sure. Your mom is having this baby for me. So if you want to be pissed, be pissed at me."

We were in the living room now. There was a naked Christmas tree in the corner with boxes of lights and ornaments sitting next to it. A few cards had been taped on the doorway to the hall, but then it looked like the project had been abandoned. It did not feel festive in there. "I *am* pissed at you. But it doesn't count. You're not my mom," she sniveled. "This just feels like such a betrayal. Mom and I have always been so close. Just the two of us, you know? And it just feels like it's never going to be the same."

"Why?" I asked, finally locating my damn handkerchief and handing it to her. "Your mom's not bringing the baby back here. You know that. There'll still be just the two of you."

"Well, it sure doesn't feel like there's just two of us when we are sitting at the kitchen table and there is this mound that used to be my mom across from me." She blew her nose.

"Yeah," I said, looking around for a place to put down the pillow. I finally propped it next to the couch. "But in two months it'll be over. The baby will be with me, you'll be at school, and when you come back this summer it'll be normal again. You and your mom can hang out together as much as you want. How much does an eighteen-year-old want to hang out with her mom anyway?"

"Maybe more than I sometimes admit," she sniffed, and handed back the handkerchief. "I missed her a lot this fall. It's complicated between parents and kids. You'll see."

I looked at her. She was so much like Lacy. Not in looks. But in personality. They were both so damn reactive. And guileless. And easy to like. "How do you know it's complicated? You've never been a mom."

"Yeah, but I've been a kid who had a great mom," she said, picking up the magazines that were all over the couch and stacking them on the table.

"If you think she's so great, then why are you being such a quote total asshole unquote with her?"

"Because that's what us kids do, Charlie. Better get used to it." Then pointing to the five-foot pillow, she said, "Why are you being so nice to her? She told me the only person she fights with more than me is you."

"I don't know. She's the mother of my baby. Plus, I like her."

Jessica leaned over and pulled up the pillow, setting part of it across her lap. "It's so weird to think of having a half brother or sister."

"Is that how you think of it?"

"Sometimes. I try not to, but after all these years of being an only kid, and all those years after my dad got remarried and I would have given anything for a kid brother or sister, it's a little creepy to realize that now there is going to be one. Only I won't ever know him. Or her."

"Do you want to?"

She was quiet for a minute. "I don't know. I haven't thought about it. Not seriously. I think it would make Mom crazy."

"Probably. But that's dodging the question. How would it make *you* feel to be part of the baby's life?" I already knew how it would make me feel. Great. It would be only great to have her around.

One of the rollers fell out as she shook her head. She caught it. "I don't know, Charlie, I really don't."

I tore off a piece of paper from one of the magazines she'd stacked and wrote my address and phone number on it. "Here, if you decide you'd like to find out." I got up and she walked me to the door. When she opened it, I kissed her forehead and said, "Be good to her, Jess. She's doing a tough thing."

Charlie

FEBRUARY

I remember exactly what we were talking about when the producer whispered into my headset, "Some friend of yours named Lacy is on Line C. She says it's an emergency."

We were talking about the Bulls' dismal performance on the road. We were *always* talking about the Bulls. It was that rare time of year when football was over, spring training hadn't begun and Chicago was down to only two teams—the Hawks and the Bulls. That makes it sparse in the sports talk department. And that day—the twenty-third of February—was no exception. It was a sleety Chicago Wednesday. Three-thirty-six in the afternoon. We went to three minutes of spots, and I had the call transferred to another phone outside the studio. Bonnie could handle the on-air calls when the break was over.

"Lacy, where are you? You okay?" She wasn't due for another week.

"I'm at the hospital," she said in a winded voice. "I went to Filene's—even though I'm a blimp, because they're having a winter coat sale and I figured I could get a good buy for next winter—but the second I stepped into the dressing room, my stupid water broke! They're not that nice at Filene's when your water breaks on a winter coat sale day, Charlie. Anyway, I just got in a cab and came here, and this was the first I could get to the phone, because I had to fill out all these forms, so I'm thinking you'd better get here. Fast."

But we still had one more Lamaze class. It wasn't supposed to happen like this. I hadn't even gotten Lacy a beeper yet. It was going to be a graduation present. "Jesus, Lacy. This is it?"

"I think so."

I looked around the station, which was jammed with green metal desks and stacks of old sports sections from cities all over the country. It looked a lot like the city room—chaotic and inhabited by people in a hurry. "How close are your contractions?" I asked, grabbing a notepad.

"Close enough."

"This isn't repartee, Lacy. I'm supposed to write this down. How close are your contractions?"

"Four minutes. And you can forget the b.s. about calling them 'contractions'—they're pains."

"Four minutes? So we've got some time, don't we? It always takes longer the first time."

"Charlie. This is not my first time—remember?"

"Oh. Yeah. Right."

The hospital was only ten minutes away. Unless, like me, you missed the turnoff. Then it was twenty minutes away. Christ, I *was* going to be Ricky Ricardo.

By the time I found a parking place, and reached the maternity floor, Lacy had set some kind of world record in fast-forward labor. She was about ready to push. Five weeks of schlepping out to those dumbass classes, and by the time I got there, everything we'd learned was a moot point. No panting, no blowing, no ice chips. Nothing. Just a pissed and sweaty version of someone who for the last few weeks had been only pissed.

Those Lamaze classes had made her crazy. Partly because she hated to acknowledge that she was going to need some support from me during the birth, and partly because pretending we were this regular couple, when we were as about irregular as you could get, made her furious. Me, it only made sad.

"I can't stand all those personal questions the other women ask all the time," she sighed one night when we were driving home. "How long have we been together? Is this our first baby? I just feel like we drive out there to lie to strangers for two straight hours and I hate it."

And of course now that I had set foot into the hospital room she could do what millions of women do at that point, she could hate me. After all, I had invented the labor process, right?

"Nice timing, Charlie," she grunted as another contraction grabbed her.

She looked awful. She had dark stains under her eyes from the makeup, her hair was stuck to the sides of her face, and the green hospital gown was wringing wet. As I stepped toward the bed, one of the nurses flipped a sheet down over Lacy's splayed legs and said, "Are *you* the father?"

"Is this a B-movie or something? Of course *that's* the father," snarled Lacy as she yanked the sheet back off. "Come on, let's go here! I'm dying!"

"Cool down, doll," the nurse said, patting Lacy's hand and motioning me out of the way. "We're going to get you right into delivery."

"Let's get her into two," a second nurse instructed as a couple of orderlies came in. And then to me, "Come on, you need to get some scrubs and a mask. Pronto."

It was all going too fast. I grabbed Lacy's hand and walked alongside of the bed with her as the orderlies wheeled her out of the room and down the yellow hallway. Doors opened on all kinds of little family sightings—grandparents, dads, younger brothers and sisters. The closed doors must have housed other families-in-progress with the guys doing the coaching bit that I would probably never do. Another contraction hit Lacy and she groaned, "Jeeeeee-zus!"

"Christ," I said as her hand squeezed hard. "I can't imagine what that feels like."

"Think in terms of passing a basketball through your dick," she gasped about forty seconds later when it was over. Then she closed her eyes and waited for the next one.

·   ·   ·

I've got no videos and no Polaroids. But I will never forget what watching my kid being born felt like. It was raw joy. Not *feeling* raw joy. But *existing* of nothing else but raw joy. I know I cried. I think I laughed. And I kept saying over and over when I looked down at the slick, squalling human that was Jake, "This is the best thing that I will ever do."

I didn't know his name was Jake at the time. All I knew, when they set him up on Lacy's chest, was that I had just stepped into a zone of vulnerability I had never been in before. I wasn't sure I could handle it.

I sure as hell wasn't sure I could handle Lacy. She was an emotional mess. From the minute Jake came out of her, and for the first fifteen minutes of his life—she could not stop sobbing. "He's okay, isn't he? All his stuff is there, right, Charlie?" I nodded, I grinned, I even kissed her. After all the lawyers and convoluted arrangements, at that moment anyway, we looked like any couple that ever had a baby. It was very strong. Very confusing.

Then we got back to the room and she did a big one-eighty. She went ice-cold. She barely talked to me and she flat out refused to look at Jake or hold him again. When the nurses brought him in for a feeding, she snarled, "Give him to his father! That's his job!" When they wanted to know if we'd be at the diapering and bathing demonstration the next morning, she sneered, "I don't *think* so . . ."

•   •   •

I let it lie. I had no reading on her, so I backed off. And sat down to fall in love with my kid. I sure as hell wasn't going to let her craziness mess up my time with him. The nurse showed me how to hold him, and how to put in the bottle. Mostly I just watched him grimace and suck at the air while he was zonked in his little bed. He was the greatest.

It was amazing. The *being* of him. The going from nothing, not to just something, but to something that was almost an everything. The going from an act—plain old ordinary fucking—to a person. A person I was linked with for life. Pretty unbelievable.

By ten that night, when they took him away after the second feeding, I was beat. Lacy's mother had showed up around six, and that was the only time I was willing to vacate the room. Meeting her mom was more than I could handle, so before she appeared, I headed downstairs for dinner. Lacy looked a lot better when I came back up. Her mom had brought her some clean sleeping things and had done something to puff up her hair. She still wasn't talking much. Before I left, I asked if there was anything I could bring her.

"Yeah," she said softly, "Jessica's baby book."

"Is that for real, Lacy? Because I will if you want."

She didn't answer.

"Did you call Jessica when I went downstairs for dinner?" I asked, still trying my best to be conversational.

"And say what?"

"Just tell her."

"What do I tell her, Charlie?" she said, punching up her pillows. "Do I tell her, 'I had a baby'? Do I tell her,

'*You* have a half brother'? Do I tell her, '*He* has a baby'? Make that '*he* has *his* baby . . .' "

"Come on, Lacy."

"I want to leave here tomorrow," she announced.

"I already told you—I'd rather pay for the extra day. Just stay here and rest."

"I don't want to rest! I want to go home!"

"Lacy, stay. It's nice here." It was. For a hospital, it was pretty fancy. The rooms in the maternity ward had wallpaper. Plus, no one was in the next bed, so it was like having a private room. "Let them take care of you for one more day. And let me have a day at home to set up. I'm not ready for him."

"There's nothing to get ready! All you need is a box of Pampers and the crib your brother gave you! I've gotta get out of here," she said, fiddling with the bandage that covered where the IV tube had punctured her arm.

"You *will* get out! Friday morning. Lacy, look, I want to be understanding, but cut me some slack here. That'll give me time to pick my mom up at the airport tomorrow too."

"Is your mom coming? You didn't tell me that."

"You never asked," I said, suddenly exhausted. I stood up to put on my coat. The snowstorm that had kicked in earlier seemed to be winding down. "She's flying in from Miami tomorrow."

"You called her?"

"Of course."

"What did she say?"

"A little of everything. She and my old man are still

torn between being pissed and excited about this. But she could hear how happy I am too."

Her voice got little. "You *are* happy, aren't you, Charlie?"

I looked at her. Clear green eyes, black curls combed and soft-looking, her face somber. She was beautiful. What could I say? From this point forward, there would be no woman I could ever meet who would alter my life as much as Lacy had. Lacy had given me a son. And yeah, happy was part of it. But "happy" was too narrow a word to wrap around the way I felt. Even so, I was stuck with it. "Yeah, I'm happy. Grateful too. You pulled off an amazing thing."

Lacy turned away from me and faced the wall. "I need you to leave now, okay?"

The next morning I tried to get back to the hospital by noon. Sophie's plane didn't land until four, but there was a shitload of shopping to do. Enfamil, Pampers, pacifiers, terry-cloth stretch things. I hit Toys "R" Us when it opened at nine with the list my sister-in-law and I had gone over the night before. Elaine had been great. She said that once Sophie took off, she'd come in for a few days until Sarah could start. I was beginning to feel like I was on top of things. Until I got to the hospital.

When I walked in, the floor nurse saw me and pulled me aside.

"Mr. Feldman? May I see you for a minute?"

"Sure," I said, instantly terrified. "Is there a problem?"

"Not with the baby," she said. She was about fifty-five with short gray hair and small round glasses. "But we had rather a, uh, strange encounter with Ms. Gazzar this morning, and I felt maybe you should know about it."

"What is it?" She had steered me to one of those family waiting rooms with the tan vinyl chairs all hospitals have. I flashed on the one I was in when Abe was sick. When all this started.

"Well, Ms. Gazzar came to the front desk and asked if we had completed the birth certificate. I said we had and she asked to see it. And then when I handed it to her, she said the strangest thing. She asked if there was any way to take her name off of it. In thirty-five years of nursing, I've never heard such an odd request."

I assured the nurse that I'd speak to Lacy. Then I went by the nursery to see Jake. He looked a lot less dented and scrunched up than yesterday. The day before he looked like a newt, but today it was amazing—he looked just like Grandpa Louie, Abe's dad. And it wasn't just that he was bald. He had the same high forehead, and the same bump on the end of his nose. Granted, Jake's was more a preview bump than a bona fide one, but there was no mistaking this baby for anyone but a Feldman. Maybe it was stupid, but seeing that made me feel terrific. It was going to be great. Jake and me. And a whole world ahead filled with stuff he was going to love—cheeseburgers, puppies, cable. I high-fived him at the window even though he was completely out, and went down the hall to have a discussion with Lacy.

She was sitting up in bed with her eyes glued to some soap opera. "Hey," was all she said.

"Hey?" I said, ready to kill her. "Turn that damn thing off."

She didn't budge. I grabbed the remote and clicked off the tube.

She glared at me. "What's that about, Charlie?"

"I'll tell you what that's about. What the hell were you doing down at the nurses' station trying to get your name wiped off the birth certificate?"

Her eyes flashed. "I was doing exactly what I said I was going to do, Charlie. Trying to burn every bridge I can between me and your baby."

"You heard the lawyer. He told you that was illegal! What the hell were you thinking?"

"I was thinking that maybe the law had changed since last summer. And even if it hadn't, I figured that it was definitely worth a shot. Who was the big tattletale?"

"I don't know her name—the nurse with the gray hair and glasses."

"Oh, yeah. She's the one that hassled me this morning about the circumcision too." She grabbed the remote from where I tossed it on the bed and clicked the TV on again. "I told her to ask *you*."

I didn't say anything.

"You're going to have it done, aren't you?"

"I'm not sure," I snapped. Outside the door a woman was being wheeled back from delivery. Her husband was singing to her in Spanish.

"But you're Jewish! Don't you *have* to have him circumcised?"

"It's not automatic anymore, Lacy. Like everything else today, it's a *choice*. What kind of coffee do you want? What kind of beer do you want? What kind of dick do you want? Christ, my first major decision for the kid, and it's got to be his dick?"

An hour later Jake was circumcised.

About twenty-four hours after that, with his belly button still on and his foreskin now off, Jacob N. Feldman left the hospital. N. stood for No middle name. There were too many relatives to get pissed off if I chose the wrong one.

Granted, the family setup Jacob N. Feldman was going home to was not very conventional. But the family setup he left the hospital with was. Lacy was in a wheelchair—hospital rules. I walked alongside her and held Jake—Lacy's rules. We looked like a regular nuclear unit until we got into the car—my rules. But we knew where we were really headed. Two separate existences.

The day was cold and blindingly bright. The snow had melted and then frozen into a thick sheet of ice that glinted the sun right back in our eyes. I drove real carefully. Jake was asleep in the portable car seat contraption in the back and I was scared shitless about waking him. Sophie was waiting for us at my end of the line, but I had to get Lacy home first. We were both quiet. When we pulled up in front of her place, I turned off the ignition, but I didn't know what to say.

"Lacy?"

"Listen, I gotta go." She grabbed her canvas bag from the floor, pushed open the door handle, and got out on the sidewalk. Then just when I thought she was going to shut the door, she stuck her head back in and said, "Do good, Charlie." She didn't look in the backseat once.

I watched her walk up the stairs and get out her key. It didn't look as if anyone was home.

Charlie

FEBRUARY - MAY

All three of us got home fine. Jake, me, and my feelings of inadequacy. There were so damn many options for fucking-up. Bathing, feeding, burping, figuring out what the hell Jake wanted. It was the crying without subtitles that got to me. There was so damn much guesswork in it all. They should have invented kids who right off the bat could help you out with different cries—the hungry cry, the wet cry, the I'm-pissed-off-in-general cry. But it didn't happen like that.

I was lucky I had help from everyone else. For starters, Sophie had been amazing. It was like having a personal trainer in parenting. Even after she left and went back to Abe down in Florida, she called in every couple of days, sent up articles, and was there in a way that made me feel great. I knew it had been a hard thing for her to deal with, but somewhere between the baby as a concept, and Jake as a living breathing person—she bought in. Even Abe was moving toward it, slowly. It made a big difference, because I sure as hell felt out there on a limb.

Long run, I knew Jake and I would be fine. We liked all the same things—eating, sleeping, shitting. Though that first month, I liked sleeping more than he did. He liked it, he just didn't do most of it during the night. Even with Sophie there for a week, and Elaine helping out until Sarah could begin, nights were always mine. I spent plenty of them holding him and rocking him back and forth. Man, his room sure filled up fast—rattles, teddy bears, a bungee swing, a playpen. By the time late spring rolled around my freezer held equal amounts of pizzas and frozen teething rings. Nights when Jake would be cranky, I'd plug in this machine that threw rainbows on the walls, lay him out on my lap or over my shoulder, and rock him to sleep. Usually I'd sing something from my extensive dad medley—"Itsy Bitsy Spider," "Take Me Out to the Ball Game," the Michigan fight song, and "The Duke of Earl." "Duke of Earl" worked best.

However, I wasn't working great at all. Not at radio anyway. Part of the reason was lack of sleep. But mostly it was the change of focus. For the first time in twenty-five years, my job was not my life. My life was completely defined by the needs and the presence of Jake. I *had* a job. I *was* a dad. It was a major shift.

I'm not saying I didn't give a rat's ass about our show. I was plenty bummed when our station did dismally in the first ratings book. The bosses said that was standard with any new station for at least the first year. Then they rode our asses anyway.

Bonnie was great though, terrifically understanding of my situation. She had battled plenty of guilt herself about being away from her kid. But her mom lived with them. Someone from the family was always there, and that was a big plus. Particularly when her son got sick. Man, I was scared shitless to leave Jake with Sarah the first time he spiked a 103° fever. But I knew I couldn't stick around.

"You're sure you've been with kids this sick before?" I asked Sarah one Wednesday in May after Jake had scared the hell out of me all night.

"Definitely, Charlie," she said. She gave me a big smile, meant to inspire confidence. It didn't work.

"The thing is, Sarah, it's not just a reaction to his DPT shot. I already took him over to your sister and she's sure about that."

"I know, Charlie. That's the third time you've told me," she said, pushing her hands into her back jeans pockets. She usually wore a nurse's uniform, but I'd needed her early that day. She showed up in tight black jeans and a red tank top. Not your basic Florence Nightingale outfit. She must have noticed me eyeballing it.

"Sorry," she said, "I didn't have time to dry my laundry."

As if I was entitled to excuses. I was still unshaven and in my sweats. The only other thing I was wearing was a feverish baby in a sling hanging against my belly.

"Why don't you leave him in his bed, if he's sick?" Sarah asked.

"I don't know. If I put him down, he wails. This way he only whimpers." I looked down at Jake in the sling. He was still flushed and sweaty. "He likes the glow of the computer screen."

She looked at me as if I were nuts. "Here, give him to me, Charlie. You shouldn't be sitting in front of that screen with him." She scooped him out of the sling and he started to wail. "Go get ready for your show."

That was what I was doing most days when Sarah arrived. Sitting at the computer scanning for stories. Jake would be asleep in the playpen right next to me. It was generally the first chance I had to sit down all day, considering that by noon, I'd fed him two or three times, changed him five or six times, bathed him once, done one or two loads of laundry, and on a lucky day had maybe enough time to brush my teeth.

"Man," I said to Sarah, "this baby maintenance stuff is so damn time-consuming. They should sell a bumper sticker. 'Kill narcissism now, have a baby.'"

She laughed. "Hey, Charlie," she said, rocking and patting Jake so his wail had diminished to a halfhearted snivel, "why don't you joke like that on the radio?"

"How do you know what I do on the radio?"

"I leave it on sometimes so Jake can hear your voice. It's good for him."

"Who says?"

"I says," she said, feeling Jake's forehead. "Man, this little guy is burning up. But he's going to be fine. I'll cool him down with a bath. Don't worry."

That day, though, I did worry. But most of the time, I left the house feeling solid. Sometimes I'd check in during a break, and nights when I got home, after Sarah left, I'd always go into Jake's room and wake him up. I needed to be with him some. To bury my face on the top of his head and smell him. It wasn't the powder. He had a baby smell. It was more than sweet. It was clean. New. Like a car. But in a car it only lasts a couple of months. I wondered how long it lasted with a baby. Whenever it ended, I knew I was going to miss it.

I missed Lacy too. But I didn't like to think about it. It didn't buy me anything. That part was hard. The mandatory amputation. But that was what she'd insisted on, and it was what I'd signed up for. I had to figure her end was even harder. At least I had Jake.

I also had women crawling out of the woodwork. It blew me away. But Andy had been right—something about a guy with a kid got to women. The *Sleepless in Seattle* syndrome maybe. All I know is six weeks after Jake was born, the calls started coming in.

Alissa, one of the women who sold advertising for the station, invited me to "bring the baby over and fix Sunday brunch at my place." It threw me completely off guard. Before Jake was born I'd taken Alissa to dinner one night and had a pretty decent time. But when I asked her out twice after that, she'd begged off. Now all of a sudden I was interesting. I wanted to be nice to her, but this time, it was my turn to beg off. Not because I had some ax to grind, but because dating and being a new dad were an impossible combination. One was so phony. The other was so real.

Then Terry, a woman who was city side at the paper, called. She'd heard about the baby, and wanted to know if I felt like escaping one night. Said she'd treat me to a movie and dinner. Same with a financial reporter named Sally. She was a great-looking redhead who wouldn't give me the time of day when I worked at the *Sun-Times*. Now all of a sudden, I get an invitation to some dinner party she's throwing. Even Elaine, who'd given up on fixing me up years ago, called to see if I'd be interested in going out one night with her and Roger and this new friend of hers from work—a thirty-one-year-old divorced mom who had two-year-old twins.

"Thanks anyway, Elaine," I said, "but that sounds like more Brady Bunch than I can handle. Nope, right now, the only woman who'd be the perfect date for me would be someone who'd either been through menopause or had her tubes tied."

"Okay," she said with a laugh, "no harm in asking though, right?"

"None at all." The truth was, right now I was content to hang out with Jake. Sometimes Bonnie and her son Greg came over on Sundays and that was enough social life for me.

"So," I asked Elaine, "what time is the Mom-Fest next Sunday?"

"Four-thirty. See you then, okay?"

"Yup." This was going to be Jake's first Mother's Day. He might not have had a mom to be with, but he sure as hell wasn't going to miss being with his grandma and the rest of his family that day. Obviously a few Mother's Days down the line, he'd have plenty of where-is-my-mom questions. And I'd have to have plenty of answers. Maybe even find him a mom by then. But this year, it was going to be simple. Roger and Elaine wanted us all to show up for dinner. How unhappy could Sophie be surrounded by two sons and four grandchildren?

Ever since Sophie and Abe had returned from Florida, they'd come over to see Jake nearly every day. Sophie was dazzled at all the tricks Jake had learned since she'd seen him in February. Now he could almost sit up without my holding him, and his latest feat was using his fist to swipe at the mobile over his bed.

"He looks like he could develop a pretty good left jab," Abe said the first time he saw him. Man, was that ever a moment. For all the brakes Abe had on about this, when I reached into the crib and put Jake in the arms of my old man . . . it was something.

The two of them never took their eyes off each other. Abe held Jake close and walked straight over to the rocker. He sat down gingerly, began rocking back and forth, and grinned. Glowed even. Then he said the same thing to Jake that he'd said to me my whole life growing up. Giving Jake a big kiss on the head, he pronounced the classic family blessing. "Not a bad-looking guy for a Feldman."

Other than the Mom-Fest at Roger and Elaine's, the Memorial Day barbecue out at Bobby and Sherry's was Jake's first big-time social debut. I guess I felt it was some sort of dog and pony show. All of a sudden at midnight the night before, I was running a load of laundry, so Jake could wear his miniature Cubs uniform when we headed out to the burbs Monday at noon.

I didn't have Memorial Day off, but the midday guy did, so I filled in for him from ten to two while Bonnie got stuck doing our regular shift solo. Calls were thin that day and with no partner to bounce stuff off of, I was sweating bullets. Talking on holiday radio sucked even more than writing for holiday newspapers. Nobody gave a shit about either of them.

It also made it hard to get someone to watch Jake for the morning, and I wound up bringing him into the station. I couldn't bring him into the studio, so I put him into the producer's booth. That way, if he went on a crying jag, it wouldn't be broadcast all over Chicago. But the kid was a brick. Slept through the whole show. Just like the rest of the city.

I took Jake home, got him bathed, changed, and fed, and by one-thirty we were heading up the Edens to Bobby's. "What a doll," squealed Jennifer, when Jake and I walked up the driveway. A crowd had already assembled in Bobby's backyard. I had Jake in the infant seat on one arm, and eight pounds of equipment for his four hours of socializing on the other. "Please, Uncle Charlie, can I take care of him today?"

"Sure, Jennifer, that would be great. You ever baby-sit for a kid this young?"

"She's handled newborns, Charlie," Sherry said, appearing from nowhere and giving me one of those fake-out air kisses.

"Hi, Sherry. How's it going?" Sherry had gone blond since I'd seen her last. I never knew in these dye-job moments if it was better to say something or take a pass.

"It's fine," she said. "It's good to see you."

It was an interesting comment from someone who'd made a concerted effort not to see me in eight months, but I let it go. "Yeah. Well, we're glad to be here." I gave her an underline on the "we're."

"He really is darling, Charlie," she said, without even looking at him. "Here, set down your stuff and grab a beer. I think you probably know most everybody." Looking around the yard, I guessed she was right. This had been an annual event for maybe fifteen years. The people there were neighbors, some were Bobby's colleagues, a few were from Sherry's world. But all of them had one thing in common. They were mostly at the tail end of kid-rearing. Some of them had kids so old, you couldn't tell which ones were the daughters and which ones were the second wives.

"Hey, Charlie," said one of the original wives, "let's take a look at this little guy before you hand him over to the teen contingency." She peered into the infant seat. "He's terrific."

"Thanks, Donna," I said. I'd always liked her. She was tiny, with shiny brown hair pulled back in a ponytail, and still looking great in a pair of white shorts. She was the wife of one of Bobby's partners. He was a real asshole, but Donna had a good attitude. She also was a relatively successful freelance writer around town. Last year she had done a great piece on the wives of all five of the pro-team coaches in town. She'd done a terrific job of winning their confidence, reporting, and then getting out alive after writing it.

We talked a few minutes before I heard Jake wailing like a banshee from the center of the volunteer baby-sitting club. Four teenage girls were seated in a circle cooing at him. I headed over to do a diaper checkout. Jennifer handed him up to me. "I'll do it if you want, Uncle Charlie."

"Tell you what," I said, grabbing Jake and fitting him under my arm in what the baby books called the football carry. "I'll do the honors and then you can feed him. Okay, Jen?"

The afternoon was pretty uneventful. And surprisingly pleasant. It also felt different from any other afternoon I'd ever spent with Bobby and Sherry. I'd gone over there in groups of "we" before, but they'd always been dating "we's." "We's" that probably wouldn't be around next year. This was different. Jake and I were the most permanent kind of "we" you can get. It felt terrific.

Around six o'clock I started gathering up our stuff so we could take off.

"We've really missed your being here the past couple of years for this," said Sherry. I was at the kitchen sink rinsing out Jake's bottles and tossing all the equipment in the bag.

"Well, yeah, I guess I was a no-show while I was on the hockey beat. We were always in the Stanley Cup."

"You weren't last year, were you?" she asked, reaching for a towel to help me with drying them off. "I thought Bobby said you were in town and that he'd invited you to come with that television woman you were seeing."

I thought about it for a second. "Sherry, I honestly don't remember where I was last Memorial Day."

I didn't. And the whole way home on the expressway,

I didn't either. The weekend *after* Memorial Day, though, I remembered. I didn't let myself think about it much because it was so damn confusing, but I sure as hell remembered it.

Big surprise. I seemed to be living with a fifteen-pound reminder of it.

Lacy

FEBRUARY - MAY

I still didn't see what good it was going to do me in life to
know about eluvial plains. But to get this damn degree, I
had to take a lab science. Physical geography sounded a
whole lot less scientific than biology or chemistry did.
The problem was, *sounded* is one thing—*was* is another—and physical geography *was* impossible.

It was Memorial Day. I had about forty hours left
before the final, and the study break I was taking out on
the back porch was already twice as long as the study
time I'd put in at the kitchen table. Not that I was doing
particularly great at anything requiring concentration.
Ever since Charlie's baby had been born, it was like all
my recall skills had just shriveled up. So did those fabulous boobs I had, but I was prepared for that—brain
burnouts, I wasn't prepared for. I'd walk into my bedroom, and forget why I was going in there. Or I'd be

talking to Steffi, and she'd say I'd already told her that. Or my bosses would tell me to check the archives for something, and by the time I called up the archives on the computer, I'd blanked out on what I was supposed to be looking up. My life was becoming a paper trail of Post-its—they were the only way I could remember things.

The creepy part was that no one even yelled at me about it. I'd been back in the office for three whole months, but they were still all treating me with kid gloves—and I hated it. I hated that everyone felt sorry for me because I'd had this baby and then given it up for adoption. And I hated even more that they all thought my current edginess was because of that—like I hadn't been edgy before.

Even Steffi went deferential on me for a few weeks. One Saturday after I got home from the hospital she asked me to go shopping with her at Water Tower Place. For some reason or other that day it seemed like the whole mall was filled with women pushing strollers or sticking their pregnant bellies in my face.

"Are you okay?" she asked when we came out of Lord & Taylor.

"Of course I'm okay," I snapped.

"Good," she said with this newly acquired beatific smile she'd been using on me lately.

"Don't patronize me, Steffi! I can see other people with babies, and not come unglued. For Pete's sake. Will you stop presuming that deep down I am grieving, but that I'm in total denial about it?"

"Lacy, who's saying you're in total denial?"

"It's not a question of *saying* it!" I said, marching toward the escalator. "It's just that the whole world treats me these days like I must be some wounded animal or something. And I'm not—I'm just fine. And for your information, the only reason I'm staring at all these babies is because I think it's completely rude and inconsiderate for their moms to drag them around in these overheated stores where they can catch a million germs, and that maybe they might consider getting a baby-sitter and leaving the kid at home when they're going to a mall, understand?"

"Sure, Lacy, I understand," she said, still sounding like St. Steffi of the Solicitous, if you ask me.

It was the same thing with Ruthie. "Are you sure you wouldn't like to take a little more time off," she had asked after I'd been back a couple of weeks, when she'd caught me staring into the nothingness over my desk even though I had a huge batch of mail left to open. "We can bring the temp back in for a while, Lacy. Maybe it's too soon for you to tackle all this."

I looked at my desk. It had never looked that way before—piles of letters everywhere. I just didn't seem able to make any decisions on which letters were definite "yesses" and which were "noes," so my "maybe" pile was huge. And that didn't do anybody any good, because it meant I had to go back and reread all of them. But I didn't let them bring back the temp. Instead, I went in and worked that whole weekend to clear the "maybe" pile up, and get started fresh again the next Monday.

But here it was, almost June, and I still wasn't completely up to speed. Sometimes it felt as if I were doing large chunks of my life in slo-mo, and I didn't know how to get back to my old pace. The weather sure didn't help any—we'd had a freak ten-day stretch of low nineties, and it looked like today was going to be just as thick and steamy. When I'd gotten dressed, I'd tried to put on a pair of shorts, but I still had about eight pounds to go before bare thighs would be a good look. Even so, my postpartum body was easier to get rid of than my postpartum mind.

I mean I didn't think about the baby all that much—except for the times when I couldn't help it. And yeah, that was a little more often than I'd planned on. Actually, I don't think it was the biological linkup as much as the psychological one that left me occasionally feeling so . . . I don't know . . . stranded. I mean, bottom line—I had to face it—I had always been a great mom. I was involved, I was connected, and as scary and exhausting as all of it had been, I absolutely loved doing it. So it was odd—odder than I ever imagined it could be—to be sitting twenty minutes south of a house that contained a child who had resided inside me for nine months and a man who . . .

A man who what? Boy, that was a sentence I didn't know how to finish. I guess I'd been having sort of a one-way relationship with Charlie these past few months because I'd become almost an addicted listener to his show—at least when I wasn't in class. I'd sit at the kitchen table with my Lean Cuisine and my beer and turn on his program. Whether they were talking about how erratic the Bulls had been, or how pathetic the

Cubs were, or anything, it was always pretty interesting. Actually, it was even more interesting when there weren't a lot of calls. Then Charlie and Bonnie would just talk with each other—sometimes about sports and sometimes about real life. I waited for Charlie to mention that he had a kid—some sort of funny story or something—only he never did.

Actually, a horrible thing had happened with Charlie one day in mid-April. I saw him. I don't know what he was doing in the parking lot of my Target, but as I was carrying all the stuff I'd bought back to my car, I looked up and saw a man way down the aisle extracting a baby from the backseat of a maroon Volvo. He was smiling and talking to the baby while he cuddled him close and flipped a blanket all around him. It was freezing cold that day, and I had my parka hood up, so I know he didn't recognize me standing there between two cars. But I recognized him and I stood there rooted to the ground, unable to pull my eyes off the two of them.

Only actually there were four of them. Because coming around from the other side of the car was a long-haired brunette wearing a ski headband and a camel hair coat. She was holding the hand of a little kid in a snowsuit and then he reached up and grabbed Charlie's hand and the four of them walked toward the store. It was a killer moment. I mean, I knew it was probably Bonnie, and I knew he and Bonnie were friends, and I knew Charlie was smarter than to get involved with someone from work, and then I remembered how he managed to get involved with me . . .

Oh, damn, damn, damn . . .

I went right to Steffi's from the Target parking lot and made her fix me some tea. "Are you worried something's going on with them?" she asked. She'd gotten a lot less patronizing after I yelled at her in Water Tower Place, and that made it much easier to deal with her. "Because, Lacy, hard as it is for you to accept, you still don't get a vote on who Charlie brings into his life, and you can't expect that someone as attractive as he is isn't going to wind up with somebody."

"How do you know he's attractive?" I asked, slamming my sugar spoon on the counter. "You've never met him."

"His picture was on the radio-TV page one day. He's darling! Very Jewish J. Crew."

"I know . . ." I sighed. "Oh, God, I just hate how this whole thing hasn't been all that smooth and orderly as it was supposed to be."

"Oh, Lace, did you honestly think it would be? What sort of order would it have gone smoothly in?"

"Well, you know," I said, remembering how one-two-three I thought all this would be to execute. I have baby; I turn it over right away to Charlie; he's happy with his new life; I get to pursue my new life; I get things back on track with Jessica . . .

And that was another thing. Jessica and I were hardly what you could call back on track. I'd been prepared to accept that things between us were going to remain strained all during my pregnancy. Christmas had been particularly horrible—especially one night when she mentioned she was thinking of staying in touch with Charlie so she could get to know her "half sister or brother." That made me a little crazy. I mean there I was, working twenty-four/seven to mentally distance myself from this kicking, hiccuping entity inside me, and then unilaterally and with no warning, she's telling me that she's considering a lifetime relationship with him.

But then when the baby was born, she did a complete reversal—at least with me. She never even asked me how much the baby weighed or what his name was— only if it was a boy or a girl. Then nothing. I had no idea if maybe that was because she was planning to get the rest of the answers directly from Charlie, or what. I only know that to date, I haven't been able to ask her if she's contacted him, because I'm not sure how I'll deal with her answer.

I also know that Jess has managed to keep her distance from me all year—and it's hurt. It's hurt that she's pushed me off this spring each time I've said I'd like to fly east to see one of her games. "I don't play that much as a freshman yet, Mom, don't waste your money." "I have to work on a paper all weekend, it wouldn't be a good time to come." And even a couple of weeks ago on Mother's Day, I didn't hear from her until nearly six in the evening. She said she'd been in the library all day studying, but the pathetic truth is that by the time she'd gotten hold of me, I'd definitely managed to turn into a Hallmark moment deprivation victim. I mean when Steffi stopped in that afternoon, I actually heard myself say, "I already knew I wasn't going to hear from one kid, but I thought at least this one would come through."

Steffi was stunned. "Lacy?" she said, unwrapping the silver earrings I'd gotten her because we always gave each other presents on Mother's Day. "Did you just say what I think you said?"

"Yeah, I said it—but I didn't mean it the way it sounded."

"Oh," she said, coming over to hug me for the present, "you didn't mean it like a woman who was not only feeling sorry for herself, but was also acknowledging for the first time since February that there are two kids of hers on this planet?"

"Don't, Steffi," I said, hanging on to the hug, and closing my eyes just in case some stupid tears tried to push their way out. "It's just that I had no idea how terrible this would feel sometimes."

"I know, hon," she said, pushing my hair back. "I'm sorry."

"No," I said, once I got my voice as untrembly as possible, "it's true. I don't acknowledge the baby. I can't. But, God . . . sometimes I think it would have been four million times easier to have just had the baby randomly adopted. It would have been unfair to Charlie, but this knowing where the baby is living, and who the baby is living with, and having that be someone who I guess had become so much a part of my life . . . In my worst moments, on my worst days, it's just this huge double hit."

But then of course there was the fact that on my best days I was actually okay. Like today. Yup, for whatever reason, today just felt like a day when I'd turned the corner. I mean the truth was, nothing was on my mind today except how to plow through this horrible geography stuff. Around eleven o'clock the phone finally rang.

"Hey, girl."

"Hey, Josie. How many chapters do you have left?"

Josie and I had decided to take the same class together second semester. She'd been great the past couple of months. The day I came home from the hospital she called and said, "If you want to talk about it, I'm here. If you want to move past all this, let's go." I loved her for that, and I loved that we'd grown a lot closer these past months. Two nights before, she'd been over for dinner and we'd set up a study goal of ten geography chapters a night. Today was supposed to be the last stretch.

"I am done, woman. That's why I called. To make you feel rotten and lazy."

"How'd you know I was behind?" I watched while a cavalcade of ants headed toward my yellow highlighting pen.

"I didn't. I just knew you'd be where I would have been if I hadn't had insomnia last night. I finally got up and finished the last few chapters. Man, that stuff is grim! I'm not looking at it again until tomorrow. I'm going to sit out the day at the Cubs game. Wanna come with Michael and me?"

"You know I can't. I've got to do this. But thanks for calling and making me feel panicked."

"Anytime. I'll call you tomorrow and we can go over the last few chapters."

"Great."

I walked back out on the porch, but it had gotten too hot to stay out so I went back inside to fix some iced tea. I flipped on the radio to scan for a weather report, but before I could change stations I heard Charlie's voice. That was weird—he was *never* on this early, but he must have been filling in for someone because of the holiday. The thing was though, he wasn't getting any calls—none. Not to mention, he was on all alone without a partner, and you could kind of hear that he was struggling for material. Which probably explains why, about ten minutes later, I heard Charlie Feldman say something that completely somersaulted my inners. He'd been talking about the history of baseball uniforms or something, and then all of a sudden he looped into baseball uniforms for babies. Yeah, he laughed warmly, it seems there was a miniature Cubs uniform over at his house. It belonged to his three-and-a-half-month-old son—a son whose name was Jake, who had curly dark hair, who weighed fifteen pounds, who laughed when you stuck your tongue out at him, who just last week started sleeping through the night, who . . .

So much for today being one of my best days.

I bagged all attempts at studying, and sweltering as it was, grabbed my bike and took off for a head-clearing, heart-clearing ride.

It didn't help.

An hour later when I got home, I grabbed a shower, put on a blue sundress, and walked over to Steffi's. She'd asked me to come by and grill out with her and the kids and her mom. Dolores and Brian had gone to the Dells for the weekend with another couple, so I was happy to have a place to spend the afternoon.

The quads were finishing cleaning out the garage—one of the tasks they were earning money for, in order to finance tuxes and formals for the prom. Things like proms—which set any parent back—were four times the hit for Steffi. She did the best she could, but the quads were definitely expected to pitch in on big ticket items. A "Spice Girls" CD was blasting from the backyard. It made me realize how long it had been since I'd yelled at anyone to turn down the music.

I found Steffi and her mom in the kitchen, slicing things up for potato salad. The whole room smelled of heat and onions and parsley. "Frances," I said, bending over to kiss Steffi's mom, "I haven't seen you in ages. How have you been?"

"Why I'm just fine, dear," she said. Frances was the opposite of Steffi. Where Steffi was statuesque, Frances was short and chunky. Steffi ran from makeup, and Frances was always shedding powder all over her clothes. I liked Frances—but then she wasn't my mother—she wasn't on *my* case all the time. Or at least she wasn't until that afternoon. Because the next thing she said was, "You look wonderful, Lacy. I gather quite a bit has happened to you this past year."

I looked at Steffi. I knew she hadn't told her mom about the baby. There'd have been no reason to—Frances was a daily Mass woman, and my situation would have made her apoplectic, even though I wasn't her daughter, but only her daughter's best friend. "Well, it has been an unusual year," I said. And then doing my best to divert her I asked, "How was your winter in Arizona?"

It didn't work—Frances plowed forward. "When Steffi went to the store earlier I sat down with her photo album and saw all the pictures from this Christmas. You certainly looked ready to pop, dear."

I tried to smile.

"So tell me, what did you have? Another daughter, or your very first son?"

Charlie

FATHER'S DAY

It was Sunday morning and it was hot and muggy. The air conditioner in my bedroom was alternating between gasping and wheezing. It was only a matter of time until I would hear that inevitable appliance death rattle. Man, I did *not* want to think about air conditioners today . . .

Because I knew exactly what would happen. I'd spend the morning dismantling the sucker and swearing at the parts. Then by early afternoon, pissed and defeated, I'd pack up Jake, and we'd schlepp to some discount appliance store in the suburbs to drop a few hundred bucks on a new unit. Which wouldn't get installed until next week.

Perfect. My first Father's Day ever with this kid, and at almost four months old he's about to sit ringside and watch his old man get pulverized in the Mr. Fix-it department. Granted, half the guys in America who have big red toolboxes have even bigger carpenter and electrician bills, so why should I be different from any other schmuck with a screwdriver? Abe stunk at it. I stunk at it. I suppose my kid might as well deal with his genetic legacy today. Happy Father's Day, Jake.

I'd hoped as a little Father's Day offering maybe he'd shatter his world record and sleep later than he ever had in all of his hundred-plus days of life. No such luck. He'd gotten me up at the usual six-fifteen. But once he'd downed the milk/oatmeal/apricot brew I concocted for his breakfast, he seemed happy to hang around in my bed sucking on his fingers while I explained to him that the Cubs may have just lost eleven in a row, but it didn't mean squat. He had to get used to the heartache sometime.

The doorbell rang. I wondered who the hell showed up at nine o'clock on a Sunday morning. Pulling on last night's T-shirt and some shorts, I picked up Jake and plodded down the stairs. The living room was a pit. Toys had been tossed out of the playpen, the bungee swing hung lopsidedly from the door frame, and a big blob of mashed carrots had congealed into an unspeakable shape on the couch. This was not the living room of an all-adult household.

Before I could get to the door, the putz started ringing again. "For Christ's sake, hang on a minute will you?" I barked and yanked the door open.

Lacy was standing there in a white sundress and sandals. She held a big brown bag crammed with groceries. A bunch of flowers and a bag of fresh bagels were resting on the top.

"Hi," she said.

"Lacy! What the hell?"

"What the hell, what?" Her green eyes flashed both defiance and discomfort. "It's Father's Day, Charlie." Then the eyes went right to the baby. "Hey, Jake."

Me, she couldn't quite look at. She shifted the bag to her other hip, extended her free hand to Jake, and lightly ran it through his hair. Then she said, "Anyway, I thought maybe I could fix you some breakfast."

Watching her, I think the air got sucked out of my lungs. "Jesus, Lacy, give me a minute here to process this. Okay? I mean, I don't hear squat from you for four months, and wham! out of fucking nowhere you show up on Father's Day? It's a lot to register."

She nodded her head. Her hair was shorter. Maybe redder. Maybe I just didn't remember. "I know, Charlie. I know. But I just figured that it's hard on Father's Day not to have anyone say anything or do anything to acknowledge that you're being a great dad."

I didn't say a word. Not that I was speechless. I just needed her to fill in the blanks. After all this time, after all this distance, after all this silence, I needed to know what the hell had pushed this woman from Point A— slamming the door on Jake's and my existence—to Point B, standing here on my doorstep telling me I'm a great dad.

Lacy set down the bag of groceries on my stoop and took a deep breath. "You're going to make me say it, aren't you?"

"I don't know what the 'it' is you're talking about, Lacy. I wouldn't presume to predict the 'it' a person like you is thinking. Or feeling. But you're right, I am plenty interested in whatever you're about to say."

"Oh, God, Charlie, this is so hard," she said, taking a deep breath. "Do you think we could just sit on the stoop for a second?"

We settled ourselves down, and she reached toward Jake. "Can I?" she asked, holding her arms out to him.

He went right for her hair, looping his mucky fingers into her curls. She couldn't help but grin. "He's great," she said, "very guy."

"Well, yeah. It seems to be the model we got." I waited for her reaction to the "we."

There was none. Then Jake reached out for me and she handed him back. Gently. Then she wrapped her arms around her knees, rested her chin on top of them, and, still afraid to look at me, fixed her eyes on the front-yard tree. Taking a huge breath, she said, "I just can't pull it off, Charlie. I just can't not think about you, and not think about Jake, and not wonder, and not know. I mean, I've tried to do it—I've tried really hard—but it's like instead of really living my new life, all I am doing is shoving down all these thoughts and feelings that I really have about you guys."

I could have pushed. I could have forced her hand by making her label those thoughts and feelings, but the fact was, for her, for this fierce, lovely, adamant woman, what she had just said was as close to a declaration of love as a person could expect. For now, anyway. Plus, the point wasn't *what* she *said*. It was *where* she *was*. And where Lacy was, was right there on my front stoop. That was the important part.

I cupped her cheek and turned her face toward mine. "So now what?"

"I don't know," she said, looking me dead in the eye. "Do you think we can talk about that over breakfast? I mean, I bought all this stuff and like I said, I figured until Jake can do it on his own, maybe I should be in charge of making sure you get a good Father's Day breakfast." She got up from the step, smoothed down her dress, and picked up the grocery bag.

"Lacy, help me out here. Are you saying that you're showing up here every Father's Day until Jake is big enough to make me breakfast?"

"Um, hum," she said slowly, nodding her head.

"Really?" I grinned, stepping closer and handing her Jake while I took the bag out of her hands. She smelled great. "So tell me, Lacy, when can a kid start to do that? You know, fix me breakfast on his own? In a couple of years? In five years? In eighteen years?"

Lacy took a deep breath. "Well, Charlie, it depends. Some kids start later than others. Some kids can take a real long time."

This time she did smile. Then Lacy Gazzar stepped over the threshold.

Acknowledgments

Thanks to Jean Naggar, Jennifer Weltz, and Maureen Baron, for all their guidance and smartness in birthing Charlie and Lacy; to Herb Gould, who helped me understand the world of sports guys; to Terry Beacom, who explained the college sports part; to Suzy Kellet, whose life has been so frequently on loan to my writing; to Todd Musburger for the most thorough job of guardian-angeling ever; to Chris Paschen and Kathy O'Malley for listening, questioning, and best-friending; to the fabulous Tom for the excellent testosterone reads; and to Erin and Adam just 'cause I love them so completely.

About the Author

Judy Markey has written a syndicated humor column in the Chicago *Sun-Times* for fifteen years. She also co-hosts Chicago radio's top-rated midday talk show, WGN's "Kathy and Judy." She has lovely e-mail and telephone relationships with her two adult children.